'Grim and often blackly funny . . . it is impossible not to be drawn into Francie Brady's world, but Christ knows you wouldn't want him in your house . . . a shockingly intimate portrait of a mind out of kilter'   *Guardian*

'A brilliant book, so very funny as well as being heartrendingly sad'
                                                                    J. P. Donleavy

'An extraordinary study of the struggle and heartache that inevitably arise when instinct and physical need come face to face with the more refined virtues of reason and intellect. Francie is a lovable villain, a semi-sweet psychotic who elicits from the reader much the same affectionate interest that Perry Smith did in Truman Capote's *In Cold Blood*. It is precisely Mr McCabe's ability to capture the warring states of Francie's mind that elevates this book from the level of the absurd to that of art'   *New York Times*

'Startlingly original . . . a masterpiece of literary ventriloquism – a Beckett monologue with a plot by Alfred Hitchcock . . . an almost perfect novel written with wonderful assurance and a technical skill that is as great as it is unobtrusive. It is also viciously entertaining, the sort of nasty Gothic shocker that is liable to keep you up late against your better judgment'   *Washington Post*

'What he does is gruesome, what he thinks is pitiable . . . it is the rich expressiveness of Francie's account which touches. He blurts lyrical phrases that only the semi-articulate achieve – the sort of book you feel guilty enjoying'   *Daily Telegraph*

'Compelling, unashamedly horrible, memorable and sensitive'
                                                                    Times Literary Supplement

THE BUTCHER BOY

Also by Patrick McCabe in Picador

The Dead School

Breakfast on Pluto

Mondo Desperado!

Emerald Germs of Ireland

PATRICK McCABE

THE BUTCHER BOY

PICADOR CLASSIC

First published 1992 by Picador

First published in paperback 1992 by Picador

This Picador Classic edition first published 2015 by Picador
an imprint of Pan Macmillan
The Smithson, 6 Briset Street, London EC1M 5NR
EU representative: Macmillan Publishers Ireland Ltd, 1st Floor,
The Liffey Trust Centre, 117–126 Sheriff Street Upper,
Dublin 1, DO1 YC43
Associated companies throughout the world
www.panmacmillan.com

ISBN 978-1-4472-7516-9

11

A CIP catalogue record for this book is available from the British Library.

Printed and bound by CPI Group (UK) Ltd, Croydon, CR0 4YY

INTRODUCTION

I cannot think of any other opening to a novel that captures
me quite like this:

> When I was a young lad twenty or thirty or forty years ago
> I lived in a small town where they were all after me on
> account of what I done on Mrs Nugent. I was hiding out by
> the river in a hole under a tangle of briars. It was a hide me
> and Joe made. Death to all dogs who enter here, we said.
> Except us of course.

The manic pulse of tragic inevitability that courses
through the book is set in motion by this first paragraph with
such deliberate force that it surprised me to learn that these
were the last words of the novel that the author wrote. Here,
immediately, is the singular voice – playful, idiomatic, unreliable – of Francie Brady, at once implanting the reader inside
his mind.

One of the powerful ironies of the book is that the voice
exerts a control over us, in the sense that we cannot break
from it, while the narrator is himself never fully in control of
it. The syntax runs wild; the real mingles with delusion; time
gapes and contracts. Everything – the description, the detail,
the ragged storytelling – is generated through the warped
oddball consciousness of Francie. There is never a moment
when we feel that an idea has been transposed to fit into it.
We are bound to him from the get-go. Off on our travels –
'Saddle up! We're riding out! Yee-haa!'

The events of the novel take place in a small, unnamed Irish town during the late fifties and early sixties – the final part to a fevered backdrop of the Cuban missile crisis. Francie, though, does not share everybody else's trepidation about the end of the world: 'New Fears? That was a laugh. I never felt better.' He is separate, in this, in all things, from those around him, preoccupied with comics, Flash Bars, John Wayne, hacking at the ice with his friend Joe. And with the middle-class family recently returned from London – the Nugents. Central to the sorrow – and the tension – of *The Butcher Boy* is our building awareness that these fixations, as he grows older, as he slides further into mental illness, will never leave him.

One of my favourite scenes is in the Bundoran hotel where Francie sits down to eat, a few tables away from a businessman 'who looked like Humpty Dumpty's brother'.

> I wanted to leap into the air like Green Lantern or the Human Torch and land at Humpty's table. OK Humpty let's talk about your brother! I want the lowdown on these communists and I want it now!

The businessman clearly thinks that he's had his breakfast interrupted by a lunatic. Yet to the reader, there is a logic to the flow of Francie's thoughts. We get it, because we are so embedded inside his head. And there is an enjoyment in the fact that we understand at the same time the incomprehension of Humpty, and anybody else not inside Francie's head, because we recognize how we would ourselves respond to a lunatic in the restaurant. It is in that relationship between the interior and the exterior – normality; his normality – that the novel finds its humour, pathos and truth. The real is thrown into shocking light by the dramatic irony that we are viewing, through Francie, a reality that he does not always understand. Naturalistic fiction would not be able to achieve this double-edged truth. McCabe has said that 'I've always felt that naturalism or social realism only provides a third of the story . . . [it] gives you the marble but not the inscape of the statue.' Instead, what we are presented with in *The Butcher Boy*, to use the author's preferred term, is the 'social fantastic'.

I don't cry a lot. There is one portion of this novel, though (when Francie first starts working at the slaughterhouse), that brings me as close to it as anything in fiction ever has: a dramatic irony that is stretched out over twenty pages of a scenario that we gradually understand but Francie cannot, or will not. The real is so often heightened by Francie's inability, or refusal, to interpret. In one beautifully wrought scene, his uncle Alo returns from Camden for a much anticipated party. Through the deranged fog of Francie's excitement there is an intimate sadness at work. Alo comes into the presence of Mary, and an old love burns hopelessly amidst the crowd. It is in the capturing of small details, the momentary stills of 'trembling lips', of Mary 'hunched . . . up over the keyboard' that we grasp the bigger picture, one that is made all the more powerful because it is undeclared.

Early in the novel, Francie walks in on his mother's suicide attempt:

> . . . when I got into the kitchen who's there only ma standing there and a chair sideways on the table. What's that doing up there ma I says it was fuse wire belonging to da just dangling but she didn't say what it was doing there she was

just stood there picking at her nail and going to say something and then not saying it.

Those details of the 'sideways' chair, the fuse wire, the image of her 'picking at her nail', resonate with a horrible power for us – while Francie runs away delightedly, *Yee ha!*, to buy two Flash Bars and a macaroon from the shop.

And yet, running through the novel, there is the insinuation of another cognisance beneath the narrative surface. The glimpsed possibility – underneath all the obfuscating layers of fantasy, schizophrenia, alcohol and drug use – that he does understand. That he sometimes knows it 'was only me raving and didn't happen'. This buried understanding appears most often during, or shortly after, the most acutely traumatic moments of the book. He may have bombed off to the sweet shop after seeing his ma up there on the table, but a few pages later, when he is induced into a delusion by the sight of Mrs Nugent and her son Philip on the footpath, it is his own deeply repressed shame that we read in the conversation he concocts:

> Just stands there on the landing and lets the father do what he likes to her. You'd never do the like of that would you Philip? . . . Of course you know what she was doing with the fuse wire don't you Philip?

It is tempting, but perhaps too simplistic, to think of *The Butcher Boy* as part of a wave of Irish fiction expressive of an emergent, open Ireland, desirous to lay bare the ills and injustices of the post-independence period. There is, if you want to frame it in this way, a literature of the side-lined, the brutalized, the stigmatized and abandoned, which would include McCabe among its practitioners – alongside Dermot Bolger, Dermot Healy, Roddy Doyle, all forerun by the myth-busting arrival, thirty years earlier, of Edna O'Brien. I feel, instinctively, though, that placing *The Butcher Boy*, or any of these writers' books, inside a stable of thought is partly misleading. Largely because I don't imagine for a moment that *The Butcher Boy*'s author would do so himself, or that such an impulse towards a perceived movement of contemporaries could have motivated him to write the novel. It is the job of critical and social commentators to make such connections. For an author to do so would likely result in work that strikes a false, polemical, note. Personally, the novel which I cannot help but hold up against *The Butcher Boy* is John McGahern's *Amongst Women*, published two years earlier, and also focused on mid-century small-town Ireland – because of the complete opposition, formally, linguistically, of the two books: *Amongst Women* a masterpiece of constraint, its violence and history muted, suppressed; *The Butcher Boy*, on the other hand, letting loose its sentences and its violence with joyous frightening abandon.

It is somewhat more feasible to draw the connections between *The Butcher Boy* and other examples of McCabe's work. In particular, the novels published most closely to it – *Carn*, *The Dead School*, *Breakfast on Pluto* – which contain the same huddled intensity of small-town life, and of characters on the fringes through whom society is refracted, hoisted up and pinned to the wall.

Undeniably, *The Butcher Boy* exposes the cruelties of a conservative Catholic institutionalism that Francie is repeatedly returned to, made ever more vulnerable to abuse, or to his own mind, with never a suggestion of the support he so clearly requires. Nor do the people of the town offer any assistance. Mrs Connolly might come round to clean the house at one point, but Francie is from the beginning an ostracized figure, kept always at a watchful distance by a populace eager to whisper its judgements, but never to get involved in Francie's broken family unit of alcoholic father and manic-depressive mother.

Nonetheless, it is the town and its inhabitants that give so much colour to the book. There is a febrile energy to the place that Francie, inside but outside of it, is uniquely able to convey: of the children on the lane or the women gossiping in the shop; of the drunk lad (McCabe, incidentally, made a brief cameo appearance as a town drunk in the 1997 film of the novel), or Grouse Armstrong, tearing out of the slaughter-house with a string of intestines; of the Virgin Mary speaking through Mickey Traynor's daughter on the Diamond as the townspeople clamour for the end of the world.

If the town, and his parents, have given Francie anything, it is an inheritance of shame.

God's curse the fucking day I ever set eyes on you!

The desperate echo of this phrase, shouted by his father to his mother, can be heard aimed at Francie throughout the book. Shame grips him at every turn, inhibiting his development. A great part of the sadness of *The Butcher Boy* is in the realization that Francie will never become an adult. He experiences no proper childhood, no stability, from which to move on – a situation made all the more poignant by his longing for it. Over and over, we find him seeking to construct an invented history of normality: the Alo party is a roaring success; he journeys to the site of his parents' honeymoon in Bundoran and the B&B where he imagines them lying on the bedspread thinking about 'all the beautiful things in the world'. Ultimately, it is a search that only ever leads him to the replication of familial shame – drinking; attempting suicide; being taken away to 'the garage' – or to enraged confrontation with his family's antithesis, the TV advert happy Nugents.

The most sombre marker of Francie's stultified development is the growing up of his best friend Joe. In a narrative in which the passage of time is so unclear (located obliquely through real life events such as the Munich air disaster, 1958, and the Cuban missile crisis, 1962) it is Joe's educational, social and sexual development that points to the emptiness of Francie's. While Joe moves on to a mature life of his own, Francie will be forever hacking at the puddles of ice on the lane. It takes on a terrible symbolism, that lane. The image of it becomes part of a gathering army of crystalline details, every one of which has a particular symbolic meaning that is compounded by relentless iteration. Snowdrops. Pilchards. Flies. Flash Bars. Goldfish. Orange skies. To every reader who has been moved by *The Butcher Boy*, the mention of any of these words cuts straight to a deep, sad knowledge. Together, they symbolize the bars of a cage that Francie, with the collusion of all around him, makes for himself – a physical but essentially mental confinement that we take a wild pleasure from, trapped inside his head, although we know, as he knows, that he can never be let free.

I felt like laughing in his face: How can your solitary finish? That's the best laugh yet.

Ross Raisin

For the McCabes,

Brian, Eugene, Mary, and Dympna

When I was a young lad twenty or thirty or forty years ago I lived in a small town where they were all after me on account of what I done on Mrs Nugent. I was hiding out by the river in a hole under a tangle of briars. It was a hide me and Joe made. Death to all dogs who enter here, we said. Except us of course.

You could see plenty from the inside but no one could see you. Weeds and driftwood and everything floating downstream under the dark archway of the bridge. Sailing away to Timbuctoo. Good luck now weeds, I said.

Then I stuck my nose out to see what was going on. Plink – rain if you don't mind!

But I wasn't complaining. I liked rain. The hiss of the water and the earth so soft bright green plants would nearly sprout beside you. This is the life I said. I sat there staring at a waterdrop on the end of a leaf. It couldn't make up its mind whether it wanted to fall or not. It didn't matter – I was in no hurry. Take your time drop, I said – we've got all the time we want now.

We've got all the time in the world.

I could hear a plane droning far away. One time we were standing in the lane behind the houses shading our eyes from the sun and Joe says: Did you see that plane Francie? I said

1

I did. It was a tiny silver bird in the distance. What I want to know is, he said, how do they manage to get a man small enough to fit in it? I said I didn't know. I didn't know much about planes in them days.

I was thinking about Mrs Nugent standing there crying her eyes out. I said sure what's the use in crying now Nugent it was you caused all the trouble if you hadn't poked your nose in everything would have been all right. And it was true. Why would I want to harm her son Philip – I liked him. The first day he came to the school Joe says to me did you see the new fellow? Philip Nugent is his name. O, I says, I'll have to see this. He had been to a private school and he wore this blazer with gold braid and a crest on the breast pocket. He had a navy blue cap with a badge and grey socks. What do you make of that says Joe. Woh boy, I said, Philip Nugent. This is Philip Nugent, said the master, he's come to join us. Philip used to live in London but his parents are from the town and they have come back here to live. Now I want you to make him feel at home won't you? He was like Winker Watson out of the *Dandy* in this get-up of his only Winker was always up to devilment and Philip was the opposite. Every time you saw him he was investigating insects under rocks or explaining to some snottery-nosed young gawk about the boiling point of water. Me and Joe used to ask him all about this school. We said: What about these secret meetings and passwords? Tell us about the tuck shop – come on Philip but I don't think he knew what we were talking about. The best thing about him was his collection of comics. I just can't get over it, said Joe, I never seen anything like it. He had them all neatly filed away in shirt boxes not a crease or a dog-ear in sight. They looked as if they had come straight out of the shop. There were comics there we had never seen before in our lives and we thought we knew plenty about comics. Mrs Nugent says: Make sure not to damage any of those now they cost money. We said: *We won't!* – but afterwards Joe said to me: Francie we've got to have them. So you could say it was him started it and not me. We talked about it for a long time and we made our decision.

We had to have them and that was that.

We called round to Philip and had a swopping session.

We cleaned him out. I admit it. It was only a laugh. We'd have given them back if he asked for them. All he had to say was: Look chaps, I think I want my comics back and we'd have said: OK Phil.

But of course Nugent couldn't wait for that. Anyway we left Philip with his pile of junk and off we went to the hide going on about it all until the tears ran down our faces. Wait till you hear this one Joe would say one flea says to the other what do you say will we walk or take a dog. He was reading out all these jokes I couldn't stop the laughing, I was choking. We got so bad I was hitting the grass with my fists crying stop Joe stop. But we weren't laughing the next day when Nugent got on the job.

I met Joe coming across the Diamond and he says to me watch out Francie we're in the wars with Nugent. She called at our house and she'll be round to you. Sure enough I was lying on the bed upstairs and the knock comes to the front door. I could hear ma humming and the shuffle of her slippers on the lino. Ah hello Mrs Nugent come in but Nugent was in no humour for ah hello come in or any of that. She lay into ma about the comics and the whole lot and I could hear ma saying *yes yes I know I will of course!* and I was waiting for her to come flying up the stairs, get me by the ear and throw me on the step in front of Nugent and that's what she would have done if Nugent hadn't started on about the pigs. She said she knew the kind of us long before she went to England and she might have known not to let her son anywhere near the likes of me what else would you expect from a house where the father's never in, lying about the pubs from morning to night, he's no better than a pig. You needn't think we don't know what goes on in this house oh we know all right! Small wonder the boy is the way he is what chance has he got running about the town at all hours and the clothes hanging off him it doesn't take money to dress a child God love him its not his fault but if he's seen near our Philip again there'll be trouble. There'll be trouble now mark my words!

After that ma took my part and the last thing I heard was Nugent going down the lane and calling back *Pigs – sure the whole town knows that!*

Ma pulled me down the stairs and gave me the mother and father of a flaking but it took more out of her than it did out of me for her hands were trembling like leaves in the breeze she threw the stick from her and steadied herself in the kitchen saying she was sorry over and over. She said there was nobody in the world meant more to her than me. Then she put her arms around me and said it was her nerves it was them was to blame for everything. It wasn't always like this for your father and me she said. Then she looked into my eyes and said: Francie – you would never let me down would you?

4

She meant you wouldn't let me down like da did I said
no I wouldn't let her down in a hundred million years no
matter how many times she took into me with the stick. She
said she was sorry she had done that and she would never
do it again as long as she lived.

She said that was all there was in this world, people who
let you down. She said when Mrs Nugent came to the town
first there was nobody like her. I used to be up the town with
her every day she said. Then she started crying and saying
this awful place and dabbing at her eyes with a tiny bit of
tissue out of her apron pocket. But it was no use it just frit-
tered away into little pieces.

The light slanting in the window and you could hear the
children playing outside in the lane. They had set up a shop
and were paying for groceries with pebbles. They had empty
soap powder boxes and bean tins. No – its my turn one of
them said. Grouse Armstrong scratched his ear and yelped
running in and out among them.

I was thinking how right ma was – Mrs Nugent all smiles
when she met us and how are you getting on Mrs and young
Francis are you both well? It was hard to believe that all the
time what she was really saying was: *Ah hello Mrs Pig how
are you and look Philip do you see what's coming now – The
Pig Family!*

But it didn't matter for me and ma we were great pals after
that any chance I got I says to her well ma do you want any
messages up the town sometimes she did and sometimes she
didn't but I always made sure to ask her anyway. She gave

5

me my dinner and says Francie if you ever have a sweetheart you'll tell her the truth and never let her down won't you?

I says I will ma and she says I know you will son and then we'd just sit there for hours sometimes just staring into the firegrate only there never was a fire ma never bothered to light one and I wasn't sure how to go about it. I said what fire do we want its just as good sitting here staring into the ashes.

I don't know what night it was I think it was the night the town won the cup da had to be left home it was one of the railwaymen dropped him at the door. I stood on the landing but all I could hear was mumbling and coins dropping on the floor. I was going back into the room when I heard something breaking I wasn't sure what it was but it sounded like glass. Then I heard da cursing the town and everybody in it he said he could have been somebody hadn't he met Eddie Calvert who else in the town had ever met Eddie Calvert who else in the town even *knew* who Eddie Calvert was? Who? he said, *Who?* He shouted at ma: Do you hear me talking to you?

She mustn't have said anything for the next thing he was off into the speech about his father leaving them when he was seven and how nobody understood him he said she lost interest in his music long ago and she didn't care it wasn't his fault she was the way she was then he said she was mad like all the Magees, lying about the house from the day they married never did a hand's turn why wouldn't he go to the pubs she had never made a dinner for him in his life?

Something else broke crockery or something and then ma was crying: Don't blame me because you can't face the

6

truth about yourself, any chances you had you drank them away!

It went on a long time I was just standing there listening to it all I knew I should have gone down but that's no use now is it I didn't did I? I didn't go down and that's that. I was trying to listen to the cars going by on the Newtown Road and saying to myself: I can't hear anything in the kitchen now it must be all over.

But it wasn't all over and when I stopped listening to the cars I'd hear him: God's curse the fucking day I ever set eyes on you!

The next day we got out of school early on account of the town winning the cup and when ma seen me at the back door she got all flustered and started making jokes and all this. Then she got her purse down off the window and says here Francie, there's sixpence – why don't you go on round to Mary's sweetshop and buy yourself a quarter of dolly mixtures? No ma I says, I won't buy dolly mixtures but I *will* buy two Flash Bars and a macaroon bar if I can can I? Of course you can she says. Now go on go on and her face was red and patchy and hot like she'd been sitting bent over the fire only there was no fire. It was a pity but Mary's was shut so I had to come back and tell ma. I wanted to see if I could still get keeping the sixpence. But when I tried to open the door it wouldn't. I knocked at the window but all I could hear was the tap sssss. Ma must be up the stairs I said whistling and rolling the tanner round in my hand wondering would I get the Flash Bars after all or maybe six cough-no-more black toffees. Then I heard a clatter I thought I'd better get in the window to see what that was I thought maybe Grouse Armstrong or someone was in stealing the sausages again but when I got into the kitchen who's there only ma standing there and a chair sideways on the table. What's that doing up there ma I says it was fuse wire belonging to da just dangling but she didn't say what it was doing there she was just stood there picking at her nail and going to say something and then not saying it. I told her Mary's was shut could I still keep the sixpence she said I could *Yee ha!* I said and bombed off out to the border shop to get six cough-no-mores but then when I got there I said two Flash Bars and a macaroon please. When I got back ma was doubled up in the chair by the dead fire for a minute I thought she was shivering with the cold but then she looked at me and said: You know you were only five pounds weight when you were born Francie.

It wasn't too long after that ma was took off to the garage. She says to me: I'm away off up the town now Francie I have to get the baking started for your Uncle Alo's Christmas party. Right, I says, I'll just stay here and watch the telly and off she went I didn't notice the time passing until I heard Mrs Connolly at the door with da and some other women she said ma'd been standing for two hours looking in the window of the fishing tackle shop with the bag on the ground and a tin of beans rolling round the footpath. Da was flushed and when the women said they'd have to see about a nightdress he got even more flushed then Mrs Connolly said never mind Benny I'll look after it and she tapped him on the shoulder like a mother then hoisted her skirts and went off upstairs singing. He went out into the scullery then

8

I could hear him swigging whiskey in under his coat. He was waiting for them to call out through a megaphone: *Don't move! Stay right where you are! Put the whiskey down nice and easy and don't try any tricks!* A few more women came in and stood whispering by the fire. I could see Mrs Connolly pulling the zipper of her housecoat up and down going terrible terrible but I didn't care. *Take 'em to Missouri!* said John Wayne and *hee-yah!* he rode off in a thunder of hooves. They hung around for a while talking about this and that, stuff they thought da might like to hear, about the town band and the way the government was ruining the country but he wasn't any more interested than they were, he just kept on nodding he'd have nodded no matter what they said. If they had said wasn't it terrible about Mrs Lavery's daughter being eaten by wolves on the Diamond he'd have nodded and said yes indeed it was. Mrs Connolly said well I'd best be off now I've left his dinner on the stove and you know what men are like if you don't look after them. Oh now, they said, and gave her a shove, who are you telling, at least your fellow eats mine will eat nothing I give him. Oh they're a terror the men, a terror now to the living world. All was left of John was a cloud of dust and the desert pocked with hoofmarks. I've a bit of business to do said da, you'll be all right, and handed me two bob. Then off he went to see about his business Tower Bar business that is. I didn't know anything about ma and all this but Joe filled me in. I heard Mrs Connolly saying breakdown what's breakdown Joe. I says, Oh that's when you're took off to the garage, Joe told me, its when the truck comes and tows you away. That was a good one I thought, ma towed away off up the street with her coat on. Who's that, they'd say. Oh that's Mrs Brady they're taking her off to the garage.

Joe said there was some crack in this town and there sure was. Hand me down the spanner I think Mrs Brady's ankle needs tightening. Oh now, I said, what a laugh.

There was some good laughs in them days, me and Joe at the river with our noses in the water, hanging over the edge. You could see the dartboard eyes and the *what do you want me to do* faces of the fish. Hey fish, Joe would say, fish? Fuck off! What do you think of that, fish? we'd say.

Then we'd go off on our travels.

It was all going well until the telly went. Phut!

That was that then, a blank grey screen looking back at you. I fiddled with it but all I got was a blizzard of snow so I sat there looking at that in the hope that something would come on but it didn't and there was still nothing when da came home. How did it happen he says and I told him. I was just sitting there the next thing – out like a light. He pulled off his greatcoat and it fell on the floor. Right, he says, all business, let's have a look at this now. He was humming away to himself happy as Larry about it all. Then he says you know there's not as much into these televisions as the likes of Mickey Traynor makes out. He had bought it off Mickey Traynor the holy telly man that was because he sold holy pictures on the side. He fiddled about with it for a while but nothing happened then he shifted it over by the window and said it could be the aerial but it only got worse there. He hit it a thump and then what happened even the snow went. After that he started to rant and rave about Mickey. He said he might have known better than to trust the likes of Traynor, him and his holy pictures don't fool me. He'll not sell me a dud television and get away with it. He'll not pull any of his foxy stunts on Benny Brady. I'm up to the likes of Mickey Traynor make no mistake. He smacked it with his hand. *Work!* he shouted. Look at it – I should have known it'd be no good. Work! How long have we got? Six months that's how long we have it, bought and paid for with my hard-earned money. But I'll tell you this – Traynor will give me back every cent I paid him every cent by Christ he will!

He drew out and put his boot through it, the glass went everywhere. I'll fix it, he said, I'll fix it good and fucking proper.

Then he fell asleep on the sofa with one shoe hanging off.

There wasn't much I could do then I got fed up watching the birds hop along the garden wall so I went off up the street. I said to myself well that's the end of John Wayne I knew it'd lie there glass and all and nobody would ever bother coming to fix it. Ah well, I said sure Joe can always tell me what happens and it was when I was thinking that I saw Philip and Mrs Nugent coming. I knew she thought I was going to turn back when I saw them. She leaned over and said something to Philip. I knew what she was saying but I don't think she knew I knew. She crinkled up her nose and said in a dead whisper: *Just stands there on the landing and lets the father*

*do what he likes to her. You'd never do the like of that would
you Philip? You'd always stand by me wouldn't you?*

Philip nodded and smiled. She smiled happily and then it
twisted a bit and the hand went up again as she said: *Of
course you know what she was doing with the fuse wire
don't you Philip?*

She thought I was going to turn back all red when she
said that but I didn't. I just kept on walking. Ah there you
are Mrs Nugent I says with a big grin, and Philip. She looked
right through me and it was one of those looks that is supposed to make you shrivel up and die but it only made me
grin even more. I was standing in the middle of the footpath.
Mrs Nugent held on to her hat with one hand and took
Philip with the other would you let me by please she says.

Oh no I can't do that I said, you have to pay to get past.
She had all these broken nerve ends on her nose and her
eyebrows went away up nearly meeting her hair what do you
mean what on earth do you mean she said and I could see
Philip frowning with his Mr Professor face wondering was it
serious maybe, maybe something he could investigate or do
a project on. Well he could if he wanted I didn't care as long
as he paid. It was called the Pig Toll Tax. Yes, Mrs Nugent I
said, the pig toll tax it is and every time you want to get past
it costs a shilling. Her lips got so thin you really would think
they were drawn with a pencil and the skin on her forehead
was so tight I thought maybe the bones were going to burst
out. But they didn't and I says to Philip I'll tell you what
Philip you can have half. So what's that then one shilling for
Mrs Nooge, I said, and sixpence for Philip. I don't know why

12

I called her Mrs Nooge, it just came into my head. I thought it was a good thing to call her but she didn't. She got as red as a beetroot then. Yup, I said again, ya gotta pay the old tax Mrs Nooge, and I stood there with my thumbs hooked in my braces like a Western old timer. She got all heated up then oh yes hot and bothered. Philip didn't know what to do he had given up the idea of investigating the pig toll tax I think he just wanted to get away altogether but I couldn't allow that until the pig toll tax was paid, that was the rules of pig land I told them. I'm sorry I said like they always do when they're asking you for money, if you ask me its far too much but that's the way it is I'm afraid. It has to be collected *someone has to do it ha ha*. She tried to push her way past then but I got a grip of her by the sleeve of her coat and it made it all awkward for her she couldn't see what was holding her back. Her hat had tilted sideways and there was a lemon hanging down over the brim. She tried to pull away but I had a good tight hold of the sleeve and she couldn't manage it.

Durn taxes, I said, ain't fair on folks. When I looked again there was a tear in her eye but she wouldn't please me to let it out. When I saw that I let go of her sleeve and smiled. Right, I says, I'll tell you what, I'll let you by this time folks but remember now in future – make sure and have the pig toll tax ready. I stood there staring after them, she was walking faster than Philip trying to fix the lemon at the same time telling him to come on. When they were passing the cinema I shouted I ain't foolin' Mrs Nooge but I don't know if she heard me or not. The last thing I saw was Philip turning to look back but she pulled him on ahead.

––––

A fellow went by and I says to him do you know what its a bad state of affairs when people won't pay a tax to get by. Who are you he says. Brady I said.

He was wheeling a black bike with a coat thrown over the handlebars. He stopped and rested it against a pole then dug deep in the pocket of his trousers and produced a pipe and a tin of tobacco. Brady? he says, would that be Brady of the Terrace? That's right I says. O, he says, I see. You see what, I said. Your father was a great man one time, he says. He was one of the best musicians ever was in this town. He went to see Eddie Calvert, he says then. I said I wanted to hear no more about Eddie Calvert. You don't like music, he says, do you think the town will win again Saturday? I told him I wanted to hear nothing about football either. You don't think its a great thing the town won the cup? he says. No, I says. I said it was a pity they didn't lose. I see, he says, well what's this tax you're talking about, you seem to care about that. He was all on for a discussion about the government and the way things had gone. There was a smell of turf fires and buttermilk off him. He tapped the bowl of his pipe against his thigh and he says which tax would this be now.

He thought it was some outrageous tax the government had brought in and he was about to say its time they quit or they have the country destroyed when I said ah no its not the government at all. It was invented by me, and its only the people I say.

And who are you, he says.

Francie Pig the Toll Tax Man, I says and he shook his head and tapped the pipe again, that's a good laugh he says.

Laugh, I said, I don't know where you get the idea its a good laugh. Then he said tsk tsk and you're an awful man altogether. He puffed on the pipe. Pig Toll Tax, he says, that's the first time I ever heard that now. He kept opening and closing his mouth over the brown stem like a fish smoking. Oh you needn't worry your head about it I said, it has nothing to do with you. What it really should have been called was The Mrs Nugent and Nobody Else At All Tax but I didn't tell him that. I see he says well in that case I'll be on my way.

His index finger jumped off his forehead *gluck now* he said and away off up the town with the bike sideways and the wheels ticking.

I went into the shop. The whine of the bacon slicer and the shopgirl licking a pencil stub racing up and down a wobbly tower of numbers on the back of a paper bag. The women were standing over by the cornflakes saying things have got very dear. Its very hard to manage now oh it is indeed do you know how much I paid for Peter's shoes above in the shop. When they seen me coming they all stopped talking. One of them moved back and bumped against the display case. There you are ladies I said and they all went right back on their heels at the same time. What's this? I says, the woman with three heads? When I said that they weren't so bad. Flick – back come the smiles. Ah Francie, they said, there you are. Here I am I said. They leaned right over to me and in a soft top secret voice said how's your mother Francie? Oh I says she's flying she's above in the garage and it won't be long now before she's home, They're going to give her a service I says, hand me down the spanner Mike! Ha, ha, they laughed, that was a good one. Yup, says I, she has to come home shortly now to get the baking done for Uncle Alo's party.

So your Uncle Alo's coming home! they said. Christmas Eve I said, all the way from London. Would you credit that now says Mrs Connolly with a warm little shiver, and will he be staying long? Two weeks says I. Two weeks she says and smiled I was going to say do you not believe me or something Mrs Connolly but I didn't I had enough on my plate with Mrs Nugent without Connolly starting. He did well in London, Francie, your Uncle Alo, says the other woman. Then they all started it. Oh he did well surely he did indeed, a great big job and more luck to him its not easy in these big places like London. It is not! Mrs Connolly'd say and then someone else would say the same thing over again. It was like The History of Alo programme. But I didn't mind. I said now you're talking and all this. Mrs Connolly said: I saw him the last time he was home with a lovely red hankie in his breast pocket and a beautiful blue suit.

I seen him too, he was like someone in the government or something.

He was indeed. It takes the Bradys, they said.

Every time, I said.

Good man Francie, said the women.

I'll tell Alo to call down and see you when he comes home, I said, you can have a chat with him about London and all.

Do that Francie, they said. I will indeed, I said. Then I said well ladies I'm afraid I can't stay here I have to be off on my travels.

Dear dear aren't you a ticket Francie? they said.

I'm away off up the town on business to do with the toll tax.

Toll tax? I never heard tell of that now Francie. What would that be?

Oh its invented by me, I told them. But of course Nugent won't pay it. You might as well be trying to get blood out of a stone.

Nugent? says Mrs Connolly, *Mrs* Nugent?

Yes I said. Well, be it on her own head. She won't be getting by so handy the next time.

They were all ears when they heard it was to do with her.

Getting by? But getting by *where*, Francie, they kept saying.

On the footpath I said where do you think, where else would you want to get past?

The footpath? they said.

Yes, I said again, *the footpath*. You'd think the three of them had gone handicapped all of a sudden the way they were staring at me.

I could see Mrs Connolly fiddling with her brooch and saying something out of the side of her mouth.

Then she said: There's no denying it Francie, you're a rare character!

The other two were hiding behind her now I think they must have thought I was going to stick them for a few bob tax as well.

Oh now I said and off I went out the door as I went by the window I could see Mrs Connolly saying something and the other women nodding then raising their eyes to heaven.

I stood on the Diamond. A tractor went farting off home to the mountains with a trailer of muck. Who's this only Father Dominic swish swish and the creak of his polished shoes well

17

Francis he says and how are you today, drrrumm drrrumm. By God Father that's a cold one I said rubbing the hands real bogman style, Hmm, he says, it is indeed, are you waiting for someone?

No, I said, I have a bit of business to do.

Business he says, what business would that be now?

I knew what he'd say if I told him about the Pig Toll Tax. Toll Tax hmm that's very interesting now yes we'll have to see if we can put a stop to that so I told him nothing. I'm waiting for Joe Purcell, I said but I wasn't Joe was away at his uncle's.

Ah I see, says Father Dom with his two thumbs like dwarfs doing an old-time waltz in and out of his little black buttons.

How's your father? he says.

The best, I says, never better.

Good good, he says, and your mother will be home soon? She will. She'll be back on the road by Christmas.

Christmas, why that's wonderful news, he says.

Yes, I said, Alo's coming home.

He wanted to hear all about Alo.

Alo, he says. You must be proud.

I am, I said.

Christmas Eve you say.

That's right, I said.

Well with a bit of luck I'll run into your Uncle Alo. This town should be proud of him. Your mother was telling me all about him and the great job he has over in London.

Ten men under him, I said. Then he smiled at me and looked me up and down. When he was ready to leave he leaned right in towards me so I could see the wiry brown hairs up his nostrils like the inside of a mattress and he says would you not run on home now Francis like a good lad, mm?

The way he said it sounded like he was nearly going to give me a few bob if I did. I should have said yes indeed I will Father if you will just be so kind as to oblige me with a small fee of five shillings Going Home Tax. But I didn't. I just said sure Father I will indeed. But I didn't. I went off down the street and as soon as I seen him going into the presbytery I hopskipped back round by the Newtown Road. There was a drunk lad with a ripped coat lying in the doorway of the Tower singing *I wonder who's kissing her now* into a bottle. Then he'd quit for a while and say: *Uh! Uh!* for a while with his head nodding like a cloth doll you'd see in the back of a car. He shouted over at me: *Do you know me do you, do you know me?* I just stood there looking at him. I didn't want to go home and I didn't want to stand there. He kept on saying it with the eyes wild in his head do you know me do you? It was getting dark and when I looked up there was one of them moons you're not sure if its there or not and the first dusty flakes of snow were starting to fall. We're early this year they said but sure all the better. That's right I said as I caught one of them on my tongue and licked it.

Fuck me said Joe the face of that, it was a monkey banging a drum in the window of the fancy goods shop with a chin bigger than its head. Farmers drove off to the mountains with big blonde dolls saying *mama* roped to the roof racks. Tyretracks of slush webbed the streets and there was music all night long in the upstairs of the Tower. Someone was battering Nat King Cole to death and an accordion wheezing help! half strangled. There were children and a dog on the white fairgreen and the town band marched again on its fourth lap of the town as if it was condemned to wander for all eternity until all the tunes came right. It was a powder country, ice floes bobbing on the freezing water of the river.

What will youse do now fish, said Joe, youse have had it now!

We stuck our noses in it but there wasn't a dartboard eye to be seen. Sorry: Gone away, signed Fish. Our twin fishing poles sat there for days without being touched.

Back from the garage there was no holding ma, talking nineteen to the dozen whiz here one minute, there the next, it wasn't just the floor you could see your face in but everything. One minute she was up the stairs and the next she'd be standing right beside you talking then away off into something else. She said we'd never be run down in this town again we'd show them we were as good as any of them. She looked into my eyes and said: We don't want to be like the Nugents. We don't want to be like any of them! We'll show them – won't we Francie? They'll envy us yet! We're the Bradys. Francie! The Bradys!

I said we sure were. I was proud as punch. Everything was starting again and this time it was all going to work out right. Look look she says to me look what I bought she says its a record the best record in the world. I'll bet you never heard a record as good as this Francie she says. What's it called ma I says its called The Butcher Boy she says come on and we'll dance. She put it on hiss crackle and away it went. Whee off we went around the room ma knew the words inside out. The more she'd sing the redder her face'd get. We'll stop now ma I said but away we went again.

> I wish my baby it was born
> And smiling on its daddy's knee
> And me poor girl to be dead and gone
> With the long green grass growing over me.
>
> He went upstairs and the door he broke
> He found her hanging from a rope
> He took his knife and he cut her down
> And in her pocket these words he found
>
> Oh make my grave large wide and deep
> Put a marble stone at my head and feet
> And in the middle a turtle dove
> That the world may know I died for love.

It was a good song but I didn't know what was going on in it. When it was over she says what do you think of that Francie – *he went upstairs and the door he broke he found her hanging from a rope!* He wasn't so smart then the butcher boy was he. She starts telling me all about it but I didn't want to hear any more. Then whiz away she goes out to the scullery singing some other song oh no she says them days are over that's all in the past. There's no one will let Annie Brady down again Francie!

She'd leave the record off for a while then she'd go in and put it on again. Anytime you'd come in, from school or anything, it would be on. And ma singing away out in the scullery.

———

21

After all this her new name should have been Ma Whiz. One minute she'd say I see Mrs Connolly has a lovely new coat then before you had time to answer she said are they turning off the town water or something about the hospital when I was born. Then off she'd go again rolling pastry and stacking butterfly buns on tray after tray.

The house was full of cakes.

Full of cakes for Uncle Alo, I said.

That's right she says, Alo loves cakes. If that's one thing your Uncle loves its cake.

And butterfly buns, I said.

You're right, she said, I'll make some more.

It got so bad you nearly had to tunnel your way into the house with all the cakes. A few times I knew da was about to say: *Stop singing that cursed song!* But he didn't in case whiz she'd be off to the garage again. He just went off to the Tower instead and didn't come back till after closing time.

I saw Philip Nugent on his way to music with his crocodile-skin music case. He stopped outside the home bakery and waited there for a minute. Then she came out and I saw her looking towards me. She handed Philip a white cardboard box the kind they used for the cakes. She was handing it to him real slow. Poor old Nugent – she really thought I cared about her and her cake. I had to laugh. Us with enough cakes to feed an army!

It seemed like years and years ago I had cared about anything to do with Nugent. I didn't even bother going near them. I just turned on my heel and off I went, still laughing.

Mrs Nugent would have a long wait before she ever caught me worrying about the likes of her again.

Ten men under him, I said to Joe.

Joe whistled and sent a flat stone skimming down the river.

Ten, he said, ten whole men. That's hard to beat Francie.

There's going to be some party in our house that night Joe, says I.

The Alo party, says Joe.

The party to end them all, I said.

Whee-hoo! cried Joe and a big shower of spiky sunlight arrows coming through the gaps in the trees when you chinked your eyes.

The nights before Alo came I didn't sleep a wink thinking about him. We'd be coming down the street and there'd be Nugent. She'd be mad for us to talk to her. Who's that woman Alo would say to me in his English accent, she keeps looking over. I don't know, I'd say, I never seen her before in my life. Then we'd walk on until she was a speck standing in Fermanagh Street. Then it started all over again with me and Alo on the Diamond getting ready to set off once more down the street and Mrs Nugent trying to attract our attention. Please Francie, I'll give you anything she'd say. Sorry I'd say, too late. Then I'd cut her off and say: What was that you were saying Uncle Alo?

The town was quiet after the bars closed. All you could hear was Grouse Armstrong howling away.

You know what he's saying when he does that says Joe.

No, I says, what.

How the fuck do I know I don't know dog language says Joe.

I could hear voices. There was someone outside the hide. It was Buttsy from the mountains. Mrs Nugent was his sister. He was in a bad way poor old Buttsy. He looked like a priest on the cover of Africa magazine with his freckles and the carrot hair falling down over his eyes. Peepil please help me build my hospital. But all Buttsy cared about hospitals now was putting me into one. He kept shouting out: *Brady!* Then he'd light a fag and I could see his hand was shaking. Devlin kept saying to him: Don't worry Buttsy we'll find him he can't have gone far. He had a pain in his head I could tell from the way he kept rubbing over his eye. Soon, says Devlin, we'll have him and we can do what we like with him. The whole town wants him to get what he deserves. If we get our hands on him before the police I know what we'll do with him, we'll drown him Buttsy what about that? Devlin said. But Buttsy had more sense. He knew they were only wasting their time if they hadn't found me by now they weren't going to, them or the police. He just sat there by the river with his elbow on his knee and an inch of ash hanging from the fag. The bastard must have come out this way, Devlin said, poking about in the bushes with a stick. *Hey Brady!* he called again. It triple-echoed across the mountains. *If you're in them woods Brady you better come out.* But it was no use so in the end they just went back towards the town.

———

When they were gone I came out and stuck my face into the river. Hey fish I said are you there? Yoo-hoo!

Come out you bastards!

The cakes were stacked in towers on the chairs. There were some on top of the wardrobe and the washing machine. There were ones with icing and without, all decorated with hundreds and thousands and marzipan and different kinds of designs. I had a hard job keeping all the flies away. I went at them with the rolled-up Irish Press. Back, dogs! I said. I had to make sure they didn't manage to land on the icing at all because if they did you couldn't hit them in case you'd break up the cake altogether. Would you like another slice of cake Francis? said ma from the scullery. I didn't. I had already had eight. I went off up the town and anybody I met I told them about Alo. Then I came back down again: Any sign of him yet? Whiz away off again. It was the best time in the town for a long while. The breadman skipped into the shop with a tray of fresh loaves wrapped in holly paper. Children tossed pebbles and watched them ping off the fountain's big white crocus of ice. Please give a little it could help a lot the radio said. When I got home ma was wearing white gloves of flour and rolling more pastry just in case we run out she said. Then the car pulled up outside and in they came, Mary from the sweetshop and everybody popping corks and dusting snow off collars. I couldn't take my eyes off Alo. Sure enough he had the red hankie in his breast pocket and the trousers of his blue pinstripe suit had a crease would cut your hand. His steelgrey hair was neatly combed in two neat wings behind his ears. He stood proudly by the fireplace and I thought to myself Nugent? Hah! Nugent has *nobody* like him. I felt like cheering. Welcome to the cake house said ma, that's what you call this place, wiping her hands on her apron. Call it what you like, home I call it smiled Alo and gave her a big hug. Da was late but the party started anyway. Here's to Christmas and all in this room, he beamed and raised his whiskey glass.

Now you said it Alo, they said, to the man himself, Alo Brady.

Ah yes, says Alo, yes indeed and swirled the whiskey in his glass.

Where does the time go, where does it go at all?

Twenty years in Camden Town this winter, would you believe it?

You'll never come back now Alo.

Come back? What'd take him back, am I right Alo? He has it far too good over there.

Ten men under him, called ma from the scullery.

God bless all here said Alo and long may they prosper.

I still couldn't stop looking at him, the gold tiepin and his polished nails, the English voice. Nugent's was only half-English. The more you thought it the harder it was to believe that Nugent had ever been anything worth talking about. Ah yes, he went on, I'll never forget it. Euston Station, London town!

A big spot Alo, you were a long way from the town then!

Nothing only my coat and case, what have I let myself in for I said.

The streets of Piccadilly, Alo!

Now you said it. Spent the night in the YMCA. Don't talk to me!

All corners of the earth, he says!

Now you said it!

Well would you credit that!

Boys oh boys.

Twenty years to the day, he says!

Well you're here now so here's to your health and all in this room!

Cheers they said and I heard the front door click closed and then da was there they hardly noticed him at all. His eyes were small like ball bearings he just moved along the edges getting drink and saying nothing. Then they said there you are Benny and started back into the old days.

Oh if only Pete was here now.

One of the best characters in the town poor Pete.

Music? There wasn't a song he didn't know.

Don't sit under the apple tree with anyone else but me!

That was his!

To go so early, who'd have thought it?

The Good Lord, he does his harvesting and he forgets no one!

Bing! Could he sing Bing! Dear Hearts and Gentle People!

No better man to sing it!

Please God he's happy where he is now!

Alo's eyes were brightly lit what about a song he says and off we went to the sitting room. He angled his elbow on the piano and when they sang *White Christmas* you could hear him above everybody else as he put his whole heart into it. You could see the veins in his forehead as he strained for the high notes. When the song was over they lapsed into silence and their eyes glazed over.

Mary, they said, you never played better.

Oh now, says Mary, I haven't played in years.

Since Alo went away, they laughed.

Go easy on the girl or she'll play none!

Alo sang *Tyrone Among the Bushes*. Sweat spread a dark stain on his back. He raised his glass and took a bow.

You never lost it Alo, they cried, Tyrone Among the Bushes you'll not top that!

Who's next for shaving!

Then there were recitations, Dangerous Dan McGrew and Sam McGee mush mush in the Arctic snow.

By God its better than a play!

Now who, I ask you, needs the West End after that! Am I right Alo?

Now you're talking! laughed Alo.

Ma arrived with a silver teapot and on the plate a castle of butterfly buns with its turrets ready to topple.

Who's for a few buns she said or maybe you'd like some cake? I'll go and get some. I have plenty of slices cut.

No this is grand we're well fed here sit down and rest yourself never mind us!

We're an awful crowd!

Alo stood behind Mary with his hands placed on her shoulders and sang *When you were sweet sixteen*.

The clapping went on for over a minute and she didn't know where to look.

You shouldn't she said.

Alo's face was red as a beetroot and his eyes were wild.

He laughed and then went down on his hunkers, half-crouched and ready to leap an abyss. I could see him checking all the faces in the room and then when he was satisfied that everything was all right he let out a kind of a growl and out of nowhere grips her by the arm. It took her completely by surprise and she nearly fell off her stool.

And why shouldn't I me darling?

He fell into her lap and his legs swung out and up into the air.

Ma squealed and everybody cheered.

We may get the priest! they cried.

Just for a split second I thought Mary was going to throw her arms around Alo and burst into tears. She kept biting her nail and her lip was trembling just like a kid when it falls and everybody's asking are you all right are you all right?

But she didn't burst into any tears. When the laughter had died away, Alo struggled to right himself with one hand and straighten his tie with the other. As he got up his fingers lightly brushed against her cheek and she bent her head. Then someone went to say something but didn't say it. After that there was silence but Alo didn't want silence. He rushed over and poured himself a fresh drink. He called for another song.

What about the Inspector of Drains from the County Leitrim? The man himself – Percy French!

Mary hunched herself up over the keyboard so that no one would see her hands were shaking. The flies were at the cakes again and there were crumbs all over the floor where Alo's elbow had knocked a plate. But no one even noticed. There was a spot of butterfly bun cream on the triangle top of his red hankie. It was well past two and everybody was singing different songs. Would you look at the time someone said and a long low whistle glided across the room.

We'll never make Mass in the morning.

Time we were moving so, they said.

You'll stay another while, please! said Alo.

There'll be more nights, they said, man dear but it was great to see you Alo!

Let me, said ma, and went to the hall for their coats.

Well there you are, said da, standing in the doorway and smoothing his hair back from his forehead with the edge of his hand.

Now we're right, they said, or right as we'll ever be!

Alo shook hands and said goodbye. He didn't want to let go their hands when they made to go off to the car he was still holding on. They called from the car Please God it won't be so long the next time!

Mary tried to look away but a magnet pulled her eyes back until they met Alo's. He reached out to touch her on the shoulder then retracted it again like a shoplifter losing his nerve at the last minute. He didn't know what to do then so he just stood there. He was standing almost on his tiptoes. If it had been earlier they all might have whistled or hummed to get rid of the silence. Now all they did was jingle coins and fasten overcoat buttons, they couldn't think of anything else to do. Mary's lips parted to speak. I knew what she was going to say. She was going to say *it was lovely to see you* but that was exactly what Alo said and the sentences collided in mid-air. Mary tried to start again. So did Alo. Then Alo went pale and leaned forward. He kissed her softly on the hair and when she looked again he was gone. He was back inside with the whiskey bottle. Da muttered something under his breath I don't know what and the ball bearing eyes were cold steel in his head. The chickenhouse fan was droning away, the hens as happy as Larry inside their warm woodchip world of burbling beaks and swooshing seed. It was like they were saying: Well we're all right. You won't find us worrying! We're too busy burbling and waiting for our dinner!

Mary was already in the car I don't know whether she was crying or what all I could see was these blurred faces leaning over to her in the back seat.

Things get to her, said da, her time of life its not easy for a woman, you'd think he'd have more wit a man of his age.

He said it under his breath but I knew he was talking about Alo. Ma said nothing, pretended she didn't hear it but she must have because he was looking right at her when he said it.

The engine chugged into life. The car took the corner by the ash pit out onto the main road, and everything settled back into silent white.

Da just stood there like he was in some kind of a trance. He kept flicking his thumb against his forefinger. I wanted to say to him stop it, quit doing that. That was the best night ever, I said.

Its time you were in your bed, he said.

Inside Alo had opened another bottle of whiskey. He hesitated staring at the silver curls of the torn label in the palm of his hand. Da said I could sleep on the sofa so I lay there with my eyes closed but there was too much going on to sleep, it was like a firework display of all the things they had been saying. Shadows ate up the room. One last song, said Alo, and a nightcap to wind it up, what do you say Benny?

No more singing. There's been plenty of singing.

Ah now Benny, laughed Alo, don't be like that. A wee bit of singing never hurt anyone, am I right Mrs?

He started into The Old Bog Road, he said that was the one the priest had taught them in the home all those years ago. I knew as soon as he had said the word *home* that he regretted it. When you said it even when you weren't talking about orphanages, da went pale sometimes he even got up and left the room. Alo tried to cover it up by saying Will you ever forget the time we robbed the presbytery orchard?

He laughed. Then he laughed again. But it was all wrong. It was like the moment before a cracked glass shatters. When da didn't answer, he just kept on asking all sorts of questions.

He told more stories then more singing. He was singing at the top of his voice. It was the silence around da that made me ice all over. Then ma wept. He paid no heed to that either, just sat there behind a glass wall of silence. Alo had his back to the fireplace like he had when he came in first. He kept waiting for da to speak. He wanted him to speak more than anything in the world. But da would only speak when he was ready. Then I saw him look at Alo. I knew the look. He wouldn't take his eyes off him now until he had finished with him. I saw him do it to ma. They could pierce you them eyes good as any blade. Then he said it. Who do you think you're fooling Alo? Are you going to go on making a laughing stock of yourself or are you going to catch yourself on? Do you think any of them believe that shite-talk you've been going on with all night?

For the love of God Benny leave the man alone, cried ma.

Coming home here crowing about Camden Town, do you want to have us the laughing stock of the place?

Look at him with his wee red handkerchief. Did the wife iron it for you?

Not again ma cried not again please Benny!

I warned him! I told him I wanted to hear no more of it! But no, we had to have it, then on top of that carrying on with her like a schoolboy halfwit. The whole town knows that too, made a cod of himself with her. Never even had the guts to ask her out straight till it was too late. Oh Camden Town's a great place Alo, we all know that. Camden Town's the place he met the only woman he ever laid a finger on. Took her to the altar because he was afraid to ask anyone else. Twenty years his senior for the love of God. Half-blind and hates him from the day she married him!

I knew ma wanted to hold it in she didn't want any of that to start now I knew what she was afraid of she was afraid of the garage. But she didn't want to let Alo down, she would never let anyone down. She had to say it. Dear God I'm sorry Alo, she said.

But da wasn't finished yet. I knew he wasn't near finished but I just lay there and didn't say anything that's all I did I just lay there with my eyes closed pretending I was asleep.

Ten men under him, said da, that's right. Closing a gate in a backstreet factory that's what he's been at from the day he landed there, tipping his cap to his betters in his wee blue porter's suit. Oh Alo went far, make no mistake!

Ma touched Alo on the forearm he looked like a child who had soiled his trousers.

There was sweat on da's upper lip it shone like needles. He said: He was always the same, from the minute we were dumped in that Belfast kip. The same softie halfwit, sucking up to the nuns and moping about the corridors. You know what he used to tell them? Our da's coming to take us home tomorrow! Night noon and morning I had to listen to it! You'd be waiting a long time if you were to wait for Andy Brady to come and take you home! I told him to shut up! What did we care I said we'd manage on our own we needed nobody. I told him it was all over. But he wouldn't listen! Couldn't be shut up, him and his mouthing! And the rest of them taking a hand out of him every chance they got!

Ma cried out. I never seen her face da before. Don't blame it on your brother because you were put in a home! Christ Jesus Benny are you never going to come to terms with it! After all this time, is it never going to end?

The side of Alo's face jerked and for a second it seemed as if he was on the verge of saying something really daft like: Do you think it will rain? Or *Where did you get that tablecloth?*

He didn't though. What he said was: Its getting late. Maybe I'm as well get to my bed.

Then he said: I'll hardly see you before I go.

He asked ma did the bus still go from the corner. She said it did.

Da had a whiskey glass in his hand. It was trembling a little. I thought maybe he wanted to fling it from him, throw his arms around Alo and cry at the top of his voice: How about that Alo? Fairly fooled you there! That took you in hook line and sinker! Me and Alo – the years we spent in Belfast! The home? A wonderful place! The best years of our lives! Me and Alo – we loved every minute of it in there! Isn't that right old friend?

When all this came into my head I wanted to leap up and yahoo. I wanted to cry out let's have another party I'll go and get Mary and the whole thing can go right this time what do you say to that Alo is that a good idea?

But that was only me raving and didn't happen and the next thing I heard was the sound of the front door closing, you could hardly hear it at all. Ma was in a bad way now. It destroyed you that place, can't you see that? she said. You can't even talk about it, can you? Not even after all this time! Its no shame Benny that you were put in there! And even if it was, no shame should make you turn on your own brother like a dog!

He didn't like that and he turned on her then. He said at least he never had to be took off to a madhouse to disgrace the whole family. I knew then ma was never in any garage but I knew all along anyway, I knew it was a madhouse I just didn't want Nugent or anyone to hear so I said it was a garage. But then I knew too that Nugent knew all about it Mrs Connolly and the women would have told her. So I don't know what I bothered saying anything about a garage for at all. I could hear Nugent saying: Imagine him thinking he could pull the wool over my eyes!

When da said that she ran out of the room and I didn't know what to do. Da was laughing to himself he said what did he care? He clutched the whiskey glass like a weapon and poured himself another. He stood in the middle of the kitchen.

I've always gone my own way, he shouted. Everything I ever did, my way – father or no father! No thanks to Andy Brady or anyone else! Do you hear me?

He just stood there waiting for another argument to start. That was what he wanted but there was no one there to start it with. Then when it didn't happen he didn't know what to do. He just stood there holding the glass swaying, like a drugged giant in the middle of the room. *You hear me?* he roared again and some of the whiskey spilt down his trouser leg. He watched it dribble until it reached the floor parting into twin rivers on the lino. It went right across as far as the bottom of the door. He kept looking at it as if there was some hidden meaning in the pattern it was making. Then he started crying, his whole body shuddering with each sob.

I waited until he was asleep in the armchair and then I opened the front door and went out into the morning.

I was afraid because I hadn't planned it and I had never run away from home before. I should have brought a bag or something. But I didn't. As soon as I got out the front door I just started walking. I wanted to walk and walk until the soles of my boots were worn out and I could walk no more.

I was like the boy on the back of a colouring book I had. His cheeks were fat red plums and he blew a puffjet of steam from his mouth as he walked up one side of the globe and back down the other. I had a name for him. I called him The Boy Who Could Walk For Ever and that was what I wanted to do now – become him once and for all.

I left the town far behind me and came out onto the open road. The white clouds floated across the clear blue glass of the sky. I kept thinking of da and Alo standing outside the gates of the home all those years ago. How many windows do you think are there says da. Seventy-five says Alo. I'd say at least a hundred says da. The priest brought them inside through long polished corridors. The assembly hall was crowded. They were all cheering for the two new boys. The priest cleared his throat and said quiet please. I would like you to meet our two new boys he said. Bernard and Alo. Bernard and Alo who? said all the other boys. The priest smiled and rubbed his soft hands together. I was waiting for him to say *Brady* and finish it. But he didn't say Brady. He said: *Pig*.

Every day I walked until it got dark. I slept under bushes and once in a tyre. I didn't know what day it was when I reached the city. I was exhausted so I leaned against the big sign. It read: WELCOME TO DUBLIN.

The buses were green as gooseberries and a stone pillar cut the sky. This is Dublin I says to a fellow yeah its Dublin where do you think it is for the love of Jaysus. I liked the way he said that and I tried to say it myself. Jay-zuss. Who's that over there I says to this woman and she looks at me with her mouth open. A big grey statue mouthing about something in the middle of the street and birds shiting all over his head. I thought it was the president but she told me it was Daniel O'Connell. I didn't know anything about him except he was something to do with the English and all that. The way they were going across that bridge you'd think someone had said: I'm sorry but we're going to let off an atomic bomb any minute now. Bicycles going by in dozens, tick tick tick. Where were they all going. If they were all going to work there was a lot of jobs in Dublin. It was eight o'clock in the morning. There was picture houses and everything. Over I went. The Corinthian Cinema written in unlit lights. What's going on here I said. The creatures were coming to take over the planet earth because their own was finished there was nothing left on it. The shaky writing said they came from beyond the stars bringing death and destruction. I'd have to go and see them aliens when it opened up. I went into a chip shop. There was a woman with bags and half a beard muttering to herself and spilling tea on the saucer. She said she hoped the communists won she said they're no worse than the rest of them. She looked over at me and told me she had two sons. And neither of them were any good she said. I wasn't listening to her. I was thinking about how I was going to get money to see the aliens. The girl says to me what would you like. I says chips. What have you been up to she says you look like you've been dragged backwards through a ditch. Oh just walking I says. You'll need a few extra chips so she says and gives me a big heap. I could see her counting money in behind the counter. Then off she'd go into the kitchen with the door swinging behind her I could hear her going on about dances. I wished the old woman would hurry up and get out, her and her sons and her bags. Soon as she waddled off I waited for the girl to go back into the kitchen. I was in behind the counter like a bullet and I stuffed any notes I could into my pocket. Then I ran like fuck. All the way down the street I kept thinking: Hunted from town to town for a crime he didn't commit – Francie Brady – The Fugitive!

Except for one thing – I did commit it. The first thing I did was I went into a sweetshop with bullseyes and the whole lot. There was a woman there with a chain on her glasses. What did she think – someone was going to try and steal the glasses off her face? Thirty Flash Bars I said. I put them all into my pockets and ate as many of them as I could.

There was a smell of stout and a big ship pulling into the dock. I wondered was it time for the aliens yet. How would it be? I went into the Gresham Hotel and ordered a slap-up feed. Who's going to pay for this? says the waiter licking his pencil hmm hmm. I am my man I said, Mr Algernon Carruthers. I seen that in one of Philip's comics. Algernon Carruthers always on these ships going around the world and eating big dinners. Certainly Master Carruthers he says. I knew what he thought that I was one of these boy million-aires. There was a woman smiling at me. Good day madam! I said. For fuck's sake!

I bought bubblegum cards and spread them all out on a park bench. I had Frankie Avalon, John Wayne, Elvis, and a load of other ones I don't know who they were. I took buses all over the place. Whiz, buses shooting by like arrows. This is some place, this Dublin I says. Then it was time for the aliens. I stocked up at the kiosk. Are you going to eat all this yourself says the man. Oh no I says, my brothers and sisters are inside the whole family ma and da too I said and I could see him looking after me I think he knew well there was no one else in there. Come on aliens youse bastards!, I was thinking as I pushed Maltesers into my mouth one after the other.

Tinny voice the mayor squared up to the alien leader and told him he'd never get away with it. Every army on earth will fight you he says. But the alien just laughed. He had a human body that he stole off some bogman of a farmer that gave him a lift but you knew by the twisted sneer that inside he was a fat green blob with tentacles like an octopus and his face all scales. Make no mistake he says we will control the world and neither you nor anyone else in this town will stop us. It was him saying *in this town* made me think of the women and Mrs Nugent they were always saying that. Mrs Nugent said: I'll tell you one thing our Philip wouldn't do it. No son worth his salt would do what he did, disown his own family.

She looked at the women and said: No matter what they are they're still his own flesh and blood!

Mrs Connolly sighed: Ah God love them its a pity of them. I seen her the other day and she was at her wits' end. As if she didn't have enough on her plate without him running away like that!

Now you said it Mrs.

It was pouring rain. I stood on a street corner staring at this sign. It was a big neon baldy man. He was bald when the sign wasn't flashing but when the sign flashed there he was with a big head of hair. It was a great sign. Why Go Bald? It said that over and over again in all different colours. I could have stayed watching it for ever. I heard a girl singing it was in a church so I went in. She was wearing a white dress and singing a song about gardens. I never heard singing like it. The notes of the piano were clear as spring water rolling down a rock and they made me think about Joe. The first time I met him was in the lane at the back of our house. We must have been four or five at the most. He was hunkered down at the big puddle beside the chickenhouse. It had been frozen over for weeks and he was hacking away at the ice with a bit of a stick. I stood looking at him for a while and then I said to him what would you do if you won a hundred million billion trillion dollars? He didn't look up, he just went on hacking. Then he told me what he'd do and that kept us going for a long time. That was the first time I met Joe Purcell.

There was a snowdrop on the ditch that day I remember because there was only one. It was one of those days when you can nearly hear every sound in the town as clear as the girl was singing now. They were the best days, them days with Joe. They were the best days I ever knew, before da and Nugent and all this started.

I sat there for a long time I don't know how long. Then the sacristan came and wheeled the piano away. When I looked again the girl in the white dress was gone. But if you listened carefully you could still hear the song, Down By The Salley Gardens that was what it was called. I wanted to sit there until all trace of it was gone. It was like I was floating inside the coloured shaft of evening sunlight that was streaming in through the window.

I knew that I would look back some day and wonder had I ever been there in that church or did I imagine it all?

That was the way I thought about those days in the lane with Joe maybe we had never lived them at all. The priest came down and put his hand on my shoulder. He says: Do I know you?

I says no. He says why are you crying my child?

I says I'm not crying I pulled away and went out into the street. I stayed by the canal. Rat, I said, fuck off!

I leaned over the quayside wall. The brown water was streaked with strips of orange and yellow. I don't know what made me do it ma, I said. An old fellow stopped and says to me are you all right you're shaking all over. Then ma smiled and said she understood, she knew it wasn't my fault. Come home Francie she said. I'm sorry ma, I said again then she said it again, come on home, I'm waiting for you.

I will ma I said I was glad it was all over now and I would never do it, anything like that ever again.

I still had some of the chip shop money left. The man behind the counter says: Well this one here is two and six and the one on the top shelf that's a little bit dearer but better quality you'd be getting a bargain there.

How much is it? I said.

Three shillings, he says.

It was like a slice of a tree cut out and a rhyme carved into the wood and decorated all around the edges with green shamrocks. At the bottom was an old woman in a red shawl rocking by the fireside.

We sell a lot of those says your man looking at me over his glasses.

I read it a good few times. *A Mother's love's a blessing no matter where you roam.*

I put it in my pocket and off I went. I don't know the name of the towns I passed through. I didn't care what they were called all I wanted to do now was get home I was sorry I had ever left but I would never do it again.

Grouse Armstrong was asleep under a tractor but he passed no remarks when he seen me crossing the Diamond. There wasn't many about they were all in having their tea. I could see the grey glow of the tellies in the living rooms. Outside the shop the Esso sign ee-aw whingeing away as usual. There was no sign of the drunk lad in the doorway of the Tower. He was probably inside asking people if they knew him. I kept feeling inside my pocket to check if the present was still there. I don't know how I thought I was going to lose it it was hardly going to jump out of my pocket but that's what I did anyway, kept checking it. I could feel the grooves of the letters with my fingers. I was so busy thinking about that that when I turned the hotel corner at first I didn't even realize it was Mrs Nugent standing there in front of me. I had bumped into her she nearly dropped her handbag but she didn't mind, she paid no attention to it at all. O Francis, she says, and what does she do only put her hand on my arm I didn't know what she was playing at. Then O Francis she says again isn't it a pity you missed the funeral and makes the sign of the cross. Funeral I says what funeral and looked around to see was there anyone else with her some trick she was playing but there was nothing only the empty street and Grouse limping past the railway gates. I was going to say what do you want Nugent what are you putting your hand on my arm for but I couldn't get a word in she was talking away nineteen to the dozen your mother this your mother that. She wouldn't shut up about ma. What would you know about ma I was going to say only what you did on her talking behind her back you shut your mouth Nugent. But I didn't get the chance she was talking so much if you didn't know you'd think I was her lifelong friend. Then what does she do only lean right into me she was so close I could see the wiry hairs on her chin and the pink make-up and powder on her cheeks. The smell of it turned my stomach. I could barely hear what she said she dropped her voice so low. She was staring at me to see what I would do. I did nothing. I tried not to look at the stringy mouth or smell the powder. I said to myself: Do nothing Francie. I felt the present inside my pocket and said: Its OK. Everything's OK now.

I stuck the corner of the wood into the palm of my hand. She smiled again and said goodbye then crossed the road with her shopping bag bundled under her arm. She stopped outside the grocery shop and stood there looking back at me. The back door was open and the sink was full of pilchard tins. Da ate pilchards when he went on a skite. The flies were buzzing round them. There was curdled milk and books thrown round all over the place and stuff pulled out of the cupboards the dogs must have been in. I don't know how long da was standing there staring at me. There were red circles round his eyes and I could smell him. *You*, was all he said. I didn't know what he meant. But he told me. He meant *you* did it, what happened to ma. I says what are you talking about what happened to ma.

O you didn't hear? he says with a bitter smile. Then he told me they had dredged the lake near the garage and found her at the bottom of it, and says I'm off up to the Tower I might be back and I might not.

I don't know what time it was when I went round to Nugent's backyard. There wasn't a sound across the town. There was a small lamp on inside and you could see into the kitchen. It was warm and glowing. There was a table with books and a pair of spectacles on it. The table was set for breakfast in the morning. They had a butter dish with a special knife, a bluestriped jug with matching cups, all these things they had. It was as if just by being the Nugents it all came together as if by magic not a thing out of place. I shinned up the drainpipe. There was a nightlight on in there the room was full of shadows. I think Mr Nugent must have been away. Sometimes he went away on business. Philip was sleeping in his mother's bed. His head was tilted back on the pillow with his mouth open. She was sleeping soundly her chest rising and falling as if to say there's no trouble at all in my dreams I have my son beside me and my dear husband will be home tomorrow. Philip's mouth was a small whistling o. If there was a word bubble coming out of his mouth I knew what would be written in it. I love my mother more than anything in the world and I'd never do anything in the world to hurt her. I love my parents and I love my happy home. I could read the comic on the table beside his bed. It said: Adam Eterno Time Lord.

I wouldn't have minded getting a read of that comic. But comics had caused enough trouble hadn't they?

I slid down the pipe and stood in the yard. The sky was scattered with stars. I knew one thing. As long as I walked the streets under them stars there'd be only one thing anyone could say about me and that was: I hope he's proud of himself now, the pig, after what he did on his poor mother.

I wasn't sure if Philip Nugent would be going to music that day but I waited at the corner for a while and sure enough there he was with his crocodile music case swinging it absent-mindedly against his knee the way he did. He broke into a trot soon as he seen me but I ran after him and called Philip there you are, I walked along beside him talking about all sorts of things. I told him I thought his music case was one of the nicest I'd ever seen. I'd say its one of the nicest in the town, I said. Philip said thanks but I knew he was trying to quicken his step without me noticing. I said again I'd say its one of the nicest in the town and then I stopped and gripped him by the arm. No, I said, it *is* the nicest in the town! He sort of grinned and half-laughed when I said that and his cheeks turned pink. Then he said he was glad I liked it. I thought for a minute and then I said Philip do you think I could have a look at it?

He wasn't sure what to say but I kept looking at him with my big bright hopeful eyes and then he said yes yes of course. He handed it to me and I closed my eyes and ran my hands along its polished flaky surface. It really was a good music case. Then I said about the books inside. What about them Philip? I said. Can I have a look at them? Yes of course he said. He kept glancing over his shoulder and twisting the pocket of his blazer. I took the books out. They were just like his comics not a speck on any of them. You'd think those books were brand new out of the shop. Woh boy, I said. There was an ass and cart going off into green mountains on the cover of one. *Emerald Gems of Ireland* it was called. I leafed through it. I know that one!, I shouted. My da sings it! *I dreamt that I dwelt in marble halls!* How about that Philip! Are there any other good ones in it? Philip – could you sing these? Will you teach me some of them? There's some good songs in here Philip and no mistake, I said. I closed the book and I said to him, Philip how much would this book be if you were to buy it new in the shop? He frowned and was about to say he didn't know that his mother bought it for him but before he did I said yes but how much would you *say?*

He thought for a while and then he said two pounds. That's dear I said but its well worth it. I talked a bit more about the books and then I handed them back to him. The best books in the town – easy! I said. Then we walked on another bit, still talking about music. I told him da had plenty of records. I said he had hundreds, because he had. Do youse ever buy records, Philip, I said. He said they did. Who buys them, I asked and he said his da. Does your mother not buy any? I said. He shook his head and said no. When it came to records it was his da did all the buying because it was mostly him was interested in them. Oh, I said, and then I said I'll bet your ma never bought a record called The Butcher Boy did she Philip? He said she didn't. No, I said, what would she want to go and buy that for? Did you ever hear it Philip? I said. He said he didn't. Not even on the radio? I said. He said no. I said: You didn't miss much, Philip. Its the stupidest song in the world. I started laughing. Do you know what its about? I asked him but he said he didn't and shook his head. You'd think I was stupid if I told you Philip I said and looked at him wiping the tears out of my eyes for every time I thought of how stupid it was it made me laugh all over again. No I wouldn't says Philip. You would, I said, I know you would. No I wouldn't, he says. Do you know what its about Philip I said its all about a woman hanging from a rope all because this butcher boy told her lies. Did you ever hear the like of it, I said, and it sounded so daft now that I had to steady myself against the railway wall.

That wouldn't be much of a song says Philip and whatever way he said it it set me off again with the tears streaming down my face. Then I says to him: You wouldn't catch your ma paying out money for a song the like of that would you Philip?

He didn't really say anything just ran his fingers through his hair and said mm but then when I said it again he said no you wouldn't. I said I know I know you wouldn't.

I shook my head and said its some laugh have you a hanky Philip and he gave me a lend of it then on we went.

We were getting along right well and his cheeks weren't so flushed now so I started talking to him about the comics and how it had all been meant to be a joke and everything. It was all supposed to be a bit of a laugh Philip I said. We would have given the comics back to you. He said I had got him in trouble. Ah the Pig Toll Tax, I said, *that!* That was stupid.

You don't have to pay that! I laughed away as I kicked a stone on ahead. Did you ever hear anything so stupid as a pig toll tax! Paying money to get by on the street! You must be joking I said and then the two of us were laughing away at how stupid it was. Imagine if everybody had to pay it! Sure nobody would ever get anywhere. Well man dear, I said, a pig toll tax! Not at all, Philip, that was all cod! He was glad to hear that, I could tell. Then I told him about the comics I got from my aunt in America. Comics like you never seen in your whole life, I said. Not English ones, you couldn't get these in England or anywhere, oh no – only America. You just never seen the like of them Philip I told him. I have them all stashed in the chickenhouse, Philip, I said. I went there every day and what a laugh I had reading about all these superheroes. Your man comes at Green Lantern I says. Next thing bam! a big giant hammer comes flying out of his ring and splatters him. And that's only Green Lantern. There's far more than him that could do even better things than that! Nothing would do Philip now till he saw these comics. You can go to music any time I said, I might have to swop or sell these comics very soon. We went down the back way. Nobody knew about the way into the chickenhouse through the broken window at the back only me and Joe. When you got inside there you were in the dark warm world of chirps and burbles. The lightbulbs came right down from the ceiling and hung straight in front of your face. They were only maybe four feet off the floor. This is the first time I was ever in here says Philip its great. It was a secret world and he was in it, he ran his fascinated fingers along the grooves where me and Joe had carved our names in the wood we had done it all over the place.

Look at this he said, then I said I'd go and get the comics. Philip was crawling round on his hands and knees examining the cages, then he took out his music book and started making calculations along the margins of the pages with his pencil. I don't know what he was trying to figure out maybe how much space each chick had to itself or something like that. That was Philip, he'd want to know what food they ate for breakfast and how much per day and what temperature was best for them and all this. I left him there and went into the room at the back of the shed to get the comics. When I came back out he was still scribbling and muttering to himself, working out his mathematical calculations with his back to me. All I said was *Philip*, and when he turned I swung the chain but I didn't connect I missed the side of his face. I hit the flex of the lightbulb and it started swinging to and fro. The chickens flapped and squealed a bit they knew there was something wrong then I took the next swing and it thudded dully against a sack of grain I couldn't get a good look at him with the lightbulb painting these big shadow streaks as it swung. The next thing it swooped right back and I couldn't see a thing then I lost my temper and swore at him. I think he had dropped his spectacles and was crawling along the ground searching for them. I hit the ground thump thump on the carpet of woodchips. I saw him now he was right in front of me and then I heard: *Francie!*

Philip was right in front of me with one arm up saying Francie don't do it! Then all of a sudden the lightbulb steadied itself and I heard it again: Francie! It was Joe. He got a grip of me by the wrist and pushed me backwards. Philip was on the ground again but he had no idea of where he was going for he still hadn't found the specs. He just crawled and said please. Joe wrenched the chain from my grasp. It landed with a clatter against the septic tank. He cursed at me now look what you've done look what you had to go and do! I'm sorry Joe I said and I knew that was that. Joe was going to leave me and I'd be left with nobody no ma nothing.

But the thing was – Joe didn't leave me! I hadn't managed to hit Philip so he was just a bit shocked and Joe worked it so he would say he'd fallen off an apple tree and that was how he tore his blazer. But when Joe came back from leaving Philip down the street he swore more at me and said that if I ever did the like of that again they'd put me away for that was what they did with people who did things like that. He said that since the day we met hacking at the ice I was his best friend. He didn't care what his ma or da said about me or my da or the Terrace but if I did things like that it would be all ruined. I was standing with my back against the wall it felt as if I was on a cliff edge. Francie, said Joe, you have to swear that's the end of it. I did. I swore on my life that was the end of it and it would have been too only for Nugent.

After that we rode off out to the river, that was the day we built the hide. We dug a small tunnel in the ground and propped it up with pine branches then covered over the whole thing with leaves and briars and bracken. If you were passing all you saw was bushes and brambles and old leaves thrown around. But we were in there making plans, me and Joe. We built a campfire too. We blackened our faces and painted equals signs under our eyes. We mingled the blood of our forearms and said from this day on Francie Brady and

Joe Purcell are blood brothers and will be friends to the end of the world. We'll pray to the Manitou Joe said so we did. You can have a name said Joe an injun name. I was Bird Who Soars. Off I went across the sky and over the slated rooftops, gliding in between the curling scarves of chimney smoke and the bending aerials calling down to Joe far below can you see me Joe I'm up here diving with the wind stroking my eyes as I came in to land beside him but he hadn't moved, sitting there hunched up in a blanket, paring sticks and saying yamma yamma yamma, praying to the Manitou.

I sat at the window. The lane outside was deserted. There was no sign of the children but tomorrow they would be back again clumping about in oversize shoes and making tea parties with dockleaves on plates. They didn't care about all these things that people care about. All they cared about was whose turn it was next. The day after Joe and me were hacking we played marbles in the lane. That was all we cared about too. Right Francie, your turn, says Joe.

Across on the ditch a snowdrop with a bone china head curtsied and introduced its diminutive troupe. There he is again this year ma used to say about that snowdrop. The sky was the colour of oranges. I looked at my marble-white hands and wondered what it was like to be dead like the woman in the song. You'd think: the beautiful things of the world aren't much good in the end are they? I'm going to stay dead.

I thought that was probably what it was like.

———

I didn't say it!, Nugent said but she did and that was why I called down to the house. I didn't say *anything* what are you *talking about* was all she could say so I said what do you think I am Mrs Nugent, stupid? I heard you. I was walking across the Diamond and her and Philip were coming out of the shop. Philip was carrying two sliced pans, one under each arm and she had a shopping bag with coloured patches on it. I was a good bit away from them but I saw her stopping to point me out to Philip. I saw her. *There he is!* she said, *there won't be so much chat out of him from now on Philip, him and his pig toll tax!* Maybe if she had just left it at that I wouldn't have passed much remarks but she should have left Alo out of it. I just heard the tail end of it but that was enough for me. *Half-blind and hates him from the day she married him! What did I tell you Philip!*

Then off went Philip waddling with the bread and her beside him in the headscarf chuckling with the bag so I said I'd have to call down and see them after that. I took a look in the window before I knocked on the door and it was nice in there with the fire tossing shadows round the room and a brass guard with a spray of pink flowers painted on it and on top of the mahogany piano Mrs Nugent in an oval frame. She was nice-looking Mrs Nugent when she was young, with a white rose pinned to her hair and cupid's bow lips like you'd see on an old time film star not like the bits of scribbles she had now. No headscarf or overcoat with big brown buttons then, oh no. Where did that old Mrs Nugent go? Don't ask me. And Mr Nugent, he was hanging on the other wall, smiling away in his tweed coat and stripey tie. You could see by him that he had a high-up job. He had that look in his eye that said I have a high-up job. He was staring off into the distance thinking about all the high-up things he was going to do and all the people he was going to meet. I don't know if he was English but he spoke like it. He said good afternoon when everybody else said *hardy weather* or *she looks like rain*. There was a wicker basket of lilies of the valley under the picture of John F. Kennedy. And on the music stand of the piano the ass and cart going off into the mountains of Emerald Gems of Ireland. It was a nice warm room with an amber glow that reached out to you and beckoned you in. Come on in, it said, so I thought maybe I would but then knock knock and out comes Mrs Nugent. She was a long way now from the rose in her hair all right. Cupid's bow lips! What a joke! She had on a raggy old apron with forget-me-nots scattered all over it and a heart-shaped pocket bulging with clothes pegs.

I had to laugh at the furry boots.

She must have been washing for she had on rubber gloves and was pulling at the fingers. A crinkly arrow appeared over her eyes in the middle of her forehead and she said what do you want. No she said what do *you* want? I could see in the hall. There was a barometer pointing to very hot some barometer that was. They say there's going to be rain Mrs Nugent I said, rubbing my hands together all business. That won't please the farmers. What do you want she said again. Then she said it *again* and I said nothing much just called down to see how Philip is getting on. Philip is very busy with his lessons, she said. I knew he was. He was always busy with his lessons, working things out. Investigating this and that. That was the kind of Philip. That's what I said to Mrs

Nugent. Mr Professor, I said, always busy! Nugent said nothing. She was picking at one of the clothes pegs inside her pocket. Well that's the Christmas over now for another year Mrs Nugent I said but she said nothing to that. All over now, I said again, it'll be very quiet now till Patrick's day. Yes, she said.

I suppose you're glad to get it all over with, I said and folded my arms. I smiled. She picked little bits off the inside of her lip and said yes she was. Then she whispered goodbye now and made to close the door but I stuck my foot in the jamb and held it fast. Ah its for the kids really I said and sure its only once a year. Mrs Nugent wasn't so sure now what to do about that. Pick pick at the clothes peg. I just thought Philip might like to come out and have a few kicks of the ball. Me and him, Manchester United against the rest. Do you like Manchester United I asked her. Tommy Taylor and Denis Law. They're the best. The Munich Air Disaster I said. Did you ever see the like? The whole team Mrs Nugent. I seen it in the paper. All they found of Tommy Taylor was his boots. It was terrible I said. Terrible. I shook my head in dismay and Mrs Nugent must have thought it bad too for her eyes reddened and she wiped her mouth with the back of her hand and a bit of her sleeve. When he comes back in to do his lessons after a few kicks he'll be right as rain. *Philip*, I called. I knew he was in the kitchen for he always did his lessons at the table the spectacles were on. It was just beside the television and sometimes Mr Nugent sat there with him and helped him puffing away on his pipe like an ad on the television himself. *Yes I like Maltan Ready Rubbed Flake says Mr Nugent!* with the big briar stuck in his gob. I called out but he didn't hear me that time either so I called again.

A few kicks, I said. Are you coming? But still there was no
sign so I thought maybe the comics would get him out. I have
a whole load of new comics Philip I said. Can you hear me
Phil? I said. It was good saying Phil like that. Yup, me and
Phil we been old buddies for a lawwwwng time, that's what
I said. *Dandy Beano Topper Victor Hotspur Hornet Hurri-
cane Diana Bunty Judy* and *Commandos* I said all in one
breath and I was like a magician drawing an endless streamer
of coloured bunting out of my mouth. *I'll tell you what
Philip*, I said then, *I'll let you have all my Commandos for
all your Toppers now there's a fair deal what do you say Phil!*
On account of *Commandos* costing a shilling and *Toppers*
only being tuppence you couldn't get a better deal than that.
But still there was no sign of Philip so I had to go and say it
all over again. Then what does Mrs Nugent say only please
go away. Mrs Nugent I said, if you think I've come to rob
Philip of his comics that's where you're wrong, I wouldn't do
that. I just wouldn't do it. That's all over. That was supposed
to be just a joke Mrs Nugent. Look – I really am going to
give Philip my *Commandos*. Philip, I called. Then I said it yet
again *Dandy Beano* and all that. What was Philip doing in
there? Mrs Nugent's cheeks were all wet and her voice was
shaky. I thought I'd cheer her up for she really thought I was
going to rob Philip Nugent. Look Mrs Nugent I said I'm not
going to rob him! I said it loud and clear so she would
believe me. He can have every comic I ever collected. I'm
serious Mrs Nugent. He can. The whole lot. I didn't care
about comics any more. What did I care about comics? But
Mrs Nugent still didn't believe me. She just sniffled and
wouldn't look at me. Look Mrs Nugent I said and I got down
on all fours on the tarmac. I made sure to get a bit inside the

hall in case she shut the door on me and then I stuck out my face and scrunched up my nose and made my eyes as small as I could then I gave a big grunt. I thought that would cheer Mrs Nugent up. I looked up at her again. Snort. Then I laughed. What do you think of that Mrs Nooge? What a laugh it was. The more I snorted the more I laughed I really did think it was the best laugh ever especially when Philip appeared with his what's going on here face on. *Detective Inspector Philip Nooge of the Yard here!*

At first Philip didn't know what to do you don't usually expect to come out of your kitchen and see a pig wearing a jacket and trousers crawling round your front step. He was standing there with a pencil behind his ear. There was a joke but I didn't say it. Did you hear about the constipated professor? He worked it out with a pencil. I was too busy watching Philip trying to work out a professor plan. Snort! And then Philip's face. I looked right up at him. A game of football. Me and you against the rest Philip what do you say? Then I gave another snort and poor Philip didn't know what end of him was up. Snort. Then off I went laughing again. Then what did Philip do only try to push me out of the hall. Ow, Philip I said, you're getting your fingers in my eyes. I could hear his heart beating from where I was. He stuck the sole of his shoe against my shoulder. Ow I said get your big boots off me, that hurt me Philip! Then ha ha again. You're too rough I'm not playing with you! I'm only joking. Mrs Nugent kept saying Philip Philip I don't know if she knew what she was trying to say. Which would you say is the best Philip I said. Denis Law or Tommy Taylor? Philip was down on his hunkers trying to shoulder me out the door and he was as red as a beetroot huffing and puffing away there. His pencil fell on the ground. I never saw such pushing and shoving. Philip would push one way then I'd push the other. Then it'd all start again. Mrs Nugent didn't do anything, all she did was stand there fiddling with the pegs in her apron pocket and I could see that Philip was on the verge of saying will you help me ma for God's sake but he had such good manners he didn't and what happened then whatever way he turned didn't he knock the wedding photo off the wall and crack down on the floor it went with bits of glass all over the hall. Now look at what you did, she said, blaming Philip whatever she was blaming him for. Sure he couldn't help it if I was snorting around the place. Then he didn't know what he was at he starts to pick it up and she shrieks *mind the glass mind the glass you'll cut yourself* no I won't he says you will she says and then Philip starts getting all excited standing there with a handful of broken bits of glass. I gave a snort. That's pig language for watch yourself with the glass there Philip I said. Philip's forehead was wet with sweat and his eyes were more sad than frightened now.

I think it was him looking at me with them sad eyes that made me get up and say that was a good laugh but I think its about time I was back at the farmyard what do you say Mrs Nugent? But she said nothing only stood there twisting a clothes peg and saying please stop this please! Right you be now Mrs Nooge I said and hopskipped down the lane, I'll call back another day I said and I did.

And the reason I did that was because when I got to thinking about it back in the house I thought what am I worrying about Philip Nugent's sad eyes for? I had probably imagined it, he might even have been putting it on. The more I thought about it the more I said yes that's right he was just putting it on. Philip Nugent, I said to myself, you are a crafty devil, the way they say it in the comics. That old Philip Nugent, the trickster! So a couple of days later, back I went except this time I made sure they weren't in. I waited until I saw the car heading off down the lane I knew they were going to visit Buttsy up the mountains.

In I went through the back window hello Francie welcome to Nugents! Oh hello there nobody I said.

Dant-a dan! Welcome to Nugents Mr Francie Brady! Thank you I said, thank you very much. It gives me great pleasure to be here standing on these black and white tiles in the scullery, Mrs Nugent. Oh no not at all Francis we're delighted to have you. Now you must meet everyone. This is my husband and this is my son Philip but of course you know him. Except that really there'd be no fear of Mrs Nugent saying any of that she'd be on the phone to the sergeant straight away but oh no she wouldn't for she was up the mountains drinking tin mugs of tea with carrot-head Buttsy the brother in a cottage that stank of turfsmoke and horsedung. But Nugents didn't smell like that. Oh no. It smelt of freshly baked scones, that's what it smelt of. Scones just taken out of the oven that very minute. I went on the hunt for them but I could find them nowhere. I think it was just the smell of old baking days that had stuck to the place and she hadn't been making scones at all. No matter. Sniff sniff. Polish too there was plenty of that. Mrs Nugent polished everything till you could see your face in it. The kitchen table, the floor. You name it you looked at it you were in it. You had to hand it to Mrs Nugent when it came to the polishing. Flies? Oh no, not in Mrs Nugents! And any cakes there were all under lock and key where Mr Fly and his cronies couldn't get at them. You could see them in the glass case under plastic domes and there was a three-tiered stand with two pink ones and a half-eaten birthday cake on it. Those flies they must have been driven daft – looking in at them beautiful cakes and not being able to get at them. I was myself so I knew what they must have felt like. I could have broken it open but I didn't want to spoil it they looked so good in there. I'd say she made all of them herself. There was a photo on the wall of Mrs Nugent lying on the grass in a park somewhere. What came into my mind was that I never knew that Mrs Nugent had been young once as young as me. For a long time I thought she had been born the same age as she was now but of course that was stupid. In that photo she was about five. She was lying there with a big gap between her teeth and freckles all over her face like Buttsy. Hee hee she was saying to the camera. Good old Mrs Baby Nooge I thought. How many years ago was that I wondered. Could have been a hundred for all I knew. Mr Nugent's briefcase was sitting in the corner and his tweed overcoat was hanging up behind the door. I helped myself to some bread and jam and turned on the television. What was on only Voyage to The Bottom of The Sea, Admiral Nelson and his submarine gang they were getting a bad doing off a giant octopus that was hiding inside a cave where they couldn't get at him. He was a cute bastard sending out these big curling tentacles with suckers on them knocking the sub against rocks upside down and everything. All you could see was these two eyes shining away in the darkness of the cave as much as to say I have you now Mr smart alec navy men, let's see you work your way out of this one. *Dive! Dive!* snapped the admiral into a microphone but she wouldn't go down. The music was going mad. *Kill the bastard!* I shouted, I was getting excited too, *harpoon him that'll shut him up!* But the admiral wasn't as stupid as the octopus thought he was. *Right that's it all systems are go!* and the next thing these depth charges start hitting the octopus smack between the eyes boom and the squeals of him then. Pop pop out go the two eyes like lights and the tentacles flapping around like wasted elastic and the sub away up to the surface with the whole crew cheering and the admiral wiping the sweat off his face smiling OK everybody that's enough back to work. Then beep beep goes the echo sounder and away off they go happy as Larry and back to normal. Fair play to you admiral, I said, that shut him up. And it sure did, the octopus was lying at the back of the cave like a busted cushion and it would be a long time before he was suckering or tentacling again. I made myself a big mug of tea and another doorstep of bread and jam to celebrate. It was hard to beat it sitting there eating and enjoying myself. It was a grand day outside. There were a few skittery bits of cloud lying about the sky but they didn't care if they ever got anywhere. Birds, crows mostly, hanging about Nugent's window sill to see what they could see. Well well look who's in there Francie Brady. He's not supposed to be in there. Hey crows I said, fuck off and that shifted them. Ah this is the life I said I wonder have we any cheese or pickle. We certainly had – there it was in the brown jar in the fridge! And did it taste nice! It certainly did! Make no mistake – I would definitely be staying at Nugent's Hotel on my next trip to town.

———

When I had finished my snack I went upstairs to see if I could find Philip's room. No problem. Comics and a big sucker arrow lying on the bed, dunk went the arrow into the back of the door and dangled there. Then I opened the wardrobe and what did I find only Philip's school uniform the one he wore at private school in England. There it was, the navy blue cap with the crest and the braided blazer with the silver buttons. There was a pair of grey trousers with a razor crease and black polished shoes could you see your face in them you certainly could. I thought to myself, this could be a good laugh and so I put it on. I looked at myself in the mirror. I say Frawncis would you be a sport and wun down to the tuck shop for meah pleath? I did a twirl and said abtholootely old boy. I say boy what is your name pleath? Oo, I said, my name ith Philip Nuahgent!

Then I went round the house like Philip. I walked like him and everything. Mrs Nugent called up the stairs to me are you up there Philip? I said I was and she told me to come down for my tea. Down I came and she had made me a big feed of rashers and eggs and tea and the whole lot. What were you at upstairs Philip dear she said. Oh I was playing with my chemistry set mother I said. I hope you're not making any stink bombs she said. Oh no mother I said, I wouldn't do that – its naughty! Mr Nugent lowered his spectacles and looked at me over the top of the paper. That's correct son, indeed it is. I'm glad to hear you saying that. Well it thrilled me no end to hear Mr Nooge saying that. Then when I looked again he was back reading his paper.

I felt good about all this. When I was finished I said I was going back upstairs to finish my experiments but I didn't, I waltzed around the landing singing one of the *Emerald Gems* to myself O the days of the Kerry Dances O the ring of the piper's tune! and then into Mr and Mrs Nugent's room. I lay on the bed and sighed. Then I heard Philip Nugent's voice. But it was different now, all soft and calm. He said: You know what he's doing here don't you mother? He wants to be one of us. He wants his name to be Francis Nugent. That's what he's wanted all along! We know that – don't we mother?

Mrs Nugent was standing over me. Yes, Philip, she said. I know that. I've known it for a long time.

Then slowly she unbuttoned her blouse and took out her breast.

Then she said: This is for you Francis.

She put her hand behind my head and firmly pressed my face forward. Philip was still at the bottom of the bed smiling. I cried out: *Ma! Its not true!* Mrs Nugent shook her head and said: *I'm sorry Francis its too late for all that now. You should have thought of that when you made up your mind to come and live with us!*

I thought I was going to choke on the fat, lukewarm flesh. *No!*

I drew out and tried to catch Nugent on the side of the face.

I heeled over the dressing table and the mirror broke into pieces. Mrs Nugent stumbled backwards with her breast hanging. Now Philip I said and laughed. Philip had changed his tune now he was back to *please Francie*. I said: Are you talking to me Mr Pig?

When he didn't answer I said: Did you not hear me Philip Pig? Hmm?

He was twisting his fingers and so was his mother.

Or maybe you didn't know you were a pig. Is that it? Well then, I'll have to teach you. I'll make sure you won't forget again in a hurry. You too Mrs Nugent! Come on now! Come on now come on now and none of your nonsense. That was a good laugh, I said it just like the master in the school. Right today we are going to do pigs. I want you all to stick out your faces and scrunch up your noses just like snouts. That's very good Philip. I found a lipstick in one of the drawers and I wrote in big letters across the wallpaper PHILIP IS A PIG. Now, I said, isn't that good? Yes Francie said Philip. And now you Mrs Nugent. I don't think you're putting enough effort into it. Down you get now and no slacking. So Mrs Nugent got down and she looked every inch the best pig in the farmyard with the pink rump cocked in the air. Mrs Nugent, I said, astonished, that is absolutely wonderful! Thank you Francie said Mrs Nugent. So that was the pig school. I told them I didn't want to catch them walking upright anymore and if I did they would be in *very* serious trouble. Do you understand Philip? Yes he said. And you too Mrs Nugent. Its your responsibility as a sow to see that Philip behaves as a good pig should. I'm leaving it up to you. She nodded. Then we went over it one more time I got them to say it after me. I am a pig said Philip. I am a sow said Mrs Nooge. Just to recap then I said. What do pigs do? They eat pig nuts said Philip. Yes that's very good I said but what else do they do? They run around the farmyard Philip said. Yes indeed they do but what else? I tossed the lipstick up and down in my hand. Any takers at the back? Yes Mrs Nugent? They give us rashers! Yes that's very true but its not the answer I'm looking for. I waited for a long time but I could see the answer wasn't going to come. No, I said, the answer I'm looking for is – *they do poo!* Yes, pigs are forever doing poo all over the farmyard, they have the poor farmer's heart broken. They'll tell you that pigs are the cleanest animals going. Don't believe a word of it. Ask any farmer! Yes, pigs are poo animals I'm afraid and they simply will cover the place in it no matter what you do. So then, who's going to be the best pig in the pig school and show us what we're talking about then, hmm? Come on now, any takers? Oh now surely you can do better than that! That's very disappointing, nobody at all! Well I'm afraid I'll just have to volunteer someone. Right come on up here Philip and show the class. That's the boy. Good lad Philip. Watch carefully now everyone. Philip got red as a beetroot and twisted up his face as he went to work. Now, class! What would you call someone that does that? Not a boy at all – a pig! Say it everyone! Come on! Pig! Pig! Pig!

That's very good. Come on now Philip you can try even harder!

What do you think Mrs Nugent? Isn't Philip a credit?

At first Mrs Nugent was shy about what he was doing but when she saw the great effort he was making she said she was proud of him. And so you should be I said. Harder, Philip, harder!

He went at it then for all he was worth and then there it sat proud as punch on the carpet of the bedroom, the best poo ever.

It really was a big one, shaped like a submarine, tapered at the end so your hole won't close with a bang, studded with currants with a little question mark of steam curling upwards.

———

Well done, Philip, I cried, you did it! I clapped him on the back and we all stood round admiring it. It was like a rocket that had just made it back from space and we were waiting for a little brown astronaut to open a door in the side and step out waving. Philip, I said, congratulations! I was beaming with pride at Philip's performance. I wouldn't have believed he had it in him. Philip was proud as punch too. I turned to the class. Boys, I said, who's the best pig in the whole pig school? Can you tell me? Philip they all cried without a moment's hesitation. Hip hip hooray. Clap clap the class lifted the roof. Very good easy now steady I said. Now its time for Mrs Nugent to show us how well she can perform. Can she do poo as well as her son Philip? We'll soon find out! Are you ready Mrs Nugent? I was waiting for her to say yes Francis indeed I am then away she'd go hoisting up her nightdress and scrunching up her red face trying to beat Philip but I'm afraid that wasn't what happened at all.

Mrs Nugent was there all right but she wasn't in her nightdress. She was wearing her day clothes and carrying a bag of stuff she had brought back from Buttsy's.

Her mouth was hanging open and she was crying again pointing to the broken mirror and the writing on the blackboard I mean wall. I looked at Philip he was white as a ghost too what was wrong with him now, hadn't he got the prize for the pig poo what more did he want? But Mr Nugent said he was in charge now. *I'll deal with this!*, he said in his Maltan Ready Rubbed voice. Philip and Mrs Nugent went downstairs and then there was only me and him. He looked good Mr Nugent you had to say that for him. His hair was neatly combed across his high forehead in a jaunty wave and he had shiny leather patches on the sleeves of his jacket. He sported a pioneer pin too – that was a metal badge the Sacred Heart gave to you and it meant you were saying: *I've never taken a drink in my life and I have no intention of ever taking one either!* He stared me right in the eye he didn't flinch once. He didn't even raise his voice. He said: You won't get away with it this time! This time I'll see to it you're put where you belong. And you'll clean up *that* before you leave here with the police and the walls too for my wife's not going to do it. You've put her through enough. Well, that Mr Nugent, I thought. How was I supposed to run a proper pig school with these kind of interruptions? Mm? That's what I want to know I said. But not to Mr Nooge to myself. What I said to him was: Tell me Mr Nugent how's Buttsy getting along? He didn't answer me so I just went on talking away to him about all sorts of other stuff. He was standing with his back to the door in case I might make a run for it. But I couldn't be bothered running anywhere. The rocket had cooled now and the tail of steam was gone. I was thinking about the small astronaut appearing out of the door saluting with a grin on his face reporting for duty *sir* when this smack hits me right on the side of the face and there's the sergeant standing there rubbing his knuckles and saying: *Don't, don't!* Or you'll be the sorry man. Don't don't what was he talking about don't what? You'll clean it up, he seethed, make no mistake about that. Of course I'd clean it up if he wanted me to I don't know what he was getting all hot and bothered about. I brought it off down the garden in a bit of newspaper and broke it up with a stick behind the nettles. I was whist-ling. If there was a small astronaut inside it he'd had it now.

Mrs Nugent was still crying when I left but Mr Nooge put his arm around her and led her inside. When the silent films are over sometimes this hand comes out of nowhere and hangs up a sign with THE END on it. That's what it was like when we were driving away in the car. The Nooges' house standing there and the hand hanging up the sign on the door-knob as phut phut off we went.

So that was the end of Nugents, for the time being anyway.

The sergeant was going on about ma in the front seat how he'd courted her years ago when she was one of the nicest women in the town only for the tribe she had to get herself in with. Thank God she's not here to see the like of this he said.

No, I said, she's in the lake, and it was me put her there.

By Christ if you were mine I'd break every bone in your body, he said. Then he wiped his mouth and muttered: Not that you could be any different.

We sped by the convent. There was a few of the lads from the school kicking a ball up against the wall. I gave them a big wave through the window and they waved back for a minute until they seen it was me. Then what did they do only pick the ball up as if I was going to get at it or something. I waved again but they pretended not to see me. They weren't so keen on me after the time they had me on the school team that played Carrick. Oh now says the master you're a wiry wee buck you'll make a good winger. I've seen you you can move as fast as a March hare when you want to. I even scored two goals I don't know what they were talking about.

It was this big galoot on the other team. He says to me half-way through the match right you you shifty little fucker you're going to get it and what does he do only cut the legs from under me I did nothing he says to the ref and gets away with it. I was all twisted up with pain and I was limping for a good twenty minutes to look at me you'd think poor Francie Brady will never play again. That must have been what he thought for the next time I had the ball he comes strolling over to me as if he's just going to pluck it off my toe. Well he could if he wanted to he could do what he liked all I was interested in was getting him back for what he did on me so soon as he comes over I lifted the boot from behind and bang right in under between the legs and he goes down like a sack of spuds agh agh and all this. Just before the ref came over I managed to get another dig in at the butt of his back, studs and all. I was going to try the same trick what did I do but the ref took my name and put me off. The master gave out to me and wouldn't listen to my side of the story so I says fuck youse and your football after that. But I don't think they wanted me on the team anyway. I'd say that big Carrick bastard would be glad to hear that. He was so big I could nearly run in between his legs. Before I kicked the crigs off him that is.

The sergeant reminded me of the clown in Duffy's circus not the way he looked but when he talked. Especially when he was telling you all the terrible things were going to happen to you now. H'ho! he'd say. And H'haw! Just the same as Sausage the clown. H'ho yewer an awfill man altogedder, Sausage'd say and away off round the ring with his stripey legs flying. Him and the sergeant must have been born in the same town or something.

He was off again. H'ho when the priests get their hands on you there won't be so much guff outa ye h'ho. I said I'm sorry Sergeant Sausage but he stubbed the fag excitedly in the ashtray and said its too late for that me buck you shoulda thoughta that when you were in Nugent's up to your tricks! H'ho aye!

Boo hoo, Sergeant Sausage, I said.

He was so excited he didn't even notice I had called him Sergeant Sausage. There were laurel bushes all along the avenue and a gardener forking manure and muttering to himself. When we went past in the car he stood looking after us with one hand on his hip and tipping his cap back. I made a face at him through the back window and he nearly fell into the manure heap. Up she rose out of nowhere the house of a hundred windows. This is a grand spot I said. H'ho says the sergeant we'll see if you say that in six months' time! H'ha.

A man made of bubbles in charge of a school for bad boys it was hard to believe but it was true for there he was at the window his big bubble head and out he comes bouncing bounce bounce ah *Howareye!* he says to the sergeant, I never saw such a big bright white polished head as that old Father Bubble had. Howareye at all! he says again and the sergeant starts to huff and puff and try to dicky up his uniform. Oh not too bad now Father did ye have a nice trip not too bad eh Father thanks.

Ah that's grand said Bubble.

Then he looks over at me. So this is the famous Francie

Brady, he says, doing tricks with his fingers and saying hmm hmm.

Yes Father, I said, Its the one and only Francie Brady.

You speak when you're spoken to says Sausage but Bubble raised his hand and said no problem Father.

I gave Bubble a big wink good man yourself Father I said and next thing his face goes all cloudy. He's a bad article says the sergeant and I thought he was going to make a go at me.

Bubble was staring at me with these two eyes like a pair of screwdrivers. You'd do well to keep a civil tongue in your head, Mr Brady, that's what I'd say to you now. The sergeant liked that he started rubbing his hands and going six months' time six months' time!

Then the two of them just stood there glaring at me for a minute I thought they were going to light on me and start kicking me down the avenue with these mad *let's batter Francie Brady!* eyes on them. But they didn't. You just heed my advice, says Bubble, and then he sank his arms deep into these slits in his soutane and smiled at Sausage and away off talking then about football and the weather. Sausage thought the town might win the county championship oh I don't know about that says Bubble. Neither did I but I thought a good result would be: The other team – 100 goals. The town – 0. I was going to say that to see what they'd say but then I says ah I'll not bother my arse. They went on jabbering for over half an hour and left me standing there like a gawk. Then Sausage says: Well I'll be off so. He looked over at me: I'll be keeping tabs on you, he says.

Yes, Sergeant, I said.

He backed off slowly as if I was going to pull out a revolver blam blam him and Bubble one in the head apiece but I wasn't then brrm brrm phut phut and h'ho that was the end of him.

Now, says Bubble stroking his chin and staring right at me, maybe we understand each other a little bit better. What do you make of your new home, Mr Brady?

Its grand says I, good enough for pigs.

What did you say? says Bubble and he didn't like that either.

He gave my jumper a chuck.

You'll find no pigs here!, he says. But he could say what he liked I knew well it was a school for pigs.

The Incredible School for Pigs!, I said in my telly voice.

Did you hear what I said says Bubble there's no pigs! This is a school.

Indeed it is, I said – A school for pigs!

There's no pigs! he said and his voice squeaked a bit at the end it was a good laugh.

Welcome to the school for pigs, I said and pulled away from him.

Don't worry, he says, you're not the first and you won't be the last!

He was rolling up his sleeves. He didn't say the first what. I cupped my hand and the echo glided in low under the laurels.

Little pigs! Little pigs! Open up! I cried.

He tried to get a hold of me but I was too slippery for him and when I went down on all fours he couldn't manage it at all. I crawled around him and that near drove him mad. I let a few snorts out of me. There was an old priest above at a window. I went up on my hind legs and begged a bit for him. Snort I said and a big grin.

Then Bubble caught me a rap on the side of the head and I saw stars. That's nothing to what you'll get, he said. I was glad he did it. I wanted him to give me a proper hiding.

I said all sorts of things to get him to do it. I said welcome to the pig school. I stuck my face right up to his and scrunched it up into a snout. I snorted. Go on, I said and I stuck my chin out. But instead of laying into me he backed off and just looked at me with the screwdriver eyes. He wasn't afraid or anything. He was just looking and taking it all in so then I stopped. Are you quite finished now he said and I said I was. I was exhausted and I had a headache. All these crows on the telephone wires. What are you looking at cunts, I thought. Then he says get inside out of that and no more of your lip. I went upstairs to the dormitory where there was a saint on every window-sill, such a shower of dying-looking bastards I never seen. Bubble was right behind me as I humped the case. I pointed to Our Lady. She's in a bad way I said to him, she needs to suck a zube. He said nothing only to be down at Benediction in half an hour and up at six the next morning for footing turf in the bog. There was a little Jesus over on the window across from my bed. He was looking over at me. Poor poor Francie Brady he was saying: Isn't it a terrible pity too? I went over to him and says: *Isn't what a terrible pity?*

Oh oh er er I'm only saying he says. No, I says, you didn't answer me – Isn't *what* a terrible pity?

All right then I says have it your way so crack, off the side of the washbasin and down into the plughole goes his little head just sitting there sideways looking up glug glug. There was a gaping hole in my stomach for I knew Joe would have heard all about Nugent's by now. I had let him down. I had nobody now that was for sure and it was all my own fault. I wouldn't blame him for not writing to me, why should he after what I'd done on him? I broke my promise and that was that. I tried to get at my wrists with the jaggy bit of the statue. I managed to get at bits but it was doing no damage you could still be at it in a hundred years' time the way it was going. Then over comes this bogman fellow here's my head and my arse is coming. *What are you doing oh my God luck he's broke Our Lord if the priest sees you with that he'll kill you!* I looked at him with the statue in my hand. There was a little red Elizabethan collar round the neck of it where I'd been hacking with it. I never seen the like of that bogman. He had this big tuft of hair sticking up and two other bits like indicators on either side. *O you're goanta bee in terrible trubble* he says. His scarecrow trousers stopped at the ankles and he stood there hunched up with his bony arse cocked in the air like he was carrying an invisible bag of spuds on his back. I wouldn't like to be you he said again but I was fed up of him by then so I made a go at him with what was left of the statue and off he went as white as a ghost nearly skittering himself. Then I threw No-Head in the bin and lay down on the bed.

Whee-hoo said Joe and the toboggan came thundering down the white blanket of the fairgreen. Them was the days, I said to Joe, we had peace then. The coloured orb of the marble sat in the cradle of his thumb. He looked at me puzzled. Whose turn is it Francie? Is it my turn? I said it was, even if it wasn't.

The marble rolled along the hard clay in a trail of light.

That old Joe. I didn't know what to do when the letter came. I told everyone about it. All they said was: Huh? but I didn't care. I was speechless. But one thing was for sure. I wasn't going to be getting in trouble ever again. From now on I would be studying for the Francie Brady Not a Bad Bastard Any More Diploma so I could get out of the school for pigs and bogmen. Me and Joe would ride out to the river and there we'd stay. I had found a good place for myself when I wanted to be away from the bony arses following you around and asking questions, it was the boilerhouse down behind the kitchens, and I went in there and read the letter over and over. Whumph!, went the big stove, glowing away with a carnival of sparks going hell for leather in the pit of its big belly. I sat on a pile of bags, old sacks and read:

Dear Francie you eejit what are you doing. I told you about Mrs Nugent but you wouldn't listen what were you doing in their house? Were you trying to burn it down there's all sorts of stories Francie. I asked Philip but he won't tell me. Philip is OK Francie if you ever touch him again you'll put yourself in trouble bad trouble. He really is OK. He doesn't want any trouble with anyone. He told me. We shouldn't have robbed the comics Francie it was wrong. There's a carnival here now it stays open till twelve. You can win all sorts of things. Bears, anything. Did you ever see Laramie Shoot-Out? You aim the rifle and up comes the sheriff. He's made of cardboard. He draws first but if you hit him you get five more goes. We were round there last Saturday. The rifle range – its brilliant! Philip Nugent got two bullseyes so he won a goldfish. He gave it to me because they have one already. I put it in the window. We're going round again next weekend. If I win anything I will send it on. Philip says he has a special plan to work on the slot machines so I might. Write soon Joe.

I kept thinking about the goldfish. What did Philip Nugent think he was doing? I just couldn't believe it. He was nothing to do with us. I wished I could get the goldfish back off Joe. But what did Joe *take* it for? Why didn't he say: Sorry Philip you're nothing to do with us.

Then it came to me: he was only doing it to make peace between us all so that there would be no trouble and when I came home me and Joe would just carry on the way we always had. I just hoped that Philip Nugent didn't think he was going to be hanging round with us just because Joe took a goldfish off him. Because if he did he was going to be sorely disappointed. Me and Joe had things to do. Tracking in the mountains, huts to build. If Philip Nugent wanted to pray to the Manitou he would have to form his own blood brother gang. For his own sake I hoped he didn't think that he was all in with us now. But he wouldn't. I knew Joe would put him right and there would be no problem. It was just as well it was Joe, I thought, instead of someone who would just tell him to shove off or something soon as I appeared home and make him feel real bad about it. That was the kind of Joe. He would explain it all gently and clearly to him so that he wouldn't be hurt. He was good at that Joe, taking things easy and explaining them, just like the way he did with me after the chickenhouse and all that.

The main thing was for me to get out of this School For Pigs so we could get back into action. I was as light as a feather when I had all that thought out. I said hello to the bogmen and everything. That night I wrote to Joe and told him that it was all changed now. There was going to be no more trouble with Francie Brady. It was all over. I was glad to hear that he had taken the goldfish off Philip I said there was no point in us being enemies. From now on the Nugents can go where they like I said. We were going to have too many things to do and places to be. If I met them on the street I would salute them and say hello but that would be it. I would go on ahead about my business from now on. The Francie Brady trouble days with Nugent and all that, they were over. Kaput. Trouble days – all over Joe, I said.

Then I licked the envelope and sealed it. I smiled and left it on the window-sill for posting in the morning.

But the minute I left it down, I thought: *But what about the goldfish?* What did he have to *take* it for?

I woke up in the middle of the night. I had been dreaming about Mrs Nugent. She was out in the scullery baking scones. The house was full of baking smells. She called in: Is anybody ready for some more scones?

Yes I am said Philip and then he said what about you Joseph?

I felt the blood draining from my face when I saw Joe looking up. He was doing his lessons with Philip. He smiled and said: Yes please. They're quite beautiful Mrs Nugent.

Thank you Joseph, called Mrs Nugent.

That was the end of the sleep for that night I couldn't sleep any more thinking of what Philip was saying to Joe. It wasn't that they were talking about me or anything. That was the funny part. In the dream they didn't even know who I was. The next day I said to myself: I never want to dream that dream again.

In the nights I would lie there hatching all my plans and schemes for when I got out. It was hard to hatch anything with all them bogmen around me. Soon as the lights went out, wheeze wheeze. Quit breathing youse bastards!, I wanted to say but you never knew when Bubble was lurking down below with his torch. I'd build a raft that was the first thing and send her sailing down the river. Off we'd go, who knew where we'd wind up? A tree house, what about that? That was good. Joe above pacing up and down on guard blam with the Winchester Die dogs of crows! There was a warehouse up at the old railway, we could make a Nazi Headquarters there. I was as bad as the sparks in the boiler-house stove with all these notions tearing about in my head. You'd only be half-finished with one idea and the next thing here would come along another one, no I'm a better idea what about me it would say. One thing for sure, it would be a long time before I bothered Philip Nugent again. I was glad now that Joe had taken the goldfish. It cleared everything up and now we could all start from the beginning again. Philip could live his life and we could live ours. The beautiful things of the world, I had been wrong about them. They meant everything. They were the only things that meant anything. That was what I thought now. I fell asleep and dreamed I was

Bird Who Soars gliding through the snow-covered mountains of Winter.

Every day after that off we'd tramp to the bogs with Bubble at the head throwing big cheery smiles at the people of the town standing there gawping after us like we'd marched through the streets without our trousers. The women whispered there they go the poor orphans. I had a mind to turn round and shout hey fuckface I'm no orphan but then I remembered I was studying hard to get the Francie Brady Not a Bad Bastard Any More Diploma at the end of the year so I clammed up and gave her a sad, ashamed look instead. As soon as we got out into the open countryside Bubble relaxed and started swinging his arms and singing *Michael Row The Boat Ashore* and the bogmen sang *Allel-oo-yah!* all delighted trying to get Bubble to look at them. They said to me isn't Father such and such great. I forget his real name now but it was Bubble they were talking about. Oh yes I said he's an absolutely wonderful singer. Yes, said the bogs, he's my favourite priest in the whole school. Then off they'd go trying to get up to the front to talk to him. But Bubble was all right. I liked the way he always gripped the sleeve of his soutane as he jaunted on alleloooo-ya!, with a red country face on him like a Beauty of Bath apple from all the walking. We'd dig all day long and Bubble would tell us stories about the old days when he was young and the English were killing everybody and the old people used to tell stories around the fire and you were lucky if you got one slice of soda bread to feed the whole family. But what harm did it do us? That's right, says one of the bogmen, being killed did nobody any harm. For fuck's sake!

Ah no I was talking about the soda bread says Bubble ha ha. There's nothing like a nice big slice of soda bread Father I said, wiping my brow and heeling a few sods onto the stack. He paused for a minute and licked his lips. He looked at me with his eyes all misty. Running with butter he said. Now you said it Father, I said and went back to my work, whistling away. I could see the bogmen giving me dirty looks because I was talking to Bubble. I smiled at them. Do you know what a good big slice of soda bread is good for I was going to say. Oh we know, they'd say. For making hardy men out of young country fellows like ourselves? No, for driving up your big bogman arses I'd say. But I didn't say it at all. I just smiled again and made out I had a pain in my back. *Gosh, my dear fellows*, I said, this is hard work indeed. The look on their boggy faces. They didn't know what to say. Oo-er, yes, they said, or something like that. As if they could pretend they were posh, the dirty bog-trotters!

One day Bubble took me up to his study and said to me: I'm glad you're learning manners.

Yes Father, I said.

Then what does he do he goes all misty-eyed again and stares off out the window making a speech about all the boys who had passed through the school in his time there. I've seen them come and go he said, since the first day I came in here as a fresh young curate myself. I remember that day well, Francis, it was all so new to me then. Then he starts into another story about tyres burning the day of his ordination and his mother weeping with happiness. Ah, yes, he said, shaking his head and away off into some other story. Ah yes but I wasn't listening to a word he said I was too busy watching a Flash Bar wrapper that was flapping about over the ambulatory and thinking to myself I wouldn't mind sinking my choppers into a Flash Bar right this minute. In we'd go with a half crown to the shop. Thirty Flash Bars please. Eh? your man would say. Then off we'd go hardly able to walk with all these bars and eat the whole lot one after the other out the railway lines, me and Joe. Big strings of toffee and a beard of chocolate all over your face. Bubble was on about your man who had founded the school. That's his picture there he said. He had a big breeze block of a head and a pair of eyebrows like two slugs trying to stand up. I wouldn't have fancied a scrap with him. You could tell he was a bogman too. It was him founded the school for bogmen with bony arses then was it, I said. I did like fuck. When the speech was over Bubble smiled again and said it was nice to talk to you Francie, keep up the good work, Oh yes, I thought to myself, I certainly will, after all I have to walk out of here with that Francie Brady Not a Bad Bastard Any More Diploma, Father Bubble.

After that they put me serving Mass. What a laugh that was. Me and Father Sullivan up before the birds getting into all these starchy togs inside in the sacristy, they'd freeze the goolies off you. Black as pitch outside and not a soul stirring. I'd carry the cruets and stuff and off we'd go me and Father Sullivan like two big whispers moving along the corridor to the chapel rustle rustle. Domine, exaudi orationem meam, he'd say with the hands outspread. I was supposed to say Et clamor meus ad te veniat. Et fucky wucky ticky tocky that was what I said instead. But it didn't matter as long as you muttered something. Father Sull never listened anyway. They said he wasn't right since he was on the missions. I don't know what happened some Balubas put him in a pot or something and ever since he'd been walking round with a face on him the colour of stirabout never slept a wink roaming around the corridors at night in his soft shoes all you'd see at the window was this yellow face looking out.

It was around that time I started the long walks and the holy voices. Bubble says to me what are you doing going on all these long walks down to the low field by yourself?

I told him I thought Our Lady was talking to me. I read that in a book about this holy Italian boy. He was out in a field looking after the sheep next thing what does he hear only this soft voice coming out of nowhere you are my chosen messenger the world is going to end and all this. One minute he's an Italian bogman with nothing on him only one of his father's coats the next he's a famous priest going round the world writing books and being carried around in a sedan chair saying the Queen of Angels chose me. Well I thought – you've had your turn Father Italian Sheep man so fuck off now about your business here comes Francie Brady hello Our Lady I said. Well Francie she says how's things. Not so bad I said.

Lord be praised, said Bubble and I thought he was going to take off into heaven on the spot. I could feel his eyes on me as I floated down to the low field.

I knelt on the soggy turf for penance. I looked up and there she was over by the handball alley. I wasn't sure what to say to her ah its yourself or did you have a nice trip or something like that. I didn't know so I said nothing at all. She had some voice, that Blessed Virgin Mary. You could listen to it all night. It was like all the softest women in the world mixed up in a huge big baking bowl and there you have Our Lady at the end of it.

She had a rosary entwined around her pearly white hands and she said that it gladdened her that I had chosen to be good.

I said no problem, Our Lady.

I told Father Sullivan all about it and he said I had unlocked something very precious.

The next day I got talking to a few more, St Joseph and the Angel Gabriel and a few others I don't know the name of. The more the merrier. I went through Father Sullivan's books and found out dozens of the fuckers. St Barnabas, St Philomena. We could have had six matches going at once in the low field there was that many.

The bogmen were raging. I don't see why she's appearing to you, they said, what's so special about you?

I told them to fuck off, what did they think she had nothing better to do than appear to a bunch of mucksavage bastards like them.

It was hard to beat that old sacristy and the chapel in the mornings, the twirl of candle smoke and the secret echo of the pews, all the sounds of the morning not born right yet.

It wasn't very long after that that Father Tiddly arrived at the school. But of course that's the joke for he had been there all along. Yes – Father Sullivan! We were in the sacristy and if there was one thing Father Sull loved to hear it was my stories of the saints in the low field. But there were two saints he adored most of all and they were St Catherine and St Teresa of the Roses who came down from heaven on a cloud of pink flowers. Any time you mentioned them he got all weepy and joined his hands praying. They had never come to the low field at all but he kept asking me about them so I had to make up a few yarns about them and all the things they said to me. I was in the middle of one of these stories when I look up and what's old Sull doing only smoothing my hair back from my eyes and stroking away at my forehead with his pale cold hand. Look at you, he said, my serving boy. Introibo ad Altare Dei I said I don't know why and the next thing what does Sull do only plant this big slobbery wet kiss right on my lips. Then he said please, tell me the story of St Teresa of the Roses again. So I did, all about the petals falling out of the sky and the smell of perfume what was the perfume like he kept saying. I nearly said look Father do you want me to tell the story or not because if you do will you please stop interrupting? But I didn't for you never knew with Father Tiddly he might start crying or anything. When I told the story sweatbeads as big as berries popped out on his forehead and when it was over he started muttering and fumbling around the place going this way and going that way and going nowhere at the same time. It wasn't until the third or fourth time I told this story about the roses that he began the Tiddly Show. I thought it was a great laugh with all the prizes you could win out of it. Are you all right Francis he'd say. Oh I'm grand Father and dropped my eyelids shyly like Our Lady did. Sit up here he said and slapped his knees. So up I went. What does Tiddly do then only take out his mickey and start rubbing it up and down and jogging me on his knee. Then his whole body vibrates and he bends away over I thought he was going to break off in two halves. I'd be in a right fix if that happened. What would Bubble have to say about that? Just what is going on here? Why is one half of Father Sullivan lying over by the bookcase and the other half still in the chair? Have you something to do with this Mr Brady? Back to your old ways are you? I might have known! But it didn't happen like that lucky enough. Tiddly just crumpled up like a paper bag and lay there hiding his eyes and saying no. I told him not to be worrying his head but he wouldn't come out from behind those hands. Sob sob that was old Sull I mean Tiddly. I read a book while I was waiting for him to come out. Once or twice I caught him peeping through the cage of his fingers but he was in again just as quick. What a book that was! Your man going about the streets of Dublin all tied up with chains under his coat and saying I'm sorry Jesus for all the bad things I done. Matt Talbot, that was his name. The things he got up to in that book. He goes out to the butcher's and buys a kipper. Boils it up in the kettle. And then what does he do? Gives the fish to the cat and drinks the water himself all because of his past sins. What a headcase! He used to buy all the timbermen drink in the pub. Oh here comes Talbot, they'd say, now we're right for a few jars. And sure enough Matt would fork out for the lot. Good man Matt they'd say you're a good one. Then the foreman says to Matt: Fuck off Talbot there's no more work for you around this yard. Poor old Matt. Off he goes to the pub and they're all in there drinking. Any chance of a drink says Matt. No, I'm sorry, haven't a bob. Sorry Matt. That's what they all said. So poor old Matt, off he went in the rain and then back to his dingy old room just him and the cat and not a tosser between them. I know what I'll do he says. I'll start sleeping on floorboards and wearing chains. Then God will forgive me for all the drinking and bad things I done. Will you God? Oh yes says God as long as the planks are good and hard. So out with the planks and on with the chains and away goes Matt through the rainy streets until one day he drops down dead and who finds him only the nuns eek sister! Look here's a man its a holy martyr all chains! I was chortling away at this when Tiddly says dear God I'm sorry Francis. I said it was all right have you any fags? I think if I had said you ought to be ashamed of yourself Tiddly would have gone up through the skylight on the spot and pegged himself off the roof. So I said nothing and just sat there with my mickey snoozing on my thigh smoking fags and reading about Matt and all the saints. Blessed Oliver Plunkett! Chopped in quarters! For fuck's sake!

You're my best little girl says Tiddly and went away off spluttering at his desk.

He said he could see the beautiful things of the world shining through my eyes.

Is that where they are now, I said. I told him about the children in the lane and the sky the colour of oranges. I should have kept my mouth shut about them. I was only halfway through and when I looked up there he is with the tears running down his face. He kissed me on the hand over and over. Tell me again tell me about them again – please Francis! I thought his eyes were going to come right out, plop on the carpet oh for fuck's sake now what what we going to do – if Bubble finds these!

He gave me three fags for that was all he had left. I knew he would have given me all the fags in Carroll's factory if he had them. The way he looked at you that old Tiddly with his big sad squiggle of a mouth. It was like the coyote after the road runner has made a complete cod out of him.

But he wasn't that much of a cod. He told Bubble he was almost one hundred per cent sure I had a vocation for the priesthood and he was giving me guidance. Bubble was over the moon. He stopped me in the ambulatory and says: Look at Saint Augustine!

Yes, Father, I said and bowed my head. Yes Father, I said softly, whoever St Augustine was, there was nothing about him in my saint book. If God does call you it is your duty not to be afraid. Remember that we are here at all times. That is what we priests are for after all. We're not ogres Francis! Yes Father I said, I know that. I could feel him staring after me purring away happily to himself as I headed off to the low field to talk to the saints and smoke a fag and get stuck into the packet of Rolo that Tiddly had given me.

Then the next time he starts this breathing into my ear. He said I smelt like St Teresa's roses and he'd give me as many Rolos as I wanted if I told him the worst bad thing I ever did. I told him things about the town but he kept saying no no worse than that and I could feel his hand trembling under me. No matter what I told him it still wasn't bad enough. No he says you must have something worse than that something you are afraid to tell anyone something you are so ashamed of you don't want anyone in the wide world to know about. I told him to stop I didn't want him to do it I didn't want him to say it anymore. But he wouldn't stop. I could barely hear him but he was still saying something you could never forgive yourself for a terrible thing Francis a terrible thing please tell me I said stop it! But he wouldn't then I heard ma again it wasn't your fault Francie I got a grip of him by the wrist I just grabbed on to it and sank my teeth in he went white and cried out No Francie!, I said *stop it don't ever say it again!*

I didn't go near him after that. I never wanted to see him again him and his smells and his breathing and his terrible things. But the bite only made Tiddly more mad for me than ever. He took me out to a cafe in his car and he says I love you.

OK Tiddly, I said but no more questions ever again yes Francis he says anything you say.

Da arrived one day bumbling up the avenue in his greatcoat like Al Capone. I knew by him that the sight of the place put the fear of God in him it reminded him of the Belfast school for pigs. He had a half-bottle of Jameson in the pocket of his coat. I could see the neck of it sticking out. His eyes wouldn't settle in his head, they kept darting about. I knew it was the priests looking down at him. They were saying to him: Well Mr Pig, are *you* back again? I thought we got rid of you forty years ago!

That was what they were saying to him and why he lowered his eyes and reached in his pocket to get a grip of the whiskey bottle he pulled it out helplessly like a child's rattle. There was a smell of wax polish in the reception room, and a big oaken table with short fat legs like a wooden elephant. Bubble arrived in he hid the whiskey just in time. He stood beside me smiling with his soft hands crossed over his stomach and looked down at me with that stupid face he put on when parents or policemen or anyone came round. It was half-priest, half-cow. O he's coming along grand he said even though nobody asked him. All da was worried about was he'd be caught red handed with the whiskey and get kicked out into the laurel bushes and told never to come back. Up at seven every morning saying Mass, never gives back answers, O he's a credit Mr Brady. Then he dropped his voice and said you know Mr Brady I've seen them come and go and then he was away off again. I stood at the window and watched the bony arse brigade circling the walk. A crow squatted on top of the goalpost uprights worm-spotting in the churned turf of the playing field. A radio was playing thinly somewhere. See the pyramids along the Nile, the song drifted, watch the sun rise on a tropic isle. I was standing there on the sunlit sand looking up at the pyramids and thinking how small I was when I heard the door click shut softly the way it did the night Alo left and the room seemed to swell to three times its normal size. He was at the whiskey again. It didn't seem to even matter now if there was anyone else in the room or not. He was following the trail of his own words as if he had no idea where it would take him, pausing only every so often to swig the whiskey out of the bottle. There was a coach trip all those years ago, to the seaside town of Bundoran in County Donegal. The war was over and everybody was happy. Every time the bus went down a hill they cheered and clapped and sang. She had fallen against his shoulder by accident. Oh dear God!, they shouted, would you look at this!

A camera clicked. We're the talk of the place!, ma cried but what did da do only put his arm around her.

They held hands along the strand and they talked about the brass band he'd started in the town and a book he was reading, the life and times of Michael Collins the revolutionary hero. Oh now what would I know about the like of that, said ma. I don't know where you get all these brains, she laughed. There was no row that day no whiskey, nothing. Three times after that they met in the same town, strolling through the dappled bedlam of the carnival to a boarding house called Over The Waves where there was music in the evenings. He was asked to sing and was she proud when he closed his eyes and gave his rendition of *I dreamt that I dwelt in Marble Halls*. They all knew us there, he said. The woman of the house, every night: I wonder could we persuade Mr Brady to give us another rendition? That's what she used to say. *You're my special guests! The lovebirds! Benny and Annie Brady.* Below the bedroom window the hush of the sea and ma I could see her lying there on the bed with him but it was a different woman, it was the ghost of what could have been ma. I didn't know how I felt when he kept going on like that, part of me wanted to turn on him and say its no good now why didn't you say that all those nights when you were down on your knees in front of her with your speeches May the curse of Christ light on you this night you lazy good for nothing tramp that was all you had to say then! But anything I was going to say like that withered as soon as it reached my lips for whatever way it happened it seemed now as if the flabby flesh had somehow slowly melted from his bones, fallen invisibly off him as he spoke. He wasn't in the room, there were no craggy priests glaring down at him, all he could see was her standing at the water's edge as he called to her, his voice tumbling across the years and the salt breeze, *Annie Annie*. And afterwards on the esplanade he held her in his arms and said to her are you prepared to live on potatoes and salt for the rest of your days and what did ma do she tossed back her wavy hair and laughed is that all you can offer a good-looking girl like me Benny Brady?

Then they both got down on their knees and said the rosary together on the rocks and I wondered how it could ever have been, that moment, with its half-heard prayers carried away and the carnival swirling in the distance, the waves lapping on the shore and da fingering the beads and looking longingly into her eyes just as he did now. You could almost hear the whisper of the dead afternoon as we stood there in the empty, lost silence of that huge room.

Shut up I said, shut up about it, something rose in me and I wanted it over. She was a good woman your mother he said, he was starting to slobber. It wasn't always like this you'll never know how much I loved that woman. I got it into my head that a couple of the bony arses were coming over to the window to gawp I told him again to shut up it was no good now, none of it. He said not to talk like that to him he had his dignity. I got down on my knees like he used to when he rolled home after a skite with his clenched fist up and one eye closed may the curse of Christ light on you this night you bitch the day I took you out of that hole of a shop in Derry was a bitter one for me. He said no son should say the like of that to his own father. Every time I thought of them standing there at the water's edge I said worse things to him and in the end he cried. I came here to see you, son, he said if you only knew. I said you have no son you put ma in a mental home. Maybe I'm better off then to have no son how could you call yourself a son after what you did. After what I did what did I do I had him by the lapel and I knew by his eyes he was afraid of me whatever way I was looking at him. *What did I do?* It was hard for him to say it, I could barely hear him I loved you like no father ever loved a son Francie that was what he said it would have been better if he drew out to hit me. I just let go of his lapel and stood there with my back to him fuck off I said fuck off and I knew I'd been alone for a long time when I heard Bubble's soft lisp well Francis wasn't that a nice surprise?

Swish swish off we went across the quadrangle together. I didn't know your father was a musician said Bubble. Oh indeed he is Father, I said, it was him set up the brass band at home and there's no better man to play a trumpet. Really, said Bubble, isn't that wonderful! Yes, it wasn't long after they got married he set up the band. They got married in Bundoran you know. Is that so? said Bubble all ears. Yes, I said, there was a boarding house there called Over the Waves, that was where they spent their honeymoon. They were always talking about going back there but they never got round to it. Everyone knew them there, all the guests. He used to sing for them in the evenings. Its a pity they never managed to go back. Perhaps they will yet Francis, he says, there's still plenty of time. Indeed there is, I said, its not often you see a singing skeleton she'll bring the house down.

———

Tiddly said wouldn't it be lovely if we could get married. I said it would be great. I could buy you flowers and chocolates and you could have dinner ready when I come home he says. Ha ha I laughed, like a girl, and did Tiddly like that! Little Miss Snowdrop, I said, Queen of All The Beautiful Things in the World!, and that nearly drove him astray in the head altogether. The sweat hopped off him. Flip, in went the Rolos.

One day I was down in the boilerhouse watching the circus of sparks putting on a show inside the big stove. I was puffing away on a Park Drive Tiddly had given me. Then I heard the voice: *I know you're in there, you can't fool me!* You needn't think I'm afraid of you, Mr Head-The-Ball Brady. I'll take you! I'm the man will take you! Your trick-acting'll not annoy me! Come on! Come on out you snaky bastard!

I heard the keys rattling and when I looked up who was it only the gardener with a big graip pointed at me and his eyes mad in his head, I have you now my buck what'll the priests have to say about this!

I went white and I said well I suppose that's me fucked but then what does he do only start chuckling to himself and lock the doors, give me a light he says. Effing sky pilots, what do I care about them! What one of them was ever any good? They wouldn't give you the steam off their piss. He said they owed him five shillings since nineteen forty. All of a sudden the whole boilerhouse smelt of weeds and fertiliser. We stood there watching the sparks' circus inside the little door of the stove. There was a touch of the bogman in that gardener too. Hate, he called it. There's great hate off that stove, he said. O, I says, powerful hate! Powerful hate altogether!

———

I'm afraid you appear to have missed this part of the grass verge, the sky pilot says to me. I had the shears in me hand! I had! He was a lucky man that day I can tell you. He was within that of getting it with the shears!, he says, and showed me a bit of his thumb squeezed between two fingers.

He bit away at the butt of the cigarette. Me, he said, who fought for this country. O yes, he says, I was in the GPO in Easter Week. All I cared about in the GPO was Michael Collins and that was only because da was reading a book about him when they were in Bundoran. *Did you know* Michael Collins, I says to him. He nearly had a stroke. *Did I know* him? Didn't he stay in our house!

He stared at me with the eyes dancing, flicking away at the fag. I said da knew about him. O aye but not as much as me, oho I knew him all right he said and hunched down looking right at me. You don't believe me? he said and gave me a thump on the arm it nearly knocked me into the fire. I do believe you I said. *You want to see the amount of rashers and black puddings that man'd eat*, he said, *small wonder he was a good soldier!*

Then he leaned back and folded his arms with the butt stuck in the corner of his mouth. His foot was tapping away waiting for me to say something. I landed a big farmer spit in the middle of my hand. By Christ!, I said, there's not many men can say that! Stayed in your house! He looked at me proud as a dog with two cocks.

Now you said it he says and dragged happily on the butt.

And I'll tell you another thing he said – I was one of the best lads with a rifle he ever seen.

Be the hokey Jasus!, I said with my mouth open.

There you have it, he said and closed one eye: But don't breathe a word. I wouldn't please the bastards.

It was nearly dark by the time he was finished blowing up Crossley Tenders and plugging Tans.

The red eye of the cigarette glowed as he pulled on it through the pink claw of his clay-caked fingers.

I'll meet you here tomorrow he says and I wondered was he another Tiddly. But I knew he wasn't. All he wanted was a Black and Tan to sit on his knee so he could shoot him in the head. Jasus he shouts there's the priest get down get down and the two of us hunkered down. When I looked at him he had his arms wrapped around his head like an octopus. All you could hear was mumble mumble oh yes indeed and the squeak of the leather shoes as they went past. *O yes,* I could hear them saying, *he certainly came into his own in the county final!* Its all right I said they're gone now. The bastards he said, peeping out through a crack in the door, if they catch me here its more than my job's worth!

So that was the way it went. Between being Tiddly's wife and keeping an eye out for the Black and Tans for the gardener I was doing all right in that old school for pigs only Tiddly had to go and fucking spoil it didn't he.

Sit up here now, he says and took me on his knee. O he says you're a picture. Ha ha I says the way he liked it and he says you'll never guess what I got for you.

I stuck my finger in my mouth and rolled my eyes mischievously.

Guess, he says. Go on, guess.

Sweets, I said.

No, its not sweets.

A book, I said, its a book.

No, he said, its not a book.

I tried all sorts of things but it was none of them. I could hear Tiddly rooting about behind the big armchair and the crackling paper of a parcel. His fingers were all over the place as he fumbled with the twine and tried to open it.

Let me, I said.

O, said Tiddly.

Tiddly's eyes were the size of jampot lids. I swooned.

O father its lovely!

It was a woman's bonnet with a long white ribbon dangling down.

I felt like laughing my arse off but poor old Tiddly wouldn't have liked that biting away at the skin of his mouth oh Francis.

What do you think says I putting it on and doing a twirl for him in front of the mirror. I went spinning round the room and Tiddly got so weak he had to steady himself against the arm of the chair.

Oo do you think – ah I'm beautiful – ah!, I says.

His bottom lip was trembling. Sit up here now he says so up I went. He puts his arm around me you've no idea how much I love you Francis he says in the nights I even dream about you. I want to know everything about you. Ten Rolos, says I. Tell me all about yourself. I told him a heap of lies and true stuff mixed in. That was a good laugh, all about the football match and the town and the drunk lad and all the things that went on but that wasn't what he wanted to know. Yes yes he says but I want to know about *you* Francis. I'll bet you live in a nice house do you? Do you live in a nice house?

He gave me a big uncle smile and that was the first time I thought to myself: I don't like you any more Tiddly.

He chucked at the ribbon of the bonnet and crinkled up his eyes. Go on, he says you can tell me. I was going to tell him nothing but he kept at it go on go on and all this. I told him we had black and white tiles in the scullery and a twenty three inch television but that wasn't enough for him he still kept at it. The more he made me say things the redder my face was getting I had said so much now I could never go back and say that I wasn't telling him about our house at all but Nugent's I had to keep going if he had stopped then it might have been all right but he didn't, he kept making me say more and more. And that's what Mrs Nugent wanted. I saw her standing there beneath a tree in the lane behind the houses not far from me and Joe's puddle. Ma came out into the yard to take in the washing. When she seen her Mrs Nugent smiled through her thin lips. Then she went over to her and leaned over the wall. Ma stumbled with the washing piled under her arm. She just kept smiling at ma. With her eyes she was saying: I'll speak when I'm ready.

And when she was, she said: Do you know what he did? He asked me to be his mother. He said he'd give anything not to be a pig. That's what he did on you Mrs Brady. That's why he came to our house! Her breast was choking me again, lukewarm in my throat. I think I hit him first he fell back and I heard him shout *Don't hurt me Francie I love you!*

There was a paper knife on his desk I seen it there plenty of times I just felt around for it and tried to cut him but I couldn't get at him *please please I love you!* was all I could hear. *Put it down!*, I heard I wasn't sure who it was I think it was Bubble and someone else I couldn't see their faces right my head swum, all I could see was ma smiling and saying to me over and over again don't worry Francie no matter what she says about you I'll never believe it I'll never disown you ever ever not the way I did you ma I said *no son no!* she said I said its true ma no she says but it was and it always would be no matter what I did.

Roast pig in the dark that was what I was when I awoke, they'd locked me in the boilerhouse. I could hear whispering outside it took me a while to make it out. *You're an awful man. It took four of them to hold you. I hear it was like trying to wrassle a weasel. Do you hear me, eh? You showed the fuckers! Hee hee!*

The circus sparks put on a show for me. Look Francie they said but I couldn't see them right I think they must have given me the needle one minute Joe and me would be standing in the lane getting ready to throw the marble, the next Bubble would be floating by like a black parachute in the wind. I could hear the music of the carnival Joe was there on his own just walking in and out of the sideshows. The big wheel turned and yellow balls bounced on watersprays. Pop went the rifles and old targets were thrown away. Beside the gallery the goldfish swam in a big glass tank. There were plastic bags for taking them home in. Then the boy doing the shooting turned around and pushed the hair back from his eyes. It was Philip Nugent, smiling and counting the number of holes in his target. He was going to say something but it wasn't his voice that came out of his mouth: *Hi! Hi! Are you in there? Ha! Ha! Do you want a fag?*

Then this fag comes rolling in under the door. I don't know how many I smoked when I was in there. Hundreds maybe. The doors opened and there's Bubble standing in the light but he wasn't his usual self tugging away at his sleeve and looking away from you when he was speaking. You didn't often see him doing that. Well my fine fellow are you ready to behave yourself yet? he says.

I knew he was afraid I was going to say no. For he had no idea what he was going to do then. But I didn't. I liked old Bubble. But Tiddly he was a different story. It'd be God help him if he ever came near me again.

Its not my job to cut effing grass verges, says the gardener. If he says it to me one more time, that's it. I'm out.

What do *you* say?

I didn't say anything, just looked at him advancing on the inch of ash with one eye closed.

Or have you quit talking altogether?

The way he said it I thought I'd be as well to say something before he took into me with the graip.

Cut no verges, I said. No verges now and that's all's about it!

He nearly burst open with excitement. He whacked his corduroys with the battered cap.

Now you said it!, he cried.

Not a one! I said.

Not a shaggin' one he says with the fag shaking, by Christ you're a good one, here have a fag he said and shook a few of them, *a fag for every fucker of a sky pilot that gets his arse kicked! Go on!*

He chuckled away as a ballerina of sparks did a twirl. Did I ever tell you about the time I sprung Michael Collins from the Bridewell jail? he says.

No, I says.

I didn't?

He licked his lips and little infantrymen ran from one eye to the other. *And what would your business be says the officer? Oh I'm a Holy Ghost Father officer, I says. Very well he says, proceed padre. So off I went and not half an hour later there's me and the head of the Irish Republican Army rattling through the streets of Dublin in a horse and cart! Good man says Collins from under a pile of turnips you'll be remembered for this!*

The light was failing outside and they were all heading towards the refectory for tea.

The more I tried to get the goldfish out of my head the more it kept coming back.

One wet day I seen Tiddly climbing into a car and he was never seen again, probably away off to the garage to rub some bogman with his mickey good luck and good fucking riddance. Bubble called me up to his study and I could see he was on for a bit of detective work. Every time he thought I wasn't looking he'd look at me over the rim of the teacup. If I turned he'd look away again quick as a flash. He was trying to think of the right words for he knew if he got the wrong ones I'd tell him nothing and maybe if he did I'd tell him nothing anyway. I sank into the big leather chair and he says do you like Scots Clan I do indeed I says. He asked me a few questions about how I was getting on now. I said OK and yes and no to them all. His face was all creased up trying to find the right way of saying things it was like trying to turn the corner on two wheels. Sometimes I just shrugged my shoulders and looked out the window. Then Bubble stands there staring out knotting the fingers together behind his back wondering what way would he start his speech. It was a different speech this time there was no jokes or any of that for he knew what I thought fuck the jokes and he was right. He said life was difficult, people had their troubles. Some of the things people did were hard to understand. A soggy football went sailing past the window and a clatter of bogmen chasing after it. He said Father Sullivan was a good man. I said nothing. He starts to tell me this story then about him going off to Dublin to visit his sister. He's been working hard lately too hard if you ask me, he says with a watery laugh. His sister will look after him I said and sipped the tea. She will he says, she's very good to him. He's lucky he has her. I didn't mean to laugh but I just had to when he said that. I was chuckling away to myself. Sister, for fuck's sake! Poor old Tiddly was probably climbing up the walls of the garage by now shouting *I love you bogman!* to some young farmer lad.

Bubble knew I was laughing but there wasn't much he could do about it. If he said: Stop laughing, I'd only go and do it worse. I'd push him out of the way and shout out the window: Hey bogmen! Did youse hear about Father Tiddly the Rolo man!

That was what Bubble was afraid of. That everybody would hear. But he didn't have to worry about that. As long as he left me alone and minded his own business I wouldn't say anything about old Father Big-Mickey I mean Tiddly. Now he was gone I didn't give a fuck. I just wanted to be left alone. I hope you're happy here says Bubble. I said I am. Then I said: I'm going now.

Yes Francis, said Bubble holding the cup with one finger up in the air. I wasn't going to tell about Tiddly. But he didn't know that. All he knew was he'd seen him lying whingeing in the corner saying I love you to me. I don't think poor old Bubble was used to seeing things like that. The last thing I seen as I went out the door was him standing there all help-less and pained-looking. He was thinking: Why can't all these bad terrible things be over so as I can sing a little happy song. Like *Michael Row The Boat Ashore* maybe!

After that the days were all the same, they just drizzled past, days without Joe without da without anything. I didn't have to worry much about getting the Francie Brady Not a Bad Bastard Any More Diploma any more after the Tiddly busi-ness for I knew they were going to let me go the first chance they got I was like a fungus growing on the walls they wanted them washed clean again.

The day I left Bubble gripped my hand and said it did his heart good. I gave him a big smile. But it was all different now it wasn't like the old days when me and him used to have jokes. He knew why I was smiling. If it did his heart good he wasn't long about letting go of the hand.

I said good luck to the gardener. He said: *Its just as well you caught me for I won't be here tomorrow. I've had it with them and their verges.* He looked right into my eyes and tapped his chest. *Its not my job*, he hissed. The last thing I seen was the soggy ball sailing up into the air.

House of a hundred windows, goodbye and good fucking riddance, I said.

I called straight down to Joe's but he wasn't there. Where is he, I said. Mr Purcell looked me up and down. I have no idea, he said and closed the door. I wondered what was eating him.

I called down to the house a few more times but there was never any answer they must have been away, at the uncle's or someplace. In the end I waited at the bottom of Church Hill and met Joe coming home from school. He was in the second year in secondary now. He was carrying a big bulging bag of books. There's some amount of books in that bag, Joe, I says laughing. There was some other lad with him I don't know who he was I told him to run on ahead. *What?* he says. I said: Run on ahead – are you deaf?

I'm back Joe, I said, back from the house of a hundred windows. I laughed myself when I said that it just sounded funny saying it there walking round the road with Joe. I didn't know where to start telling him about all these things. I told him it made no odds about the goldfish or any of that that was all in the past now. Then he looks at me and says: *What goldfish?* I hit him a thump on the shoulder. What goldfish! I says, for fuck's sake Joe!

It was the first good laugh I had had in I don't know how

long. I asked Joe how things were out at the hide. He said he hadn't been out there. Is it still covered over, I said. He said he wasn't sure it was so long since he'd been out there. I said we'll have to make sure its covered over. If the rain gets in it'll ruin it. He said it would. When will we go out and check on it then I said, this evening? He said he couldn't go out that evening. OK, I said tomorrow is fine. But he said he couldn't go out then either so it had to be at the weekend. I had a pain in my stomach waiting for that weekend to come.

Joe made a wind at a gnat, lay back on the bank of the river and I told him more about it, everything I could think of. I told him about the gardener and the Black and Tans and the bogmen and their bony arses and being locked in the boiler-house and puffing fags and talking to the saints and St Teresa. It sure is some laugh said Joe, what did they lock you in the boilerhouse for? I says oh nothing just messing around, you know. That was all I was going to say but then he says it again but what did they lock you in the boilerhouse *for*? Then I thought the best thing about friends is you can tell them anything in the whole world and once I thought that I didn't care. As soon as I started the story it ran away with itself. There were tears in my eyes and I couldn't stop laugh-ing the bonnet and Tiddly, I love you! and the whole lot. You want to see the Rolos he gave me I said, I must have ate about two thousand fucking Rolos Joe. Rolos said Joe, he gave you Rolos but what did he give you Rolos *for*? As far as I could see that was all Joe wanted to hear about. Any-time I went on with the story he kept bringing me back to that part what for, what for? I wanted him to stop going back to that. I wanted to stop talking about the whole thing.

I wanted to talk about the hide and the old days and hacking at the ice and whose turn it was to toss the marble and all that, that was what I wanted to talk about. They were the best days. You could see through them days, clear as polished glass. But Joe didn't want to. He kept going back to the other thing so in the end I told him and what does he say then he says Francie he didn't really do that did he? I said what are you talking about Joe he *did* didn't I just tell you?

The next thing I knew I was in a cold sweat because of the way Joe was looking at me. I could see the flattened spot of the grass where he'd been lying he had moved back from it. He was sitting in a different place now. He hadn't moved back too far in case I'd notice it. But I did. It was only for a split second our eyes met but he knew and I knew. Then I said: I fairly fooled you there Joe. Tiddly! Imagine someone doing the like of that! Tiddly! Rolos – for fuck's sake!

I laughed till the tears ran down my face. *I fooled you*, I cried out. I had a headache and my face was all flushed. Then Joe said it was time he was getting back he had extra homework to do for the weekend. I said OK, I would see him tomorrow and we'd go to the carnival. Sure, he said, I'll try and I watched him running back into town. I was coming in the road when I seen your man coming with the black bicycle. I says to him: There you are. How are you getting on?

He tugs down the cap and says: I'm in a bit of a hurry. I have to see about the calves.

Then off he goes with the head down. I waited there to see what he'd do and sure enough when he was about fifty yards away he stops and turns to look back. I just stood there with my legs spread like Kirk Douglas. When he saw me staring back at him what does he do only let go of the bike and down it went clattering on the road. I didn't stir I just stood there watching him trying to pick it up. He didn't make much of a fist of it once he knew I was watching. Then the shopping bag came loose off the carrier and something fell out of it I think it was potatoes. What does he do then only try to pick them up too. He was a right-looking sketch with one hand holding the handlebars and the other the spuds. I cupped my hand over my mouth: Don't forget the calves! I says and off he goes with the potatoes another few of them fell and rolled into the ditch.

Then off I went up the street but there was no one around only Grouse and papers sailing like boats down the gutters of Fermanagh Street.

But that didn't last long for soon as Buttsy and Devlin heard I was home from the school for pigs they were round to the house to interrogate me about doing the poo in Nugent's. I heard them forcing the front door the stupid bastards couldn't break into an egg. I was thinking will I tackle these bastards yet or not then I says no not yet so up the chimney I went with an old jackdaw looking down at me as much as to say what are you doing here this our property. *Come on now Brady we know you're in here*, says Buttsy. If you come out it won't be so bad. Jesus what a stink in this place said Devlin what do you expect when pigs live here says Buttsy. Look at this says Devlin rotten fish in the sink, there's rats in here there's sure to be rats. No says Buttsy only pigs. Ha ha laughs Devlin. Ha ha, that was a good laugh. When I didn't come out they lost the rag. Buttsy swore and broke something. Burn the place says Devlin. He must be here somewhere they said and then I heard them rooting about outside. They came back in and wrecked the kitchen, cursing. Then they went off, fit to be tied, we'll get the bastard sooner or later. I didn't bother coming out and the next morning there was a huge pale sun sitting in the window. That did my heart good. Ah, I says, this is going to be a good day.

Off I went down the fresh, crunchy lane. I stopped just outside the chickenhouse to see if the puddle was frozen over and sure enough it was. I felt warm all over when I seen that. There was hard twisty paper growing out of the white misted ice. I tried to dig it out with my toe but it wouldn't come so I broke off a bit of a twig and hacked away at it. When I looked up there was this young lad standing there like something off a Christmas card with a big stripey scarf round his neck and a hat with tassels on it. What are you doing here mister he says, that's our puddle. Its your puddle? I says, Yes, he says, we're in charge of it me and Brendy. OK, I says and handed him the stick I won't touch it anymore. All right then mister he says, I won't tell Brendy. All of a sudden I looked at him with his rosy cheeks and the two silver snots at his nose and what did I want to do I wanted to kiss him. Not the way Tiddly did it any of that but just because all of a sudden everything seemed so good. I said to myself: Just being here is so good I could stand here for ever.

Its your puddle now, I says to him but do you know who it used to belong to? He rubbed his face with a mitten and says no – who?

Me and Joe Purcell, I said.

Oh, he says, well youse don't own it now and goes down on one knee and starts hacking away at the bit of paper.

I went into Mickey Traynor's shop. There was a big picture of Our Lord hanging on the wall. It said: *Buy a television or else you bastard!* No it didn't it said Our Saviour looks after us all.

His daughter was on her knees saying the rosary with a whole load of saint pictures spread out on top of a radio cabinet. I met her on the street one day and she told me she hated Romans because they killed Thaddeus the Christian boy whoever the fuck Thaddeus was. Mm mm mm she says the next sorrowful mystery of the holy rosary Jesus prays in the garden. Good man Jesus but you daren't say that or Mickey'd throw you out on the street on the spot. Well Mickey I said will you ever forget the days of the old television? He stuck the pencil behind his ear what television would that be now he says. Oh the one that got broke, I says, the one da gave out yards about. Did he not come up to you about it? Naw, says Mickey, I don't remember your da coming in at all now he says and goes back to his work, poking away at the inside of another telly. Without the back on it looked like one of these cities of the future you'd see in Dan Dare. Sure bring it up and we'll have a look at it, he says. Ah no, never mind about it Mickey, says I, that was all in the old days. I'm far too busy these times to be bothered worrying my head about televisions. Well, whatever you think yourself now, says Mickey as this fart comes out of the loudspeaker. Bejasus! he says then. I laughed and off I went. It sure was good to be back in the old town. Into the shop I went and who was there only Mrs Connolly and the women but they weren't expecting me this time you could tell that all right the way they were looking at me: *But we thought you were away in the industrial school!*

H'ho no ladies, I'm back in action yes indeed a puff of smoke and here he is again the incredible Francie Brady – *How are you ladies?*

They couldn't make up their minds who was going to speak. Little coughs and all this and one looking at the other – you say hello to him. No – *you do!* It went on like that for a minute or two. I think they thought I was going to pull a machine gun out from under my coat drrr die you dogs.

I had a good laugh thinking that. When I started laughing so did they and before we knew it we were all talking away about the old days and the pigs and all that. Anything I could think of we talked about it there was so many things in my head after the school for pigs. The laughs we had in those days, I says. Oh now, they said, don't be talking! You're back for good now Francis is that right says one of them and the other two gave her a look: *Don't ask him that! For the love of God don't ask him that!*

Why not? Them old women could ask me anything they liked. I am indeed, back in the old home town. That's what Audie Murphy says on the horse looking down on the sleeping western village from the hill – it shore is good to be back in the old home town. Yup! I says. All you could see was these three smiles just hanging there in mid-air. The shopgirl never opened her mouth. No, that's not true, she did. That was *all* she did, open her mouth. She just stood there behind the counter looking at us with her mouth open. It was nice talking to them there beside the cornflakes shelf, it was as if they hadn't moved an inch since I left still saying President Kennedy was a lovely man and something would have to be done about the price of butter. It would but I had more important things to talk about than that, the old days the old pig days we could have talked for hours about all that. Will you ever forget them old pig days I says. Oh now Francie, says Mrs Connolly, don't be talking! Ha ha they said, they were good days all right. Ah well, I said, that's all over, you can't be a pig all your life isn't that right ladies?

They said it was.

I said to Mrs Connolly: Isn't that right Mrs Connolly.

That's right Francis she says, that's very true.

It is indeed I says.

Ha ha says Mrs Connolly.

Ha ha says the other women.

Oh now says I.

We could have gone on talking there for hours there was so much to say but it was getting near time for me to move on and see what else I could discover on my travels. Well good day now ladies, I said, I guess I gotta mosey on. Ha ha *mosey on!*

Mrs Connolly was saying to herself I wonder was it all right to laugh at mosey on. Of course it was. I didn't care. They could laugh themselves stupid if they wanted to. Then I says well ladies I'd best be on my way. Yes Francis, says Mrs Connolly, you have to see all your pals. I have indeed I said. The smiles I had to laugh at them too – they weren't like smiles at all more like elastic bands pulled tight. Twang! and back they'd go. But sure no matter – they could smile whatever way they liked, I wasn't going to stop them. Right so ladies, I guess ah'll jest mosey along I says we'll see you soon please God says Mrs Connolly. Yup I says. When I was going by the window I gave it a rap *Jesus!* says one of them I think it was Mrs Connolly *twang!* goes the smile and the other women – are you all right Mrs Connolly? I says to myself: I never knew there was so many things in this town would make you laugh.

. There was a tin can lying there. Flip, over the hedge it went. You never know, I might play for the town yet I thought.

The fountain wasn't frozen it was spraying away goodo on the Diamond so I sat down beside it for a while. There was one thing I knew about that fountain. They had put it there for Queen Victoria the same time as they built the Jubilee Road in honour of her visit to the town that year. Except for one thing – she never came. It was a beautiful fountain well it was then. But a lorry backed into it one night and knocked all the angels and that off it and now there was a big plaster crack running up the side of it like a cut. I dropped a spit onto a fag box and thought of all the school kids and old folks *Hooray for Queen Victoria!* Except for one thing – where the fuck is she?

I couldn't stop chuckling the more I thought of it and them all going home in a huff – we've gone and built a fountain and a new road for fuck all!

But of course that wasn't true – I could sit on it couldn't I?

And the drunk lad could piss into it on his way home from the Tower. He sure could. So well done town and Queen Victoria I said to myself.

The big wheel of the carnival turned at the far end of the town, tossing hysterical people across the sky, people pretending to be hysterical that is. Well would you believe it – who comes along then only himself, old Father Dom, flapping his skirts and the shoes like little black paws peeping out. You got on well, at the em industrial school he says, I did indeed I said and who does he know it turns out, only our old friend Tiddly. Ah yes, he says, Father Sullivan, a very good friend of mine. How is he at all at all? Oh he's the best, I said, never better. An awful man for the books!, laughed Dom. A terror!, I says, a holy terror for the books! Matt Talbot, I said. Ah yes, poor Matt Talbot, sighed Father Dom and crossed himself. He was delighted at all this me knowing Tiddly and Matt Talbot and everything so we stayed there for a long time talking drum drum on the missal the weather has got very cold now and how's your father and I wonder what we can talk about now? I never seen you looking as well Francis he said, you've got so tall! I'm glad things have worked out for you. I must drop down and say hello one of these days. Do indeed Father, I said and saluted and off he went. I was wondering did he ever sit on Tiddly's knee? Are you comfortable there Dommie? Yes Father I am are you? Ah I am, I'm grand, grand now altogether. But I knew old Dom wouldn't do that. I'd say the worst thing Dom ever did in his whole life was say to his mother: No ma – *I won't* go to the shop for you!

I closed my eyes and breathed in it was like breathing in the whole cold fresh and crunchy town. I could hear the chicken-house fan droning away steady as ever down in our lane behind the houses. One day Joe said to me: Its the best sound in the world, that fan. I said why. He said: Because you always know its there.

And he was right. If you weren't thinking of it you wouldn't hear it. But once you listened, it was always there humming away softly like a quiet machine that kept the town going.

The baker was unloading trays of bread steaming from his van. Grouse Armstrong was huddled in the library door-way and off goes the drunk across the Diamond singing into his beer bottle I wonder who's kissing her now? Then he stops and starts into Grouse do you know me do you? Uh! Uh! Grouse just opened one eye for a second and then went back to sleep. You're only a baaaastard! says your man and then tumbles away off round the Jubilee Road on rubber legs. I wasn't expecting Roche so I got a bit of a shock when I looked up and seen him standing there staring at me. Who the fuck did he think he was – Count Dracula?

Ah hello there Doctor, I said, and how are things?

He didn't say anything just looked and that was what I didn't like about Roche the way he looked at you. He was saying: I know something about you. You knew by him he'd stand there for as long as he liked without saying a word.

I don't know why the fuck I did it for he didn't ask me anything but I started into telling him everything, driving to the school with the sergeant and what a laugh it was and then the bogmen and all that. I could feel his eyes all over me making notes. I went back over a few of the stories, the gardener and that, and then I said yes doctor its changed times now. The old days is all finished. I kept waiting for him to say I'm glad to hear that Francie or that's great news, like the priest, but he didn't say anything. He said nothing and just wiped his lips with a hankie and then looked at it. What do you think of that, doc, all the old days being finished? I gave him a big grin even though my head was hurting me, it was hard no matter what you were talking about not to think about the business with Joe and all that and wondering could you fix it some way or blank it out so that it hadn't happened. He lowered his voice and I had to strain to hear what he said. He said yes, yes that's good but I could tell by the sound of it that he didn't believe me. I told him more then, about the boilerhouse and the fags but he just tapped the leather of his black bag and sucked his teeth saying mm. All of a sudden it came into my head what the hell do I care if he believes me or not who the fuck is he, doctor, some doctor, he couldn't even keep ma out of the garage, could he? I didn't care about him. He could say anything he liked. I'd tell him that – fuck him! You know nothing I said you know nothing about my ma, what the fuck do you know about her she should never have gone near you it was you put her in there in the first place what the fuck would you know Roche what would you know about anything! I was wondering would he go so far as to make a wind at me after all that but when I looked up all I seen was the door of the hotel closing and him chatting away to the receptionist through the glass. All of a sudden I thought I heard someone calling: Francie!

I thought it was Joe whee-hoo I said but it was someone I didn't know who it was. I wasn't sure what to do then or where to go then I says what am I on about I'll go down to Joe's where else would I go. I blew my nail hopping about on the step then out comes Mr Purcell. Well Mr Purcell I said is the man himself there. He looked at me for a minute then he looked over my shoulder and waved at somebody some neighbour getting out of a car with a box of groceries. No, he says, Joe isn't here. The neighbour called something and Mr Purcell laughed. Oh now, he says. They went on yapping there for a while, about the weather and all this. Ah sure the farmers will never be pleased says your man. No, says Mr Purcell, now you said it. There was a fair crowd at the match Sunday. There was. Marty Dowds had a good game. He had. Marty's shaping up to be a right wee player. He is.

I just stood there on the step waiting for your man to go in. Right he says I'll see you and then he'd start into something else cars or some other shite. Then he says right so good luck now. He waved and next thing Mr Purcell smiles and closes the door behind him it just happened he didn't slam it or anything. I'd been waiting so long I forgot what I wanted to say and when I remembered it was too late and the door was closed. I waited there on the step for a minute then I just went away.

I went round to Roche's house a few times and waited for him but he never appeared I think he must have went on holidays.

They said I had to stay at the primary school even if I was older than the rest. I didn't know any of them. My class had gone on ahead to the secondary school along with Joe. I sat at the back and did nothing. No – that's not true. I played Oxo and wrote Francis Brady was here with a penknife. The master says to me who put the Vikings back into the sea I says Daniel O'Connell come out here he says and gave me a crack of the stair rod across the arm. I'll give it to you, he says, you needn't think you'll try any of your tricks with me Brady! Leddy's the man for you, that's the only place you'll ever be any good for!

I knew why he was doing that, he heard them saying in the jakes Brady was going to batter the master. I don't know how they got that into their heads I had more to do than batter doddery old masters with whiskey noses and hands that wouldn't stop shaking so I thought the best thing to do was quit going to school altogether. They were all getting fond of this fellow Leddy. Da looks at me and says: Its either school or Leddy's! You'd be as well to make up your mind!

Leddy was the butcher who owned the slaughterhouse. There was always jobs there for no one wanted to do it. To hell with Leddy and his pigs, I said. *Its good enough for the likes of you da said lying about here morning noon and night!* and went off mumbling to the Tower.

Sometimes I'd just lie there on the sofa until Joe got out of school. After a while you didn't even notice the smell only if someone else mentioned it. There was an old chicken da took home out of the Tower after a do one night. It was all flies and maggots so I fucked that out. I think Grouse got it out of the bin the crafty bastard.

I always met Joe at the bottom of Church Hill. There was no more talk about the school for pigs or anything that went on there, that was all finished now and soon it would be all back the way it used to be.

I got things for him, not comics he didn't read them much any more, fags or sweets maybe. I got the fags from behind the bar in the hotel I knew the barman went out to change the barrel at the same time every day. I got the sweets in

Mary's but I paid for them I'd never lift anything on her. Then we'd head off out to the river. I told him I could get him anything he wanted. We had some laughs out there. It was no different to the old days. It was just the same only better. Isn't it Joe? I'd say. He said it was. I says its better than the school and exams and all that shite isn't it Joe. I asked him to put on the cowboy voices like he used to. He said he couldn't do them any more. Go on, try Joe I said. I can't do them, he said, that's a long time ago. I know it is Joe I said but I'll bet you can still do them. No, he says I can't. But I knew he could. Try it Joe I says. Then he said it – OK fellas we're ridin' out!

You see Joe, I said, you can do it!

It was just like John Wayne. You'd swear it was him. I was over the moon when he did that voice. He used to spin his silver colt and say it just like that – OK fellas we're ridin' out! Say it again Joe I said, say it again! I couldn't stop asking him to say it again. But I had to in the end for I could see him getting red under the eyes and I didn't want to annoy him anyway he'd said it enough he was tired he said he had to get back. I left him in town and then I came back out myself. I'd try doing the voice but I could never get it as good as Joe. I'd lie there on the flattened yellow grass where he had been but no matter how I tried it I always got it arseways. It didn't sound like John Wayne at all. It sounded more like the bird what do you call him – I taught I taw a puddytat.

I kept at Joe to come tracking in the mountains. We'll pray to the Manitou like we used to – it'll be a good laugh I said. Oh come on Francie – for god's sake! Joe said.

The Manitou, I said – yamma yamma yamma death to all dogs who enter here! For fuck's sake Joe!

He laughed when I said that and then he said OK it was the best day yet you'd think Nugents or the school for pigs or Tiddly and all that had never happened. We spun stones across the lake and when I looked at Joe doing that I nearly wanted to cry the feeling I got was so good. Everything was so clear and glittering and polished I said to myself: Those days in the lane. We didn't imagine them. They were just like this.

I was thinking that with my eyes closed when I heard Buttsy's voice. He was standing in front of me with his thumbs hooked in his belt.

Devlin was chewing a match and carrying a fishing rod.

Well well. If it isn't our lucky day, says Buttsy.

Devlin was rubbing away at the hands like he'd won the sweep. Buttsy looked at Joe.

I want no trouble with you, Purcell, he says. Its him we want, says Devlin. You're going to be sorry now. You're going to be sorry for what you done, Brady.

Who's going to make me sorry I says. Buttsy got all pale when I said that.

Joe says: Don't Francie. Don't start any trouble.

We'll make you sorry, says Devlin and took a swing at me. When I was ducking I twisted my ankle on a rock.

Then Buttsy drew a kick at me and knocked me to the ground.

Devlin says *Come on!* and got stuck in with his big farmer's boots. Next thing Buttsy has the hunting knife out it was trembling away in his hand. You've had it now, Brady, said Devlin, we'll gut you like a pig.

What you done on my sister, Buttsy says. Her nerves have never been the same since.

He was as white as a sheet and I could see the sweat gleaming on his forehead. Do you hear me! he says. She had to go to the doctor after what you done! Roche has her on three different kinds of tablets – *three different kinds of tablets!*

Devlin kicked me on the bad ankle. You fucking cunt, he says. When he said that I started to cry.

Ha! says Buttsy, and he got all excited then . . .

Look at him now, says Devlin.

That's more like it, says Buttsy.

You see, Devlin, I told you, says Buttsy, slipping the knife back into his pocket, coming back to himself, he can dish it out but he can't take it. I said: I know what I done was wrong Buttsy. I know! I was trying to catch Joe's eye to give him the signal but he couldn't see me he was all on edge.

Women, says Devlin, that's all he's able for, women, he can give it to the women all right but when it comes to you and me its a different story, eh Buttsy?

Then they started whispering between themselves, what they were going to do with me.

I'll do anything I said. You should have thought of that before you broke into people's houses says Devlin and hit me another dig.

For fuck's sake, would you look at him! Look at him now! There's your buddy now Purcell. There's your buddy from the Terrace!

Buttsy took out a fag and lit it.

Then he goes over to Joe and says to him: What are you

doing hanging about with him? What does your old man say?

Then Joe said it: I'm not hanging around with him. I *used* to hang around with him!

All I could see was the lit fag going up to Buttsy's mouth and his head nodding as he said something else to Joe. He was blowing out the smoke and tapping the ash then he ran his arm across his forehead and that gave me my chance bumph! He didn't know what hit him. I don't know how many times I clocked him with the rock if Devlin and Joe hadn't managed to get me off I'd have finished him off it wouldn't have cost me a thought he made Joe say it Joe wouldn't have said it only he goaded him into it. I tried to get another kick at him but they pulled me back no no! Francie! Devlin says Francie its gone far enough he was scared shitless I was going to start into him but I didn't give a fuck about Devlin I wanted to talk to Joe. I threw the rock over the ditch Joe I says what do you mean why did you say that?

The way Joe looked at me then I couldn't think at first who it reminded me of then I knew, it was Doctor Roche, looking right through you. Joe, please, I said but he wouldn't let me talk. I could feel my knees going and I had to drag the words up out of my stomach, please Joe!

But he still wouldn't listen he was backing away with his palms pressing a glass wall, No Francie, not this time, not after this!

Any time I tried to say anything he just put up his hand: No!, he said. I shouted after him Joe – come back, please! I'll do anything. Anythihg you want! But all I could see was him climbing the railway gate and when I looked again he was gone. Devlin looked at me with the lip trembling: Please Francie!

I was going to but then I said what's the use what's the fucking use I just left him there *please Francie* and Buttsy crawling along the ground uh! uh! help me yeah sure.

I went round to the carnival you'd think the swingboats were going to take off into the sky altogether. I never heard so many screeches, girls holding on to their boyfriends *Save me!* and all this. There was Jim Reeves and big pink teddybears and dodgems sparking but I didn't want to see any of that I went over to the shooting gallery to see the goldfish. I don't know how many there was in the tank. Fifty maybe. Every time they swerved there was a little flash of silver. I watched them for a good while just swimming away there. I could see these girls over by the dodgems they were just sitting there swinging their legs and giggling behind their hands. They'd look over at me and nudge each other then they'd start giggling again. There was a small blondie one and they were trying to push her over to say something to me. The older one says go on and blows this pink gumbubble the blondie one says no I won't!

They kept at this for a good while then in the end what did they do didn't the three of them come over. They stood there linking each other and you say it no you say it I didn't know where to look I was as red as a beetroot, I didn't know what they were doing or what to say to them. They knew my face was going red and I knew they were laughing at that too. Look at him, he's going all red. What's he going all red for? I thought that's what they were thinking but I think now maybe they weren't thinking it at all. All they wanted to talk about was Joe. They said: You're a friend of Joe Purcell's aren't you? Do you want to know something? She likes him!

They pushed the blondie one again and she fell against me. I tried to say watch or are you OK or something but I started stuttering but it didn't matter they were away off again chuckling and giggling about Joe.

The house was littered with bottles when I got home. Da was asleep on the sofa with the trumpet beside him and there was some old lad with a cap sitting in a chair. We had a great chat tonight about the old days, all the old Tower bar crowd he says tell your father not to be worrying his head what Roche says the Bradys are tough men, hard men. It takes more than a pain in the chest to annoy them. Am I right Francie? he says. I said he was. I didn't know what the fuck he was talking about, him and Roche I wanted to hear no more about Roche. Then he fell asleep with his head hanging on his chest like a cloth doll. I wanted to sleep now too. I knew that in a couple of days everything would be all right again. We'd have some laughs then me and Joe. I couldn't wait to see him taking off Buttsy. Uh! Uh! *Help me!*

There sure is some laughs in this town Joe I'd say. Then we'd stick our faces into the water and tell the fish what they could do with themselves. I didn't think I'd sleep with all the things that had been going on. But I did. I slept like a top. I went curving through my dreams yamma yamma yamma right over the rooftops of the town and when I got back to the lake Joe was hunched there smiling and he looks at me and says: So what if we had an argument? We're still blood brothers ain't we?

Yup, I said, and we always will. That's the way it was meant to be Francie boy!

I left it for a few days so that it would all be forgotten then I called to the house and says to Mr Purcell is Joe there. No, he says, he's gone away to his uncle's for the weekend he won't be back till Monday. O I says I'll call back Monday then even though I was nearly sure I seen him at the curtain upstairs. I didn't say that because there was no sense in causing any trouble. Very well says Mr Purcell I'll tell him. Thank you I said then off I went. But the thing was I didn't see him on Monday either because now Mr Purcell took him home in the car and all I could see was him going past behind the steamed-up glass I never saw him looking out to see if I was at the corner or anything.

Da said to me: I was talking to Leddy this morning then starts spluttering into this big hankie the size of a sheet.

I didn't bother waiting to hear what he was talking to him about.

Another day I met Leddy himself coming flopping down the street in his wellies you could smell the pig dung half an hour before you saw him at all. I believe you might be coming round to give me a bit of a hand he says. Look at Leddy I thought, talk about pigs! Whatever about us, he was one for sure. He'd been working with them that long he'd turned into one. He had a big pink face and a scrunched-up snout. There was enough pigs round there without me I said.

I'd had it with pigs. But I said thanks anyway. Right says Leddy suit yourself and off he goes flop flop flop down the street.

I called round to Joe's again. There you are Mr Purcell I says, I was wondering would the man himself be about? Mr Purcell didn't say anything for a minute or two just stood there biting the inside of his lip and then he says: Didn't you call here this morning? I did I says. And what did my wife tell you? O she said Joe was busy helping her in the kitchen I think. Well you think right he said and he'll be busy all evening now if you don't mind. And what does he start to do then only close the door. It was the first time Mr Purcell had ever spoke like that to me. I was just standing there staring at the blue paint of this door and I didn't know what to think about it all. The next time I called Mrs Purcell answered it and when I asked her was Joe coming out to the river she said he was at music. Music, I said, I didn't know he did music where is he at music? Up at the convent she said, where they all go to music. The convent I said, I didn't know he went to music Mrs Purcell. He never went to music before did he? No, she says, he didn't. She was starting to close the door now too. There was a petrol truck trying to turn at the end of the lane. I watched it for a minute and then I says to Mrs Purcell OK then Mrs Purcell I must call down after and maybe he'll be here then. Very well Francis she says looking out through a crack then the door closed softly with a click. I stood there standing back from the way she said very well Francis and looking at it like the way you'd hold an envelope up to the light to see if there was anything in it. When I thought to myself: What she means is I hope he doesn't call down here ever again. I felt like I'd swallowed a chicken bone it kept moving around in my throat and I couldn't get it out. I looked up at the bedroom windows to see if there was anybody looking down. But there wasn't of course. That was just rubbish, me thinking that. Just because I thought I saw him there one other time didn't mean he'd be there again if he was there the first time that is. I went off down the lane I was going to go for a walk but then I doubled back because I couldn't figure out how Joe was doing music if he hadn't a piano he must be doing guitar. But the nuns don't teach guitar. I shone the glass of the sitting room window with the sleeve of my jumper and sure enough there it was, a new mahogany piano and sitting there on the music stand the music book with the ass and cart on the front going off into misty green mountains. I couldn't read it but I knew what it was – *Emerald Gems of Ireland*.

Philip was swinging the music case as he went by Mrs Connolly's hedge singing to himself. I just came out from behind the gate and says well Philip. He starts the twisting again only this time at the handle of the music case and I think he said hello Francis. I said Francie, not Francis. Francie, he said, and then *he* got all red. I wasn't sure how to start I thought of a couple of different things to say but none of them sounded right. In the end I just said: You gave Joe Purcell your music book, didn't you?

He said what and raised his eyebrows so I said it again. No I didn't he said. Well, I said, I'm afraid you did but all he would say then was I *didn't*. If you didn't I said, it would be in the music case then wouldn't it? Yes he says but he wasn't really listening to me. He was twisting the handle and looking past me again. Let me look in the case then and we'll see, I said and then we'll know for sure. Can I have it then Philip? He handed the case to me and looked away. I ran my fingers over its polished flakes I loved the way they peeled off and stuck to your fingers the way old paint does. He had a good lot of books in there, songs you'd never heard of before. There was one of a man singing to the moon with two palm trees behind him and another Bluebells in Spring with all these flowers swaying in the breeze and a girl in a blue dress la dee dee through the fields. Study in F, that was another one. There was a pen at the bottom of the case too. I spread them all out on the ground to make sure. Oh fuck I said I'm sorry Philip. There was a patch of water I didn't see and one of them got a bit wet. It was the Study in F. I told Philip I was sorry over and over but he kept saying it was all right. I don't want to get you in trouble I said. No no, he said, no. I checked them a good few times after that and then I said: Its not here Philip. He said I don't know maybe its at home Francie I don't know. I said no Philip it isn't at home and you know it isn't because you gave it to Joe Purcell maybe for a lend but you still gave it to him. Oh Francie please he said. I said all you have to do is tell me you might as well for I seen it in his house its on the piano. I don't know Francie he starts again he could have bought his own, or maybe I did give it to him I don't know. You don't know now if you gave it to him or not I said. He said again maybe but I said look there's no sense in saying maybe Philip. That's the book you gave him for I seen it in this very case there's an ass and cart on the front of it and mountains. And you gave it to Joe Purcell and now you're saying you didn't.

You gave it to him didn't you? Maybe it was only for a lend but you still gave it to him didn't you? All you have to do is tell me Philip that's all I want to know. Then he splutters yes yes yes and sniffles a bit. I had wanted him to say it all right but then when he did I didn't like it. What I was going to say at first was well there we are that's all that over, all you had to do was say that in the first place. But that wasn't what I said in the end. I said: What did you do that for? He says I just gave it to him Francie the music teacher said. Then it came into my head, Joe and Francie standing there in the music teacher's room. There you are Joe said Philip handing him the book. Thank you very much said Joe. And Philip smiling away. I said to Philip: This is all to do with the gold-fish isn't it? Then what does he say only: What goldfish? I don't know what you mean Francie.

When I looked at him saying that straight into my face, I thought: Please, Philip. Don't go like your mother.

I explained everything to him. It was all right him giving Joe the goldfish when I was away in the school. But that was all over now. Its no use thinking by giving music books to Joe that you can get in with us, Philip. It wouldn't be fair to tell you lies. I asked him did he understand what I meant? He said he did and although he was disappointed I knew it was better for him to know.

I'll tell you what Philip, I said. Some day we're going tracking in the mountains you can come, OK? Only don't tell her. You know what she'll do. He said yes. I gathered up the books and put them in the case. Then I walked along a bit of the way with him. I said goodbye to him at the street corner and said I would see him soon. Then I went home.

———

When I got home there wasn't a whisper in the house only for the flies, nothing only da in the armchair by the radio. I was talking away to him about Philip and how it was better to be straight with people and not keep them hanging on. I made tea and I asked him did he want some. I said: What are you doing there? Looking out at the snowdrop? I said even if Philip wants to come out to the river with me and Joe, as long as he understands that its always going to be me and Joe in the end. I thought maybe da'd had a Tower bar *do you remember the old days* party for the house was littered with bottles and the trumpet lying over by the skirting board so I reckoned he just wasn't fit to answer me. I gave his shoulder a bit of a shake and when the hankie fell out of his pocket I saw that it was all dried blood. Oh da, I said, I didn't know and I felt his forehead it was cold as ice. I said: Don't worry da. I'll look after you. I'll see that you're all right. I might have let you down before but not this time! Oh no – not this time! Us Bradys – we'll show them! We'll show them we stick together!

I saw him smiling when I said that. I pulled his chair into the fire and said sit in there da go on now. I built it up good and high I used anything I could find in the yard it was the first time there had been a fire in the house for as long as I could remember. It was good, flickering away there and the shadows swarming all over the ceiling. I rooted about and found bread and toasted it on a fork then we had tea all we did was just sit there that was all we wanted to do. Da looked at me and when I seen those eyes so sad and hurt I wanted to say: I love you da.

They said to me: You won't leave me son.

I said: I won't da. I'll never leave you.

This time its going to be all right – isn't it son?

I said it was. We're going to be a happy family son. I knew we would be in the end. I said we were. I'd make sure we were, I said. It was all up to me now. Me and nobody else. Then he said to me *the trumpet find the trumpet*. I lifted it and polished it up until it was shining just like it used to. Then I put it away in its felted case just like he did, laying it to rest like an infant after a long day. *Don't let them touch my trumpet Francie!* he said.

I told him he didn't have to worry, his worrying days were over. Your worrying days are over, da, I said.

I touched the back of his hand.

Thanks Francie, he said and I was so happy that we were able to say these things to one another that I cried, the tears just came streaming down as I sat there with my head resting on his shoulder.

The next day I says its up to me now its all up to me and nobody else they'll soon see what the Bradys are made of!

I went up the town and into the shop, shopping basket and all. I could see Mrs Connolly pointing to it and the other women crinkling up their foreheads its not too often you see Francie Brady with a shopping basket. Indeed it isn't ladies I said but you'll be seeing it plenty from now on, I'm going to be a busy man! I don't know where to start with all these jobs Mrs Connolly, I says.

I think she thought I was joking for a minute but when she seen I wasn't laughing her face changed and she went all serious oh yes she says no one likes doing them but they have to be done ha ha. That's right says the other women that's very true. When I got my things I said well ladies I can't delay have to get back to the grindstone oh now Francie they said its near time we went home ourselves we'd stand here gossiping half the day if we were let. Ha ha I said.

When I was cleaning out the coalhouse what did I find only the old television. I put it sitting on the table in the same place it used to be. By the time I was finished the shed was spotless. Now what will I do I said. I made da tea and tidied the upstairs. I always made sure never to miss Friday Night Is Music Night!

That was da's favourite programme. He used always come home from the Tower to listen to it and dare you talk while it was on. Ladies and gentlemen – here is your host, Mr Ian-Priestly Mitchell!

No matter what I did Jeyes Fluid or anything there was still a bit of a stink and flies about after the pilchards so I went back up the street and got flypapers they were supposed to be better than the sprays and as well as that you could see how many you got.

Every so often I checked the flypapers and counted them. It didn't take long. In no time at all I had eleven. I went up to get another paper just in case that one got full up too quick. Well well says Father Dom. Francis he says you're a man with things to do I think that's the fifth time I've seen you go up and down that street today. Who did Dom think he was – Fabian of the Yard? Oh yes Father I'm doing a bit of Spring cleaning below in the house I need this and that you know yourself. What's that you have there he says don't tell me you're smoking. Oh no says I its a flypaper that's all you won't catch me at the smoking Father. Not yet anyhow he says. Mm mm he says you've quit going to school altogether I see, would that be right Francis? Yes I said I've quit the school now and that's it. Isn't that a pity now, he says, for they'll tell you the schooling stands to you. I suppose it does ah well that's the way then I said I had to go into the Tower for a few bottles of stout. You're not at the drinking Francis, don't tell me you're at the drinking. Ah no, Father, I says, just a few bottles for the boss. Oh I see he says all relieved, they're for the man himself. Indeed they are I said and said good luck to him and off he floated till he met some woman Father come here till I tell you. After the stout that was the end of the money. There was none left in da's pockets and nothing in the bin only a crust. I sat with da thinking was there anything I could do then in the end I went round to Leddy. Don't worry da, I said, I'll start early in the mornings and get home early in the evening. It'll be OK, you'll see.

He looked at me and he said: You won't leave me son?

But he didn't have to worry. I wasn't going to leave him. I wasn't going to let ma and da or anyone down ever again.

There's the man that wants no more truck with pigs, he says. I'd like a job Mr Leddy I said. The smell of piss and shit and dirty guts you never seen the like of it. At the side of the slaughterhouse there was a concrete pit where they just threw out the manure and the guts and the offal and let it pile away up. The Pit of Guts, that's what I called that place. Grouse Armstrong was trailing a big sheet of white skin with innards attached to it across the yard stopping the odd time to tear and paw at it. There was steam coming up out of the pit and it was crawling with bluebottles. It was moving, you'd think it'd get up and just walk across the yard and away. Every two seconds Leddy'd draw in this big deep breath with the sound of snots like paper tearing. I dare say you weren't in too many places like this he says then I could see by him he was thinking so this is the famous Francie Brady well we'll soon see how tough he is we'll soon see how tough he is when he's inside Leddy's slaughterhouse. But I smiled away and every time he told me something about it I said that's very interesting and the worse he got about all the things I'd have to do in the place, the better I said it was. You'll have to be up and out at the crack of dawn he says, what do you think of that? I said that's fine Mr Leddy. Any man thinks this work is easy needs his head examined – you want to be tough to work here! Indeed you do Mr Leddy I said and I could see he liked me calling him that so I kept on doing it. It wouldn't have been a good idea to say I suppose you should know all these things considering you are a pig yourself with your big pink pig head but I would have liked to say it the way he was going on. Like he was some kind of visiting professor down from the Cutting Up Pigs University. The more he talked the more he wanted to talk. Pigs, by Mr Leddy. That was what I thought but I kept on nodding away. O yes. And Hmm. If you don't pull your weight he says its down that road straight away I've no time for wasters. O you'll have no trouble with me Mr Leddy I says. Good he says for I daresay they're not falling over themselves giving *you* jobs about this town. Now he says what about this fellow and this little pig looks out at me through the bars, what do you think of him? I says O he's lovely but I forgot myself for that wasn't what Leddy wanted me to say. Lovely he says, you think he's lovely. Good he says and scoops him up in his arms. Now he says take a good look at him. He was as pink as a baby's bottom and he said to me with his big eyes: I'm not a big pig yet I don't understand anything. Please – will you not let any harm come to me? And his front trotters dangling over Leddy's tattoo it was a snaked sword. Isn't he lovely says Leddy again he sure is he sure is and next thing what has he in his hand only a gun not a real gun it was a captive bolt pistol and what does he do only stick it into the baby pig's head and bid-dunk!, right into his skull goes the bolt and such a squeal. Then down on the concrete plop and not a squeak out of him all you could see was him saying you said you'd mind me and you didn't. Then Leddy looks at me haw haw haw and all this as much as to say whaddya think John Wayne huh betcha didn't expect that! Huh! he says, huh? He was all excited and the bottom lip was starting to go I knew he wasn't as tough as he let on, all he was saying was don't try any of your tricks on me Brady, just the same as the master. But it was a good one all the same. What d'you think now, eh? he says. Very good, top marks Mr Leddy, top marks from the Shooting Piglets University. Or I could say why oh why did you have to do such a terrible thing to him he never harmed anyone in his whole life you're a cruel cruel man Mr Leddy! and throw myself down on top of the poor little dead little baby pig lying there with his mouth open.

But I didn't bother with that, instead I went over to the pen and caught another fellow by the trotters he was even younger than the first. He was in a bad way altogether for he'd seen the whole thing. His eyes, *please please don't kill me I'll do anything!* What about this lad I said, he's a chancy-looking customer. Give me the pistol there Mr Leddy and I'll put a bit of manners on him. Leddy stood back with his hand on his hip and laughed. You're a good one Brady if you think I'll fall for that he says. But fair fucks to you for trying. You've a while to do here yet before you'll be able to face the like of that ha ha. Ah no, I says, Mr Leddy, not at all. It wouldn't be fair on this little fellow to leave him all alone now that his poor old friend is gone. So give me over the gun now and we'll see what we can do for him. You must think I came up the Shannon in a bubble laughs Leddy. I heard about your carry-on he says but you won't put one over on Jimmy Leddy. I was in Bangkok he says when Benny Brady hadn't even plucked your mother. I didn't like him saying that I didn't like it one bit watch what you're saying about my mother Leddy but I had promised da so I said nothing about it I just said I know, you've seen it all, you've been all over the world but let me have a look at it anyway. The piglet wouldn't sit at rest, twisting and wriggling please Francie Francie please let me go. He hands me the pistol, here he says have a look at it but be careful, I says don't worry Mr Leddy. I looked at it for a while there wasn't much to it the baby pig was still looking up at me with the ear flapping over one eye please Francie? Well any other time I would have let him down or put him back in but I wanted Leddy to take me on straight away and I had things to buy for the house and everything so I just shrugged and I don't know what all Leddy's huffing and puffing was about. One squeal and a buck as the bolt went in and I just threw him down on the floor beside the other fellow. Leddy was rubbing his tattoo, biting his lip and staring at me. Behind him a row of pigs in muslin shirts. And a lump of a cow on a table with ribs like a half-built boat. Just you and me get one thing straight he says as I handed the pistol back to him. Then he stared me out of it and said: You'll do what I tell you, Brady.

Whatever you say Captain Pig I said. No I didn't I said can I start now Mr Leddy?

Be in here nine o'clock tomorrow he says and eyes me up and down still rubbing the tattoo. Good luck now Mr Leddy I said and kick started in the air whee-hoo away off like the clappers down the street. I was well and truly in charge now. I felt good. I've got a job da I said. Fair play to you, son, he said, I knew you were a good one. I was in business now I thought. I felt like I owned the whole town.

I met the women and I said did you hear did you hear I got a job in Leddy's! They said it was great news. Indeed it is ladies, I said, wait till you see one of these days I'll be changing my name to Mr Algernon Carruthers Brady. They didn't know what I was talking about but they laughed anyway. Oh now they says, you're an awful character, Mr Algernon Carruthers Brady! Did you ever hear the like of it!

There you are now ladies, I said, can't stop to talk have to be off now I don't know what end of me's up with all the things I have to do.

You'll be a busy man from now on with all this working, they said.

I sure will, I said, but you know yourselves it has to be done!

And you're the man to do it Francie!

Now you have it ladies – its all up to me now!

Goodbye now Francie and the three hands waving like leaves in the breeze.

Every day I'd collect my brock cart from the farmyard and off I'd go round the houses and hotels gathering scraps of potato skins and rotten food. Brock they called that and Francie the brock man collected it. When Leddy wasn't there I said to the swinging pigs: OK Porky its the end of the road. Then I'd say blam! and take the fat head off them with the captive bolt pistol. Take 'em to Missouri men, I'd shout. O please don't kill me I'm too fat to run away! Too bad, Piggy! Blam! Pinky and Perky – eat lead!

Next thing what does Leddy say only you're not the worst of them you can give me a hand behind the counter in the shop. So there you are! The way things turn out! Francie Brady The Butcher Boy! Oho but this time it was different, this old Butcher Boy was happy as Larry and you wouldn't find him letting people down, no sir! Now, there you are missus! There's just over a pound and a half there is that all right? Oh yes that's fine Francis thank you very much. The next thing then was the deliveries, off I'd go on my messenger bike with J. Leddy Victualler painted on the side. Away off out the mountains and the bogs and the country lanes ting-a-ling here he comes The Butcher Boy whistling away in his stripey blue apron always in good humour. Not a bad day now, ma'am. Not too bad Francie thank God. Hello there you old bogman I mean Mr Farmer. Have you got the hay in yet? You're hard at it! Indeed I am!

Goodbye now! Ting-a-ling! Whistle whistle bark bark – *clear off dog!* Morning guv! Same again next week? Wot's that then? Two pounds of pork chops, a couple of kidneys and a sirloin roast. Oh and a couple of bones for Bonzo! No problem no problem at all guv! Ta-ra then!

And off he goes bump bump bump. Cor strike a light darlin' I says to this woman hanging out her washing.

She screws up her face: Eh? she says.

There you are again, Francie, Lord bless us you're all over the place! the women'd say. Indeed I am I'd say and twirl the meat parcels across the marble top.

There you are says the amazing Father Dom sorry Father can't stop to talk it was a different story now I reckoned with all these jobs I was important now and I had no time to waste gossiping. But especially to the likes of Roche who stopped me one day with the black bag and just stands there looking at me, out of nowhere again of course. Look Roche, I wanted to say to him, if you want to spoil things go off and spoil them on somebody else. I'm a busy man and I have things to do. I'm in charge and I have no time for fooling about and talking shite to the likes of you so go on now about your business and leave people to do their work in peace. That was what I wanted to say to black eyebrows Roche.

I was fed up of him and everything to do with him and I'd tell him that too. But I didn't and what the fuck does he do then only come over and I got a big red face on me I don't know why he just stands there. I heard you were working for Leddy.

I am, I says, what's wrong with that?

I'm not saying there's anything wrong with it I'm only asking he said.

I wanted to say: Well don't ask Roche, *Don't ask!*

Do you like it down there he says, twirl twirl the timer on his watch.

Yes I says, ten bob a week.

And what do you do with that?

I knew he was trying to trick me into saying I buy bottles of stout for da so I said: I put it in the post office Doctor.

Very wise he says.

Hmm.

What I wanted to talk to you about was your father – he was supposed to come up and see me and he never did.

O I says, was he?

Will you tell him to drop in this evening maybe or tomorrow?

Oh I will I says, I'll tell him that.

You won't forget?

No, I says. I won't and then he says it again you won't forget and I could see him looking me up and down the worst thing about that is you start thinking ah there's nothing no sweat on my forehead and that's what makes the sweat come. There was beads on my forehead. I could feel them and the more I felt them the bigger they got they felt as big as berries and that was what made me blurt out O no doctor I forgot he's gone over to England to visit Uncle Alo.

What? he says and frowns, he's *what*?

It was too late for me to take it back or turn it into a joke so I had to go on ahead with it I had to make up a whole story.

I see, he says, and he was looking me up and down twice as much now. I had to put my hand in my pocket to stop it shaking for I knew if it started he'd see it he saw fucking everything didn't he?

Then he rubs his chin and says: Right so. Well – when he

gets back tell him I want to see him straight away. Its very important.

OK, doctor I said and saluted as much as to say: There's not a bother on me. But I knew by Roche that it didn't look like there wasn't a bother on me. It didn't look like that at all.

I said to myself I won't go back to Leddy's yet I'll take the cart out the road a bit and sit down and have a think about things then I'll be all right and I would have been if I hadn't of seen Joe just as I was going by the cafe. The window was open and the music was blaring out. He was sitting in between the blondie one and some other one laughing away and who was on the other side of her only Philip Nugent. He was explaining something to her, drawing away in the air with his hands. Joe was smoking a fag, nodding when the blondie one said something. She shook the hair back out of her eyes and went ha ha at something he said. Then she rested her chin on her hand and tapped her cigarette. Philip Nugent was drumming in time to the music on the formica table. I just stood there staring in the window and the song kept going round and round in my head: *When you move in right up close to me, that's when I get the shakes all over me!* Then I saw Joe's lips move he said I'll put on another song will I and the blondie one nodded. I knew no matter what Joe said she'd have agreed O yes that's right Joe. When he stood up we were looking at one another face to face through the window. If it had been anybody else I would have given them my butcher boy wink and a big grin but it wasn't anybody else it was Joe and for the first time in my life I didn't know what to say to him. He sort of jerked his head the way you would to someone you half-knew or someone you didn't even know at all then he walked up to the jukebox and bent over it drumming on the sides with his fingers. I kept waiting for him to look back down and say come on in or something but he didn't he just kept on drumming and mouthing the words of the songs to himself. The only thing that happened was the blondie one looked up and seen me and what does she do then only cover her face with her hand and say something to the other girl and Philip Nugent. The other girl looked up to get a look at me but I was gone.

At the weekend Leddy said to me I'll say this for you Brady you're a fair man to work whatever else they may say about you here's a ten bob note and whee-hoo, off I went like a bullet to the Tower and bought some bottles of stout and then I went into the shop and got a whole pound of corned beef. All da used to ask me to get was a quarter at a time and would his eyes light up when he saw all this. I was going to give it all to him! Why wouldn't I? I still had plenty of money left. I could buy the whole tin if I wanted to. I could say to the shopgirl: See that tin of corned beef? Give me it all!

And she'd have to give it to me. On the way up the street I seen Joe and the blondie one coming across the Diamond on their way down to the carnival. I went in behind a car in case I'd have to pass them but I needn't have worried for they met the other girl and some of her friends hi! shouts the other one and then they all went off together let them what did I care about them I had my own business to take care of right Francie I said let's mosey and in I went to the shop, I was just wondering what Joe was saying to her, maybe he was talking to her about music he was hardly talking to her about John Wayne. John Wayne – for fuck's sake!

I says to the shopgirl I wanted corned beef. You must be going to make a fair few sandwiches says the shopgirl no I said no! I'm not making any sandwiches. What are you talking about – sandwiches? I said. The shopgirl was red and she said I was only saying you don't have to shout at me. It made me all nervy and I dropped the corned beef on the way out of the shop. What were they looking at? Mrs Connolly was pretending not to but I could see her turning away at the last minute pretending to squeeze a pan loaf saying is this fresh? What are you looking at Connolly I wanted to say to her if you've got something to say why don't you say it. But just in time I said to myself no don't say that its all right maybe she wasn't looking at you after all. I knew I shouldn't have said anything to the shopgirl either. But I could hardly go back in and say I didn't mean to say any of that about the sandwiches. I *am* going to make sandwiches. But they mustn't have noticed or forgot all about it for it was OK the next time I seen them they said nothing about it. I cut them all up into triangles and put them on a plate and everything. What do you think of the sandwiches da? I said. Will I make more? I will – I'll make some more. I was humming away happily as I spread the butter on the bread. There was a snowdrop on the ditch. I said to da about the snowdrop and the children playing in the lane: They do make a difference these beautiful things da. It is good having them. I stared at the snowdrop for hours and listened to the radio. Friday Night is Music Night. Here it is again da I said and he smiled. Sometimes I'd go into the shop and get thirty Flash Bars. Thirty for half a crown. It was good value. I stuffed them all into my mouth one after the other. Anytime me and Joe got a half crown. Straight into Mary's – thirty Flash Bars please. Mary could hardly carry them all. I looked at myself in the mirror after it. A chocolate beard. For fuck's sake! Sometimes I went round the lane to see if the children were playing near the puddle. You see that puddle? I'd say then I'd tell them all about Joe and me.

Your man with the scarf and the tassels says: You told us all about that before. Quit telling us the same story!

I climbed in the back of the chickenhouse and just stood in there in that woodchip world listening to the scrabbling of the claws on tin and the fan purring away keeping the town going. When we were in there me and Joe used to think: Nothing can ever go wrong.

But it wasn't like that any more.

I had five flypapers altogether now. I kept them in the cupboard where all the old clothes were. The best of all was
the brass band da I'd say, playing in the chapel yard at
Christmas what do you say? He said it sure was. All the
things people would say to you. Please God we'll all be here
this time next year and all this. We had some good laughs
too about ma and the things she used to say. There he is
again this year she'd say, my snowdrop. I'd sit there in the
dark and all you could see was the green bead of light
twinking in the radio and hear the drone of the fan outside
in the lane. You could hear the carnival music at the far end
of the town it must have been the same for them all those
years ago in Bundoran, standing there with the smell of chips
all along the strand. The music was different in them days
On The Sunny Side of The Street that was the one they
played as the wheel turned and ma cried save me Benny save
me we play that one with the town band said da as he twined
his fingers round hers. They were just standing there now
listening to the hush of the sea. There was nothing else to
listen to now that the carnival was all locked up. Ssh, said
the sea. That was all it said. Ssh. We're going to be happy
Benny aren't we? she said. Yes, he said, we're going to be the
two happiest people in the whole world. He held her then
and they kissed. You wouldn't really think of ma and da
kissing but they did and the moon was so close to ma as she

lay back in his arms that she could have reached up and put it in her pocket.

They went back to the boarding house where the woman had left the key under the mat for them. She said: For the man who sang my favourite song for me – *I dreamt that I dwelt in marble halls!*

Did you sing that for the landlady da, I asked.

I did he says, do you know what she used to call us?

What da? I says.

The lovebirds, says da.

I thought of them lying there together on the pink candle-wick bedspread and I knew they were both thinking of the same things, all the beautiful things in the world.

What else had changed since I started working with Leddy, the town.

It had turned into a big ocean liner that had been lying sunk at the bottom of the ocean and now was rising up out of the waves all glittering with lights and flags ready to sail wherever I wanted to go. If I could have gone down to Joe's house to tell him all about this it would have been good it would have been the best ever. Anything you want Joe I'd say to myself on the way to his house you can have it now because I'm going to buy it for you. We could go up on the deck and I'd show it to him, all spread out before him and say whatever you want Joe its all yours. You could see the lights of far off cities from it even. Where do you want to go Joe? You're the boss. I'd swoop away off over the roofs with bundles of ten bob notes and drop them all over the town like confetti. It would be good if it could have happened like that with Joe but it wouldn't so it was no use thinking about it.

I was going into the Tower to get some stout to go with the sandwiches and when I was coming out I seen Mr Purcell getting out of his car. The bottles wouldn't stop clinking quit clinking bottles I said I stood there in the alleyway where I couldn't be seen. Mr Purcell closed the car door and folded his raincoat. Then Joe was standing there beside him just looking up and down the street. Then who gets out the other side only Philip Nugent, I went cold all over when I saw him, the hair down over his eyes. Then he goes over and stands beside Joe, opens a book and starts showing him something in it and the two of them laughing away. Mr Nugent opened the other door and then Mrs Nugent got out. He says let me help you there we are. After that they all went inside Purcell's house and closed the door. It was starting to rain. I crossed the street and hunkered down at the window. I could see the grey glow of the television as it was turned on in the sitting room. Joe was pointing at something. Then Philip Nugent appeared, tossing back his hair. Look look Joe was saying, its Johnny Kidd and The Pirates. All I could see were the shadowy shapes but I could hear the twanging guitars. I felt bad because I didn't know about them or songs or any of that. I said to myself: All you know about is John Wayne Francie. It was hard to make out the other voices with the noise of the telly. Mr Nugent and Mr Purcell were talking about gardening and setting seed potatoes. Very true very true indeed said Mr Nugent. Then he said something about grubs on his potatoes. Mrs Purcell was in great humour, talking away to Mrs Nugent. For a minute I didn't catch on that it was me and Joe she was talking about at all, I got it mixed up with the woman on the telly. It was the best thing ever happened to our Joe said Mrs Purcell he had us worried sick running about with that other fellow. O Joseph is a grand lad now said Mrs Nugent, the best, we're very fond of him. They're mad into this music says Mrs Purcell but sure I suppose aren't all the teenagers?

Indeed they are says Mrs Nugent. Well let them enjoy

their freedom now, that's what I say, weren't we young once ourselves Mrs?

We were, we were indeed Mrs now you said it. Let them enjoy it now for they won't have the time next year. Next year is when the serious study starts. There'll be no gallivanting then!

Mrs Purcell folded her arms.

O that reminds me, says Mrs Nugent, do you remember I was telling you about St Vincent's College?

Then Joe and Philip left the room and went upstairs and the song starts again when you move in right up close to me, I think it was a real guitar. I think Philip was playing it. Then I seen Mrs Nugent coming in with a plate. She stood in the middle of the room and said: Would you like some scones Mrs Purcell?

It was only when I got home I realized I had forgot the bottles and when I went back they were gone. The Purcells' car was gone too and the street was black and deserted, all you could hear was the wind blowing a tin can across the Diamond.

The next day I asked Leddy about it but he said to fuck up and quit raving what did he know about snowdrops and orange skies. After that I thought maybe he was right fuck snowdrops and skies and the children and fucking everything. So that night I said to da I won't be home till late you'll be all right won't you then off I went to the Tower Bar and I says to the ten bob note we're not going home until every penny's gone then off up on the deck of the ocean liner we're off I says and I don't care where we're going. Whee-hoo! I shouted as I stumbled and fell up the street full to the gills with whiskey. The drunk lad let a few roars at me – *Do you know me do you?*

I swayed there for a bit with my shoulder up and shouts back at him Do you know *me* do you?

No he says do you know *me*? and we went on like that for a good while until the pair of us were falling across the Diamond singing *I wonder who's kissing her now?*

I stood on the steps of the bank and shouted Brady the Pig Man up she flew and the cock flattened her!

Fair dues said the drunk lad you're a good one Brady! We went into every pub in the town. The pig men are here I shouts and got down on all fours with the drunk riding on my back singing I wonder who's kissing her now. They gave us plenty of cheers when we did that. I didn't know pigs could sing says this lad laughing. Well you know now I says, and they can drink whiskey too so come on. Snort, says I, and down the hatch.

If the drunk lad wasn't around I'd lie in the doorway of the Tower singing into the neck of the beer bottle.

I went to the dances but I knew they wouldn't dance with me. I'm sorry but I don't dance with pigs they'd say. What did I care? Did they think I cared? There was this one in a pink cardigan holding her twenty fags and looking away when she seen me coming. The drunk lad kept saying go on go on ask her I says I will will you get out of my way for fuck's sake he kept pulling at me. Excuse me I says to her would you like to dance? She was wearing a black hairband and she made on to fix it then she says no I'm with my friends. I could see the drunk lad laughing away look at Brady would you look at Brady he says. I knew he was still looking at me so I says to her: Why didn't you bring your knitting? and she got as red as a beetroot. I went away laughing my arse off. The drunk lad thought this was the best yet. Jesus, he says, you're the best man in this town – *did you bring your knitting!* He told this to everyone he saw. After that there was no end to what I said to the women. They wouldn't say *no thanks* to me again for I wouldn't give them the chance. The drunk lad told me all about women. *They're all the one when they're on the flat of their back!* he says. *H'ho would ye look at that* he says, *I'd give her the johnny and no mistake! I'm the man would slip the boy in there double quick!* Sometimes we sat on the stage and shouted up at the musicians: Youse can play fuck all! The bands wore white suits and sang I Love My Mother and Take Me Back to Dixie. They didn't sell drink in the hall so me and the drunk lad brought our own. The bouncer says you can't drink here but I says why not. Because I say so that's why he says. I looked at him and laughed. He had a broken nose and a face like a scalded prawn. I don't like people laughing he says. *Out!* No, says I, then the drunk lad says Jesus don't say that to him he was in the army. He got a hold of me and threw me round the hall, he kicked me along like a ball of newspaper and the women going ee ee. He got me outside and laid into me with kicks. I'd fly this way and that all I could see was a blur of lights and the guitars twanging away at the national anthem. He got me against the boot of a car spits on his lip and his pudgy fist up against my chin. If you show your face round here again Brady this'll be nothing to what you'll get. Yes, I said, boo hoo. But I always went back the week after and there we'd be again slugging the Johnny Walker and the bouncer on his way over hey hey and what the fuck did I tell you last week Brady? Leddy used to say to me where did you get all them bruises for the love of Christ look at you. Oh I'd say, I tripped over a straw and a hen kicked me. Other times I'd go off to different dancehalls round the place and hang about at the back till I saw someone that thought he was a good man in a row. He'd be dancing away with his girlfriend shouting into her ear about liking Cliff Richard or saying the guitar player in the band was his cousin or some other pack of lies then I'd dunt against him and he'd say watch where you're going. I might say nothing at all or I might just look at him with a big stupid face on me you'd think I was going to burst out laughing. What are you looking at he'd say again then but I'd still say nothing just scratch my nose or pick it, anything at all. Then he'd lose the rag because he thought the girl was saying to him *well are you going to let him say that to you or are you going to do something about it* then he'd tear into me. But it wasn't like with the bouncer, I wouldn't let him kick me around. By the time the fight was over they were always on the floor crawling round help me and the women losing their minds. Come on you fucker I'd say again standing over them with my fist clenched but they'd just lie there. It'd be nearly bright by the time I got home and there was no sense in going to sleep so I'd just sit there with da thinking about things one thing I thought was dumb people must have black holes in their stomachs from not being able to cry out.

———

Every weekend now me and the drunk lad went off up the town da didn't mind I always made sure to put a blanket round him and make sure and tell him where I was going he said if you see any of the Tower Bar crowd tell them I was asking for them. I said I would then off I went. We went up to the Diamond Bar and he says I know you and you know me with his arm round me. Dink donk went the music take me back to Mayo the land where I was born. You're only a pack of baaastaaards! shouts the drunk lad. There was darts and this government is the worst yet and will you have another ah I won't ah you will and here is the news crisis in Cuba it all twisted in and out of itself till I got a pain in my head on top of everything else where are you going he shouts come back! I went out to the river and in the backroads. I went up to the cafe to see if there was anyone in there but it was all locked up with the lights out. I wanted to stand on the Diamond and cry out: *Can you hear me?* but I didn't know what it was I wanted them to hear. Then I went round the back of the chemist's shop and got in. It was good in there. I said to myself: What are all these cameras doing in here? Cameras – why aren't you in a camera shop not a chemists!

I had a good laugh at that. I laughed so much I thought I'd better see if a few of these tablets can help me to stop laughing. There were all kinds in little fat brown jars. They were like little footballers in two-tone jerseys. What were they called? I don't know. Flip, in they went faster than Tiddly's Rolos. Next thing you'd be all woozy as if you were turning into treacle. There was this girl in the photograph something to do with sun tan oil, walking across the white powder sand with a towel in her hand. She smiled at me and said: Francie, then her lips made a soft silent pop. I could feel the heat of the sun coming through the waving palm trees behind her. I felt so sleepy. She said: Its a pity you can't stay.

Yes, I said that's the thing I'd like to do most in the world is stay with you.

I know, she said, only for your Uncle Alo's coming home. If she hadn't said it I don't think I'd have remembered at all. You'd better hurry Francie! she says. Go on! Go on now! Quickly! You don't want to let him down do you?

I was skating about the shop like a spit on a range getting nowhere. I'll have to think, I said. Then it dawned on me that there wasn't a thing in the house. I climbed back out the window and for a minute I didn't know whether it was a street at all or what it was I'd lost the name for it. But then it was all right its OK Francie down the street you go. Whiz, away I went. I knocked up the home bakery but not a sound so in I went round the back. I filled my arms with cakes as many as I could carry. I searched up and down for butterfly buns but not a sign. The best I could find was creamy cones. I thought: He'll like them so I'll get a dozen.

I got into the shed at the back of the Tower for some whiskey. I was glowing with all this excitement. For fuck's sake! Imagine me forgetting that! The hundreds and thousands! So I had to go back to the bakery to get them! I took down the flypaper and put up a new one. There was no shortage of flypapers. There was a smell the dogs must have been in again so I had to go back up to the chemists now too. I took anything I could lay my hands on. I got perfume and air freshener and talcum powder and that got rid of it. You couldn't have people coming into a house with a smell the like of that. The perfume and powder made a big difference. I stacked up all the cakes into a big castle ready to topple. House of Cakes. I squeezed da's arm. Not long now, I says, whizzing up and down the kitchen and looking out the window down the lane. Still no sign. I drank some whiskey. Next thing what did I hear only the sound of a car door closing. Da! I shouted. I was all hot and red and bothered but it was great. There you are! I says as they all trooped in. They were all red-cheeked too with the snow speckled on their overcoats and their arms out will you look who it is they says Francie Brady a happy Christmas to all in this house! And who's there at the front only Mary all smiles. Any sign of Alo? she says. She had a half pound bag of dolly mixtures with her. No, not yet Mary, I says but it won't be long now. Do you know what Francie I just can't wait to see him she says, I'll bet you didn't know I was in love with him. I'll bet you didn't know that!

That's where you're wrong, Mary, I said. I did know – I knew all along!

Twenty years in Camden this winter now who'd have believed it the corks popped and we all got round the piano and waited for him. Just where has that brother of mine got to says da, dear oh dear but he's an awful man! Give us a song Mary while we're waiting he said right she says and flexed her fingers then away off into *Tyrone Among The Bushes*. I sang a bit of it then whiz away off to get another drink. I was just opening the bottle when who's there in the doorway only Alo in his blue suit and the red handkerchief in his breast pocket. Alo, says da, the man himself and threw his arms around him. Let me look at you he says and then they were off into their stories. I'll tell you a better one says da, will you ever forget the time we robbed the presbytery orchard? Do you remember that Alo? Do I remember says Alo, will I ever forget? More tea, says I, and help yourselves to the cakes there's plenty more. Alo put his hands on Mary's shoulders and sang *When you were sweet sixteen*. Then what does Mary do only stand up and throw her arms around him. Oh Alo, she says, I love you. I want you to marry me. Hooray and they all cheered and clapped. Is everyone all right for cakes I called from the scullery. That's Alo! said da. Alo stood there holding Mary and looking into her eyes. I looked outside and the snow was coming down. I thought I heard the children playing outside but they couldn't be it was too late. Right who's for another song says Alo and cleared his throat. I was going to say more cakes anyone but I'd said that already. I wondered was the puddle in the lane frozen over. Of course it was. Mary was sitting on Alo's knee stroking his face as he sang. The hum of the voices filled the kitchen. I flew round the place chatting to them all and saying more cakes are you enjoying yourselves isn't it great to see Alo home? Ten men under him, I said. I clapped and clapped and cried hooray.

I didn't know who the sergeant was at first. I just looked out and he was standing in the yard with his long raincoat on. He was staring in at me too. His face was kind of fuzzed like he was underwater. I just about knew it was him and no more.

Alo said to Mary: Just a minute and came over to me. He reached out and said: Its all right Francie.

I said Please Alo, can you help me?

But he couldn't help me because it wasn't Alo. It was Doctor Roche.

Oh Alo, I said. I didn't see the others leave. They had gone without saying goodbye. I looked around for da but he was gone too. The flies were at the cakes on the piano.

I could feel a cold hand touching me. It was cold as Da's forehead. There were all kind of voices they went by like strands of smoke.

Alo, I said.

The sergeant was saying something to another policeman. He said: Maggots – they're right through him.

The other policeman said: Sweet Mother of Christ.

Its all right Francie said Doctor Roche. I didn't mean to do any harm, I said. I know he said and he rolled up my sleeve. It was only a tiny pinprick and then I was lying back on a bed of snowdrops.

There you are said Joe, I was looking for you. I could hear the whisper of water close by.

Its the river, I said. Joe didn't even turn around.

Of course its the river he says. What did you expect – the Rio Grande?

That fucking bastard Sergeant Sausage! He did it again! Had he nothing better to do than drive around the county dropping me in these skips? I think – ah I'll just get out the car and durr-ive Francie Brady off to another kiphouse with a hundred windows how do you like it now, Francie? H'ho! H'ha! They'll put manners on you there!

There was a stench of musty drawers and Jeyes Fluid mixed. The last thing I seen was Bubble standing by the window at the bottom of a long line of beds. He was flicking his fingers behind his back. Then he turned slowly and stared right at me. On his shoulders a huge alien's head like a wasp. The funny thing was – it still looked like Bubble. You would know it was him even though it was a wasp with these furred tentacles coming out of it. Oh fuck! I cried out. I didn't know whether to be afraid or not. He wasn't moving. He was just standing there looking. I looked around to see if anyone else was afraid. But there was only me and Bubble I mean Father Alien. Then I fell asleep again. When I woke up he was gone and there was only a shaft of the most brilliant sunlight slanting in the same window. I could see the sharp edges and the outline of everything clear as crystal. Then I heard music. It was a song I knew. Whee-hoo! I couldn't make it out right but I knew it was something to do with the snowdrop and the cries of the children playing in the lane. It kind of said: You might be wrong about all that Francie. Maybe all these things are beautiful and worth having. Listen to the music and you'll see what I mean. It surged, it was music with wings. Bird Who Soars Music and what it said was nothing bad would ever happen again. It filled me with such ecstasy I skimmed the chimney pots over the town crying out for da and ma to tell them. Its going to be all right after all I cried. I could see the snowdrop on the ditch with my bird's eye. The children were blobs of colour clumping about in enormous shoes below in the lane, setting the toy tea-things on a wooden crate. Tassels was hacking away at the ice on the frozen puddle. I spun sideways and the black hole that had been in the pit of my stomach was full of light. I landed on a branch and watched him for a minute. Then I says: Any sign of your pal Brendy? The man who's in charge of the puddle?

He got some land when I said that. What does he do only drop stick and all and tear off down the lane. Hi! Hi! boys, he shouts do youse know what I seen up in that tree? A talking bird!

For fuck's sake!

Another day him and Brendy were there and I says to them, What would you do if you won a hundred million trillion dollars?

Hmm says the other lad and puts his finger to his lips. They weren't bothered now about me being a talking bird because they were used to me. I wanted to cheer. I lit off the branch and away off again into the sky and what colour was it?

It was the colour of oranges.

The next time I woke up the alien or the wasp or whatever it was was back again only this time with Leddy's face. Well fuck this for a racket I said but it went on for a good while and there was nothing I could do about it.

One time I tried to get up out of the bed I was fed up with the way things were going but this big lad in a white coat and arms like tree trunks says ah ah not so fast and stuck me back in.

I was lying there for hundreds of weeks. Or maybe months. In the end the doctor came over to me and says: You can get up and move about now for a while now if you like. I went down to the window to see about this wasp-alien but there was no sign of him or it or whatever the fuck you'd call it. This old lad in a dressing gown comes over to me and closes one eye; You needn't think you'll pull the wool over my eyes you Cavan cunt he says. Before I had a chance to say *I'm not from Cavan* or sweet fuck all to him whiz he's away off down the other end of the ward pointing at me and whispering behind his hand to this fellow with hair sticking up like burnt twigs. He was nodding away to beat the band. Oh yes. Yes indeed. That's very true he was saying or something like that.

Some days I went off with the doctors to this room with two pictures in it John F. Kennedy and Our Lady. Well well we meet again I says and gave her the wink. You're a long way now from the low field in the old school for pigs I says and she started laughing. They were all interested to hear about this. And who else did you see? Oh the whole shooting match I says. St Teresa of the Roses the lot. There was this specky lad looked like Walter the swot out of Dennis the Menace in the *Beano* he was mad to get information to write down. Scribble scribble away with his tongue stuck in the corner of his mouth. They couldn't get enough of all these saints. Have you got a fag says I and I told them more. Me and Our Lady we go back a long way I said. Its not every shitehawk she'll appear to you know. Yes yes indeed scribble scribble. Then they asked me about dreams. Did you have any dreams they said. O I did I says, I did indeed. More fags. And what did you dream about. Wasps says I, with Bubble's face. Or Bubble with wasps' faces. Then they started on about Bubble so I had to give them a whole lot about him. The worse it was the better they liked it so I put in a whole lot about Bubble stinging me and biting my head off Father Alien says

you must die earthling dog! And then he laughed and all this.
It was a good laugh. I know what I'd give Bubble if he tried
that. Fuck off Bubble you waspy bastard! I'd say. Just let him
try it.

Snip!

Let's see you conquer the world now Father!

That was a good one. I thought Walter was going to go
off the edge of the table he was writing so fast. They asked
me about Tiddly but I always brought them back to the
funny bits about Bubble and the gardener. I started on him.
I told them he had dead bodies in the boilerhouse but I don't
know if they investigated him. Maybe they sent Fabian of the
Yard around. I thought that was good too so I told them
more about it, young people from the town were mysteri-
ously disappearing in the town and that it was him he was
cutting them up with his graip and stacking them behind the
boiler. But I must have made a hames of that for they didn't
want to hear any more about him all they wanted to do now
was talk about Tiddly. O yes Father Sullivan is a very nice
man, I says, its just a pity the Balubas put him in the pot.
You liked the industrial school did you they said. Indeed I
did, especially on Thursdays because we got two sausages
each for dinner. You used to say Mass for Father Sullivan
isn't that right it is indeed. You liked him? I certainly did. A
very holy man, I said, he prays to St Teresa of the Roses. Very
good then they'd say well that will do for today. Other days
they took me off to other garages and stuck me in a big chair
with this helmet on my head and wires coming out all over
the place. I liked that. That was the best of the lot sitting
in that chair. And all these starchy bastards of students with

clipboards gawking at you *I hope he doesn't leap up out of the chair and chop us up!*

But I paid no heed to them I was too busy being Adam Eterno The Time Lord in that big chair. They could scribble all they liked I was away off through hyperspace. Hello there Egyptians I'd say pyramids and all. Adam can't come today so its me instead – Francie from the Terrace. Good man Francie they'd say with these wee hats and snakes on them. Or Romans. Leave that Christian alone, lion, I'd say. Oh thanks thanks Francie says the Christian. No problem, pal then off I'd go to see how the cowboys were getting on.

Where do they be taking you says the old fellow with the eyebrow up. You needn't think you're not seen. Then he looks down to the other end of the ward and the other fellows there nodding away. I told him to travel through the wastes of space and time like in Dan Dare that's where they're taking me and he looks at me. What? he says so I told him again and that didn't please him at all. He got a grip of me by the jumper and he says: I knew it. I knew you were a Cavan cunt from the minute I set eyes on you. You needn't think you'll come in here to make a cod out of me. Go on you cur! he shouts, I took better men than you!

The tree trunks had to haul him off me. I dusted myself down and complained to them. This is a disgrace, I said, a person can't walk around without being attacked.

Another day he comes over: So its a disgrace is it! Being attack-did is a disgrace.

―――

162

Attack-did! *Attack-did!*

Well – I heard, he says. They're going to give you the treat-
ment. There won't be so much lip out of you when they take
you off and put the holes in your head. Know what they do
then? They take your brains out. I know! I've been here long
enough. I seen the last fellow. He used to stand at the
window all day long eating bits of paper. Do you like paper?
Well you better start getting to like it. He won't be so smart
then he shouts down to Twighead at the bottom of the ward.
He rubbed his hands with glee.

I had a good laugh at that. Taking your brains out, for fuck's
sake. But that was before I woke up one day and there's
Walter at the end of the bed talking away in whispers about
me but I heard: *Its best for him in the end!* I knew it was no
use saying anything to him. I ran out of the ward and went
straight to the office. There was a meeting going on but I
didn't care. I told them: You can't touch me! I said. You can't
lay a finger on me! I want out of here!

I made a run for it but it was no use. Now Francis and
another jab in the arse it must have been a big jab this time
all I could say was mm mm as they carried me down the
stairs.

We can do it now says the doctor and holds up the
syringe to the light. Yes indeed says Walter and looks at me
then I look down and what has he got in his hand only a drill
you'd use to put up shelves.

Can you move your head a little please Francis?

Brrrrrrrrrrrrrrrrrrrrrrrrrrrrrrrrrrrrrrrrrrrrrrrrrrrrrrrrrrrr.

There. That's better he said in a soft voice. Hand me the cotton wool please doctor.

Then there was a knock at the door and who pops his head in only Joe.

Is Francie here? C'mon Francie we're ridin' out. We've got to move fast!

A pony whinnied.

OK Joe I said and threw the white sheet off me.

That's what you think says Joe and I could hear the blondie one laughing outside the door.

Joe, I called, Joe!

So you're the Time Lord says the Roman, prepare to die and I swung away up hanging by the heel.

Joe I called again but the room was empty.

I could hear the hush of the sea.

I looked down and saw Mrs Connolly. She watched me swinging to and fro smiling away with her arms folded. Come on down out of that she says so down I got. The other women looked at me from the bottom of the shop. How are you today Francie Mrs Connolly said.

I'm fine I said.

Mrs Connolly folded her arms. Ah, she said and the women smiled.

I'll bet you didn't know Francie – I'll bet you didn't know I had something for you.

No Mrs Connolly I didn't I said.

Aha but I have! she says. What do you think of that!

Its good Mrs Connolly I said.

Ah *isn't* he lovely she said again.

Are you going to sing a little song for me? Is he going to sing a little song for us ladies?

They said: Are you Francis?

A little song and the special prize is all yours! says Mrs Connolly.

She was hiding it behind her back.

Well – what are you going to sing? Will you sing my favourite for me? You know how much I like that one. Mm?

Yes Mrs Connolly I said.

I was just standing there with my knees together and my head down all shy. I was like something you'd see on a snakes and ladders board.

Hooray!, said Mrs Connolly. Quiet now ladies! Away you go Francis!

I did a few Irish dancing steps that the nuns taught us hopperty skip round the shop and singing:

I am a little Baby Pig I'll have you all to know
With the pinkest little floppy ears and a tail that curls up so
I like to trot around the town and have myself some fun
And I'll be a little porky pig till my trotting days are done!

When I was finished I was all hot and out of breath thank you thank you says Mrs Connolly and the women clapping away: He's better than the London Palladium!

Then Mrs Connolly put up her hand. Ssh, she says and out of nowhere a fat red polished apple.

Oh! the women gasped.

It just sat in the middle of Mrs Connolly's palm.

What-do-you-think-of-*that*! she says with her eyes twinkling.

Its lovely, I said.

Would you like to have a bite of it? she said.

Yes Mrs Connolly I said, I sure would and nodding away I could taste it in my mouth already.

What do you say ladies? Will I give him a bite of it?

Then the women started mm mm well and all this and had a big discussion.

Yes, they said then – if he picks it up like a pig!

Mrs Connolly rubbed it on her sleeve and said: Well Francis – *will* you pick it up like a pig?

I said I would and she went down on one knee and rolled it slowly along the rubber mat. I tried to grip it with my teeth but down on all fours like that it was too hard to get at it. You'd think you had it then down it'd go again and every time it did the women cheered. Oh! they said, he's dropped it again. Then they clapped and cheered and said: Come on Francie you can do it! But I couldn't do it. It was too hard. Can I use one hand? I said. One trotter you mean, they said. Uh-uh, sorry. That's against the rules. I don't know how many times I dropped it. Ten or eleven maybe. In the end Mrs Connolly took pity on me and handed me the apple.

Ah you poor little pig, she says, God love you. Can you not even pick up an apple?

Don't worry Francie!, the women said, its all yours now! Go on – eat it!

I didn't want to eat it while they were looking at me but I had to. They kept saying: And another bite now!

They did that until I was down to the core. Then Mrs Connolly went over to the window and looked out. *Here they come!* she said and they all started talking together again about the weather and how hard it was to manage with the price of everything. I didn't know who it was they were waiting for I just stood there watching the flesh of the apple browning in my hand. Then I looked up and saw who it was Ma and Da Pig standing there. The women went quiet when they came in and Mrs Connolly smiled over at ma. Then she coughed and dabbed her nose with a tissue. She leaned over to the woman beside her and whispered: We should see the father and mother of a row between these two in a minute!

They waited there looking them up and down. They were saying: Come on! Say something we want to see a row!

But there was no row. Ma and Da Pig didn't say anything just stood there roast red, afraid to speak or look anyone in the eye.

Oh please! Let there be a row! Mrs Connolly was thinking. She squeezed the tissue up in her hand.

We've waited here all this time for nothing – there isn't going to be a row after all!

And there wasn't. The row didn't start until we got outside. Ma Pig was near to tears.

Why didn't you *do* something? Why didn't you *say* something? she cried.

Me? Da Pig snapped, why is it always me?

He went hoarse arguing and he went from red to pure white. Then the two of them turned on me.

Why did you take the apple you stupid little pig? they said. I stuttered and stammered. I didn't know what to say. I didn't know why I had taken the stupid apple. The whole town was out to watch us going up Church Hill. Hello there Pigs, called Doctor Roche, that's not a bad day!

He locked his car and went into the hotel saying: They're a grand family those pigs!

There were so many people waving and calling to us that we were exhausted by the time we got to the Tower. There was nobody in the bar only us. There was a smell of old porter and a whiff coming from the men's toilets, it was a bar of dead years. The barman knew it was us without even looking up he rubbed his hands with a cloth and said well pigs what can I get you?

Da Pig told him and he poured the drinks. He said it was a cold enough day. Da Pig said it was and nobody said anything more after that. There was a picture of a whiskery season balancing a bottle of stout on its nose I looked at that for a long time. Ma just sat there with her chin in on her chest afraid to look up. Every time Da Pig raised his little finger the barman filled up his glass. It was dark outside when he came back from the toilet. He clattered against the stool and the barman said: You'd be as well to get him home.

Yes, said ma, and the barman kept his eyes on us until we got up and took him out. Ma said try your best son then she put one of his arms around her shoulders and I took the other then off we went with his legs trailing and the two wee piggy eyes set away back in a ball of pink skin, and them all standing at their doors with their arms folded look there they go that's them crossing the Diamond. Hey! Hey! Hullo! Pigs! Pigs! Yoo-hoo!

Ah look aren't they great, the Mammy Pig, the Daddy Pig and Baby Pig, three little piggies huffing and puffing all the way home!

Will you forgive me I was going to say yes da but I was away off swinging by the heel again and the Roman soldier with the sword who was it only Leddy he flicked away the butt of his cigarette and said something to me but I couldn't make out what it was then he just raised the sword and brought it down and cut me in two halves.

One half could see the other but they were both just dangling there on the meat rack.

Then who comes out of the shadows only Joe but he didn't see me just walked on out through the doorway of the slaughterhouse into the light.

When I woke there's Walter you're going to be all right Francie he says and the nurse holds out more tablets. Doc, I said, that bastard down there says you're going to put holes in my head. Your man must have heard me for I seen him away out the door like a light. There was no more Time Lord or any of that stuff after they gave me tablets. An odd time they'd take me down to the room and hand me bits of paper all blotted with ink. What do you think about that says the doc. You won't be writing any more messages on that paper I says. Why not says the doc lifting the specs. Its destroyed I says, look at it. Hmm hmm. In the school for docs that's what they taught them. Lift your specs and repeat after me – hmm hmm!

For a while I was all jiggy, stuffed up inside with hedgehog needles but the tablets must have done the trick for one day when I seen your man outside in the grounds I went after him. *Hey*, I shouts, *cunthooks!* He let on he didn't hear me and starts walking real fast in behind the kitchens. But I went round the far side and what a land he got when he seen me in front of him. I'll give you fucking holes in the head now you bastard! I said. I was only taking a hand at him I wouldn't have done anything but what does he start then only all this stuff about Cavan people. *There's not one of them he says wouldn't give you the last halfpenny out of their pocket. The best men ever walked in this hospital he says are the Cavan men!* Then he looks up at me with these big eyes, *you're not going to batter me are you?* But I wasn't. I wasn't going to do anything I was off to make baskets and paint pictures for that was what they had me at now. Only what I made, I don't know whether you'd call them baskets or not. That's a good basket says this fellow beside me not a screed of hair on his head. Then out of nowhere he starts on about women. What do they do he says they take you down a long garden path and away in behind a tree. Then they say do you remember the day you rang me on the telephone and I laughed and you laughed and then ma laughed and we were all laughing. That was a good day! That's women for you!

It is, I says. Some basket it was he was making, I thought mine was bad. All bits of sticks stuck out of it all over the place. When we went to Mass what does he do when the priest is holding up the Eucharist. He stands up and shouts at the top of his voice – Good man yourself! Now you have it – *run!* Into the back of the net with her! By Christ this year's team is the best yet!

You'll have to take these says Walter then there won't be a bother on you. It was like when the warden shakes hands with the prisoner and says goodbye at the gates and goes back in smiling thinking how great his job is until he hears the next day the prisoner has just chopped up a few more people. But it wasn't like that at all for I had no intention of chopping up anyone. I was off home and no more about Cavan bastards or baskets or holes in the head or any of that stuff. I'd had it with all that carry-on. Me and Walter were shaking hands and for a minute I forgot myself and says in a deep Yank voice waal Doc I guess this is goodbye. I quit that fairly sharpish when I seen Walter looking at me and wondering should he change his mind and whip me back in for more tablets and maybe the drill this time. No thanks Walter. Well goodbye Francie, we'll see you again soon. He said they'd be over to see me every month or so to see what I was up to. He said I'd be having a good few visitors over the next while to see what was going to happen. What, off to the school for pigs again I says, out to fuck with that Doc, I mean no thanks Doc. Ah no he says you won't be going back there. Best thing to do is wait and see Francis. Right so Doc and off I went down the hill in the coach. Whee! I shouts, Take 'em to Missouri men and this old crab looks at me out from behind her *Woman's Weekly*.

Go and shave your tache Missus I shouts and what a face! But what did I care! Wheee away down the hill and your mickey going *man that's great keep doing that.*

Well I just couldn't believe it. Pilchards? Not one to be seen. Flies? Gone forever. Tiles – you could see your face in them. And the smell of polish! The whole house had been cleaned, a million times cleaner than ever I could have made it! I went away off up the street and who did I meet only Mrs Connolly with a grin swinging between her ears like a skipping rope. Well Francis did you see the house? I certainly did Mrs

Connolly I said. She touched me on the forearm and says don't you worry your head now Francis, I'll be in and out to give it the odd dusting for you.

I said thank you very much Mrs Connolly and what did she say then only ah God love you sure who have you now they're all gone I thought what did she have to say that for what did you have to say that for?

I looked at her for a minute but then I said no I'll say nothing I just said thanks again Mrs Connolly its very good of you to be so kind. Ah sure wouldn't any decent neighbour do the same? she said and gives me this look you'd think she was dying for a shite but was holding it in. Once I seen her and the women talking to Mrs Cleary from the Terrace after she came home from hospital with the baby that looked like something out of a horror film. It had a claw instead of a hand. She was saying ah God love you to her too and tickling the baby inside the blanket saying sure isn't she a lovely little baba altogether I'll be down to the house this evening with them bits of clothes and odds and ends of our Sheila's I promised you. All you could hear was Mrs Cleary saying thanks oh thank you very much I don't know how many times she said thank you and Mrs Connolly ah sure not at all its the least we can do when Mrs Cleary went I heard her saying poor Mrs Cleary God love her I don't think she knows what end of her is up half the time, I seen two of her other wains running about the street last night at eight o'clock and them with hardly a stitch on them!

She's just not able, God love her, the other women said.

They all stood there looking after her as she went down the street then Mrs Connolly said its not right God forgive me I dread to think what my Sean would say if I came home from hospital with a thing the like of that!

And they just stood there, the three heads nodding away.

Hey! Hey! shouts the drunk lad when he seen me. He was counting change at the door of the Diamond Bar. He comes running over: All I need is three halfpence.

Sorry, I says, the Francie Brady Bank is closed. Eh? he says blinking in the light.

Closed for business I says and walked off.

Go on he shouts after me you're only a baaaaaastard!

I walked round the house I don't know how many times I liked the smell of the polish that much. Flowers and everything on the mantelpiece. I could see my face in the sink too. H'ho I thought, It'll be a long time before there'll be pilchards in that sink again! Yes sir! There's gonna be a lot of changes round here!

Then what did I do only get myself all dressed up there was a white jacket in the window of the drapery shop like what you'd see Cliff Richard wearing and a shirt with one of these bootlace ties. I looked at myself in the mirror. The tie was real John Wayne style but I says there's to be no more about John Wayne or any of that, that's all over. Everything's changed now its all new things. Then I brushed the jacket and headed down to the cafe.

I was going to go right in and say hello to Joe and them all sitting there and if they wanted me to sit beside them then all the better I would and I'd tell them and Joe everything that had happened in the garage and everything if they wanted me to that is. I'd say: Hello Philip – how are you getting on with the music?

He'd say fine.

Then I'd smile and sing a bit of the song: *When you move in right up close to me!*

I knew a good bit of it now from hearing it on the radio.

Then I'd get up and walk down to the jukebox. I'd lean over it for a minute and drum my fingers on the sides thinking over what I was going to put on. If the blondie one or the other one looked down at me I'd grin at her or maybe wink. Then the record would be selected and on it would come. I bought fags so that I would be able to flip one out for her when I sat back down again. You could just sit there thinking and looking at everybody passing outside on the street as the smoke curled up to the ceiling. You could mouth the words as you were sitting there. *Shaking all over!*, and then the guitar bit.

I didn't even have to think about it, I just pushed the door it swung right open and in I went. I thought they'd be sitting over by the window under the Elvis Presley poster but there was just the owner in a nylon coat reading a newspaper there was nobody else there, all you could hear was the hissing of the coffee machine and someone rattling pans in the kitchens. Yes please says your man without even looking up. What? I said I didn't hear him at first then I said its all right I was just looking for somebody I don't think he heard me either. I closed the door behind me and went back down the street. I went round to the carnival but there was no sign of them there either, there wasn't a sinner about and nearly half the sideshows had been closed or moved on. They were playing the same Jim Reeves record over and over again and you could hardly hear it it was so scratched. I hung about the streets until nearly midnight but there was no one around. The only thing I seen was the drunk lad being thrown out of the Tower. He hammered on the door to try and get back in you could hear him all over the town. I turned and went home before he seen me but I didn't sleep I just sat at the window looking out.

I went round to Leddy the next day. Where do you think you're going in that get-up he says, you can clear off from about here. But I didn't clear off I told him all about the garage and everything I couldn't quit talking and in the end he got fed up he says go on then take that brock barrow and go off round to the hotel and collect what they have they must have plenty by now. Right Mr Leddy I says thanks for taking me back. There's thousands wouldn't he says and went off inside then off I went down the street whistling and wheeling my cart Francie Brady the Brock King of the Town. Hello there I'd say. Ah good man Francie. And not a bad day now. No thank God. And Francie you're home. I am indeed. Ting-a-ling a-ling. Stone the crows its our old mate Francie! 'Ello dearies! Pound o' mince, there you go! Cor luvaduck!

Who's that gone by on the bike? What's he talking about – ducks?

The next day I got dressed up again and went back down to the cafe I knew they'd *have* to be in sooner or later. I sat in their place and put the song on. I lit a fag and then I lit another one. It was good looking at the street through the twisty horns of smoke. I put the song over and over but there was still no sign of them. I smoked a good few fags. I smoked maybe twenty or thirty. I came back the next day and did the same again. And I came back the day after that. It was dark when I was going home. The owner was sweeping up. He was an Italian.

He said: Ees quiet now. Not so much people around now.

I said there wasn't. He said it was no good in the town in the winter. I said Joe and the girls and Philip why are they not coming in?

He didn't know who I was talking about for a minute. Then he breaks into a big smile. Ah, Joseph!, he says – and Philip! Yes yes yes!

Then he starts shaking his head and trying to poke a Kit Kat wrapper out from under the seat with the brush.

No, he says, I am afraid we have not seen them for a long time. They are away. They were good customers of mine. I miss them.

I said: What are you talking about, away?

I don't know, he says, away, that is all I know.

I went to light up a fag but there was none left only an empty box. I said to him have you any fags no he says I do not sell cigarettes we are closing now please.

I must have asked him for fags again.

He says: *I told you! Cigarettes, I do not sell them! Now please!* He opened the door.

One fag then, I says, *I'll give you a tanner.*

Please! he says.

I kept thinking I was going to meet Joe or the blondie one or some of them on the street so I didn't want to take the jacket off just in case. Leddy started into me over it – for the love of Christ he says and all this but I says what do you care what I wear all you care about is me collecting the brock as long as I do that what do you care if I come in in a cowboy hat! Oh for fuck's sake! he says and in the end he just threw the fag into the gutter and says: Do it then do what you fucking well like I'm past talking to you God's curse the day I took you in in the first place!

I said: Don't worry, I'll work twice as hard now that I'm back you won't have any complaints about me Mr Leddy!

After that I didn't wait for him to tell me to do anything. I was cleaning and hosing and chopping and sawing and packing, anything there was to be done it was done hours before Leddy knew it had to be done. I worked until the sweat ran out of me. Then when I was finished I'd be away off to see if I could see Joe for I said to myself that the cafe man was talking through his arse go back to Italy I said. A couple of times I thought I saw them but it was just some other girl with blonde hair. Every night I left the brock cart back in the slaughterhouse yard beside the Pit of Guts and locked up. There was one thing Leddy was right about and that was I had ruined my good jacket all right for when I was heeling a bin into the cart stew or some stuff went all over me. I was wondering should I go back down and clean it before I went near Joe's for that was what I had decided to do I couldn't stick the empty streets and the waiting any more. Then I thought: What would you want to clean it for – do you think Joe cares if your coat is a bit dirty? What are you talking about Francie – Joe Purcell? He's your friend for God's sake! He's your best friend!

I says what the hell am I at at all, thinking that about the jacket. You think some stupid things. It must have been my time in the garage I said. Then I went off down to Joe's house.

There was a light on in the front room I thought Joe was probably at his books we could listen to records after what records do you want Joe I'll get them. Cliff Richard! He was the only one I knew. But Joe would know plenty more it wouldn't be long before I knew the whole lot. *When you move in right up close to me!* I says and pasted back my hair. I scraped off as much of the stew as I could then I knocked on the door grinning from ear to ear like I'd won the Sweep hello there Mr Purcell I said I was wondering if the man himself was in. Mr Purcell looked straight at me and jerked back a little bit then he said *what?* So I had to go and say it all over again. And he began to smile as if I was telling him a joke or something. He scratched his forehead and stared past me like he was trying to catch the attention of somebody passing on the other side of the street. Then he says: Sure Joe is away at boarding school he's away in Bundoran at Saint Vincent's College this past six months. I was going to say O of course that's right I forgot about that but I couldn't for this brr was starting in my head like the noise the telly used to make if you fell asleep at night watching it. So I didn't say that at all and then the door clicked shut real soft, all these doors clicking shut and it was starting to rain.

I was still standing there watching the gutters fill up and wondering what I was going to do when I seen Mrs Connolly going by on the far side of the street with Mrs Nugent. She was carrying the umbrella and giving Mrs Nugent a good share of it so she didn't get wet. They stopped at the hotel corner and I seen Mrs Connolly's hand going up over her mouth. Mrs Nugent nodded away. She was saying: That's right. Oh you don't have to tell me Mrs Connolly! *You don't have to tell me!*

Then they parted and there was nothing only the rain sweeping over the town and the fires glowing in the sitting rooms and the smell of frying and the grey jumpy rays of television screens behind the curtains.

I went out to the river it was bulging nearly ready to burst its banks you could be eyeball to eyeball with the fish. I was shivering with the cold and the wet. I pulled at the grass along the edge of the bank and counted all the people that were gone on me now.

1. Da
2. Ma
3. Alo
4. Joe

When I said Joe's name all of a sudden I burst out laughing. For fuck's sake! I said, Joe gone! How the fuck would Joe be gone!

That was the best yet.

It was still raining when I called at Mrs Connolly's house. The rain was dribbling into my mouth. When she opened the door I could smell rashers and I think chips. I could see them all inside sitting by the fire and they were eating scones I heard one of them saying anybody for scones? *Me!* I'll have the whole plate if you don't mind. But I didn't say that I said nothing of the sort for I had business with Connolly. There was a barometer too, like Nugents. Mild weather it said, some barometer that was. She smiled at me and wiped her hands on her apron ah hello there Francie she said. Then up goes the *what do you want* eyebrow? I put my foot in against the door in case she'd try to close it before I was finished. The rain was all salty now it was in my eyes and it was getting on my nerves she says what can I do for you Francie and I says oh its just about my father ah yes your poor father she says may the Lord have mercy on his soul. She starts fiddling with her fingers and looking down when she said that so I said no no Have Mercy or any of that Mrs Connolly why did you not mind your own business this is the thing and she looks at me and starts stuttering. Mind my own business? What do you mean what are you talking about? I said you know very well what I'm talking about and she tries the Mrs Nugent trick pushing a tear out into the eye nobody did more for your poor father than me Francie I made all the arrangements for the funeral when nobody else would I cleaned and scrubbed God knows I did and my husband says what were you doing that for and I did it because I had pity on your dear departed father God rest him nobody knows the work that I put into that house. Then she starts sniffling and I says who asked you to clean that's the trouble with the people in this town they can't mind their own business can they *they can't mind their own fucking business!*

I raised my voice when I said that and then who's standing there only some lad with a moustache I don't know who he was what does he say you he says the best thing you can do is get away from this house as fast as you can before I do this before I do that all these things he was going to do. I told Connolly to keep away from our house if I seen her back near it it wouldn't be good for her and I meant it. Moustache took a swipe at me when I said that but I managed to get a hold of his wrist and I held it good and hard until I was finished saying what I had to say to say you just stay out of my way Connolly its nothing to do with you and it never was and I'll tell you another thing I says *I'll tell you another thing!* There was snots on her nose and she was blubbering please please. Moustache was half-bent over, I never saw anyone look so stupid with his hair hanging down in his eyes he didn't know what to say fuck off or I beg you to leave me alone, so in the end he said nothing just hung there like a halfwit all red because of his big talk. I'll tell you another thing Connolly I said I don't want any of your apples either! Do you hear me – *I don't want any of your apples! I don't need any of your fucking apples!*

Then I let go of his wrist and said you remember that and I left the pair of them standing I wanted no more to do with them. I went off through the town. I wasn't too sure what I was at, I kept thinking that's Connolly dealt with what will I do now. But there was nothing much else I could do so I went off and bought some fags. I lit one and stood there smoking it. Then all of a sudden I heard Joe calling me from the alley near the cinema. *Joe!* I said and dropped the fag Joe I says is that you? Francie c'mere a minute he said but when I went over there was no sign of him. Then what did I see only the Nugents' car going by skitting water onto the footpath and Mr Nugent leaning over to wipe the windscreen holding the pipe in the other hand. Mrs Nugent was driving. I didn't know she could drive. Next thing the car slows and pulls up outside Purcells. I went round the back and stood on the far side of the road behind a parked lorry to see what was going on. Before Mrs Nugent got out she rooted around in the back and took something out a box or something. Then Mr Nugent rang the bell.

Philip wasn't there. Where was he? Then there's Mr Purcell and Mrs Purcell looking over his shoulder ah hello there this is a surprise. After that what does Nugent do only hold up the box I could see it better now it was all wrapped up it wasn't a box at all it was a present. When I looked again the door was closed and the light was on in the front room. I could see Mr Nugent handing glasses around and throwing back his head someone was telling a funny story. Oh now, he said, I couldn't hear him but I knew by his face that was what he was saying. All I could hear was rain gurgling from a broken downpipe behind me and in the end I could stick it no longer. When Mr Purcell opened the door he was bleary-eyed and rubbing them and he was in his pyjamas and dressing gown whatever he was at now. I could hear Nugent inside *who is it who is it*. Someone had turned the light off in the front room I don't know which of them it was. There wasn't a sound in the place. I said to him what's the party for Mr Purcell and he says party what party. The party, I says, the present and all. Party he says I don't know what you're talking about. I said to him look Mr Purcell I just wish you'd stop all this I just want to know if its something to do with Joe that's all is it a coming home party is that what it is? But he wouldn't tell me he just kept saying what party and what are you talking about or what is wrong with you. I think that was it I knew then that he wasn't going to tell me anything and when I heard Mrs Purcell who is it who is it or what on earth is going on its one o'clock in the morning and I just said I'm sorry Mr Purcell I'm fed up with people interfering and not telling me things all I asked you was to tell me about the party and you won't tell me well that's all right Mr Purcell its your house but you didn't have to tell me lies. He says *I didn't tell you lies!*, but I didn't want to hear any more of it I said you did Mr Purcell I'm sorry but you did. I said you never used to do that Mr Purcell I used to be able to call down for Joe and you would say sure he can come out and play with you Francie why couldn't he? You never told me lies or anything like that in them days its true isn't it?

His face changed it got all sort of pained and I liked him then it was like the old Mr Purcell he was trying to tell me something but he didn't know how. But it didn't matter for I knew what it was he was trying to say. It was all OK until she came along wasn't it Mr Purcell? It was fine until Mrs Nugent started interfering and causing trouble. That's the only reason she's giving you presents – isn't it Mr Purcell?

I looked him straight in the eye and I said: Its true isn't it?

His eyes looked kind of sad and he said: Francie.

I knew he wanted to say something else to me but couldn't because he knew Mrs Nugent was listening inside the sitting room.

I put my finger to my lips. I wanted him to know that I understood. He rubbed over his eye as if he had a headache and I knew by the way he looked at me it was his way of saying sorry. I smiled. It was good of Mr Purcell to do that. I had known all along the Purcells hadn't meant it to happen the way it did.

If only the Nugents hadn't come to the town, if only they had left us alone, that was all they had to do.

I didn't go home I walked around all night thinking what I was going to do. I slept for a while in the chickenhouse a thousand eyes wondered who's this sleeping in our woodchip world chick chicks I was going to say its me Francie but I was too tired.

When I woke up would you believe it the flies were at me now. Fuck off away from the stew I said and bam, got three of the bastards, two black splats on the lapel of my jacket, what do you think of that boys, I mean flies.

I had ten bob so I went round to the carnival to the shooting gallery. All you had to do was get three bullseyes in a row and you got the goldfish. There was a whole bunch of them swimming around with their bony mouths going here we are here we are. I steadied the butt against my shoulder and pulled the trigger *ping!*, I missed with the first one but everybody does, I thought the rifle range man was looking at me and thinking: That wasn't much of a shot. I turned around to give him a dirty look but he had his back to me and was talking away to some woman. Now I'm right I said, here we go, three bullseyes in a row. I wonder how long it took Nugent to get them probably spent a fortune. Here we go I said but I missed again. I don't know what was wrong. I got a fifty but that was no good. I said to the rifle man: You have these guns rigged haven't you?

I knew that was what they did. They bent the barrel a tiny bit off so you would never hit the bullseye. You made sure to give Philip one of the good ones didn't you, I said. *What?* he says and starts laughing. I was going to go round to Leddy and ask him for another ten bob but then I thought: Why the fuck should I? Joe Purcell doesn't care if I bring him a goldfish. I said to myself: What the fuck are you at Francie – *goldfish?*

The rifle man had his hands spread on the counter staring at me: Well do you want another go or don't you?

I started laughing. No, I don't. You and your goldfish, I said. You and Philip Nugent are well met.

I must be going soft in the head I thought, worrying about goldfish. When I walked into that old school in Bundoran to see Joe, what was he going to say? Oh hello Francie – I hope you brought the goldfish!

He was. He was in his eyeball! Me and Joe had better things to do with our time than worry about goldfish.

Goldfish! we said, fuck off!

I went up to the convent school and took a bike from the shed the girls always left them behind. I lit a fag and hopped up on the saddle. I says to myself: So the John Wayne stuff is over is it? We'll soon see about that! Indeed we will! Puff puff and the fag goes flying over the ditch. Freewheel freewheel tick tick tick and away off down Church Hill. *Take 'em to Missouri, men!*

Ting-a-ling-a-ling! Ting-a-ling-a-ling!

Off into the wind puffing fags and whistling away – My old man's a dustman he wears a dustman's hat! Hello there dandelions, fuck off! Chop go the heads with a cut of the stick excuse me just what do you think you're doing clip clip chop chop aaargh! what the fuck is going on where's our heads? Hee-yup!, I said and away again. An old woman emptying tea leaves into a drain hello there young fellow did you hear any more news she says. Any more news I says more news about what? Ach!, she says and scratches her backside, the communists ah says I what would I know about communists h'ho you won't be saying that when Mr Baldy Khrushchev presses the button. And he's going to press it. Make no mistake!

She closed one eye. You think he won't?

She started laughing away to herself oho yes but I'm afraid its too late them that hasn't their peace made its no use them running whingeing now. I told them that below in the shop get out the beads now says I for this time next week it'll be too late. We're not afraid of Khrushchev they says. But be Christ they're afraid now! *Its no joke now me son!* she says. Come on in and we'll say the rosary and then you'll have a mug of tea before you set off on your travels!

Right missus I said and down we went on our knees. Thou O Lord wilt open my lips she says please dear Jesus save us from all harm don't let the world come to an end. She had her eyes closed she passed no remarks on me all I said was mm mm and icky backy wacky talk like what I used to do for Tiddly. In the name of the father and of the son and of the Holy Ghost Amen she says and says you're a very holy boy son now sit up there till I stick on this kettle right ma'am says I. This is a grand house I says to myself. Black kettle on the hob and a settle bed in the corner and looking out from under it Mr Chinese Eyes the cat glaring what are you doing here who the hell asked you in fuck off from about here this is *my* house! Here you are now she says man dear I said that's the best cut of bread ever and sank my teeth into it, gurgle more tea into the cup. Come on now she says there's more where that came from and maybe something a wee bit stronger when you've finished that if you're able for it. Then off she goes chuckling under the stairs and comes back with a bottle in a brown paper bag. You'll have a drop she says the cat was in a bad way when he heard that. When we had that drank we took more. Where are you off to she says Bundoran says I. *Bundoran*, she says, *where the fleas ate the missioner!*

Have another drop me son, its not the first time a sup of John Jameson passed your lips.

Then she throws open the window and shouts out: Go on Khrushchev you baldy fucker! JFK is the man for you!

She told me she had six daughters and a son called Packy in England. He did well says I, he has a big job, hasn't he? He has, she says, oh our Packy did well for himself but how did *you* know that? Ten men under him says I and off she went looking for more whiskey all delighted and banging into things. I'm off to see Joe Purcell says I, Joe Purcell she says and who would he be. You can't beat a good friend she says, that was the first day I met him the day at the ice says I. You're the lucky man she says, there's not many of us in this world has friends the like of that. I know says I. Well there you are so you're off to see him now well more luck to you I wish I had a friend the like of that instead of that humpy get there standing at the door. What? says I and when I looked round who was standing there only this farmer in turned-down wellingtons pulling at his cap well he says that's that they've said no by this time next week there won't be a bullock left standing in that field we've had it every man woman child and beast in this townland!

It was just as well he turned up for when I looked out it was starting to get dark be the fuck says I its time I was off. The farmer looks at me and her with his mouth open. Good luck now ma'am says I all you could hear was *indeed I did have a glasheen of whiskey and neither you nor Baldy Khrushchev nor anyone else'll stop me!*

I nearly ran into the ditch three or four times look out says I but there wasn't a sinner to be seen Khrushchev hasn't much work to do about this place its done already I said next thing down the hill whee and off out into the open country again cows looking over ditches, where are you off to Francie mind your own business you nosey heifer bastards, watch out dandelions here I come! I couldn't stop laughing with all the whiskey inside me and the wind in my face and the pebbles skitting on all sides end of the world I says what are they talking about this is the beginning of the world, not the end.

Am I right Joe?

Yup! Francie boy says Joe.

Khrushchev hadn't much work to do in Bundoran either all you could see was two bits of newspaper wrestling in the middle of the main street, one boat in the harbour and nothing in the carnival park only a caravan with no wheels and a skinny mongrel tied to a fence. The houses were grey and blue and wet and in a sulk for the winter. Boo hoo nobody comes to stay in us any more. I wondered where it was they said the rosary. I dropped a spit into a rock pool, spidery tentacles and all these coral colours shifting in there. Are you prepared to live on potatoes and salt for the rest of your days, Annie? Is that the best you can offer a girl Benny Brady?

They were lying there on the candlewick bedspread and they could hear people drifting home from the dancehall until it got bright. Outside the window the sea ssh ssh was all you could hear. I knew what the boarding house was called. Over the Waves. I didn't know where it was but did that matter? Ting-a-ling! It wouldn't take old Mr Snort long to find a boarding house, no sir. Excuse me sir I need your assistance with a small matter. Yes my dear fellow how can I help you?

Algernon Carruthers. Tick tick tick whee along the beach shingle clattering against the spokes. Frawnthith my boy I do believe its time we ate.

I went into the hotel and sat down all plink plonk xylophone sounds and cutlery rattling far away. Well says the girl what would you like everything I says. What do you mean everything I says rashers eggs sausages beans and tea all that. She scribbles in the notebook. You're a hungry customer she says. I am, I said, sticking the napkin into my collar, I could eat a live hen.

There was a businessman with a bald head and glasses sitting down the other end. He looked like Humpty Dumpty's brother. I thought maybe he was in town leading the investigation. I know who did it! I seen them pushing your brother! I'd tell him. But he was leading no investigation. He was just reading the *Irish Times*. I could see what was on the front of it from where I was sitting. Crisis in Cuba – New Fears. New Fears? That was a laugh. I never felt better. If they said to me: Go on out and shoot all the communists for us Francie! I would have said: Sure bud.

I says to Humpty: I'm the man to do it! I'll knock a bit of sense into them. Oho yes! Make no mistake about that! He lifted his glasses and looked down at me. I think I must have looked a bit of a sketch with the stew and all on my good jacket and the smell of brock I don't know if he could get that or not. But I could get it myself so I'd say he could. But what did I care? Brock? What has that got to do with it now? Fuck Brock!

I wanted to leap into the air like Green Lantern or the Human Torch and land at Humpty's table. OK Humpty let's talk about your brother! I want the lowdown on these communists and I want it now!

But that was time enough. I didn't want to give old Humpty a heart attack. I stuffed the napkin into my collar and says: Oho but they're the curs, they're the bad wicked animals but Humpty never let on he heard me. But they've met their match this time. Oh yes, yes indeed. They've gone too far this time! John F. Kennedy. I said it like John Wayne, John Ayuff Kennedy. Yup! I said, they shore hay-yuv!

He gave the newspaper a stiff shake and up goes the glasses will you please keep quiet can't you see I'm trying to read.

The girl brought his breakfast and he folded up the newspaper what does he do then only lick his lips. Ah! he says, all delighted now. Then I pointed to it and laughed I says a good feed you can't beat it but he didn't say anything all I could hear was the clink of his fork munch munch.

Then I said: This is the place! This is it!

He looks at me with a rasher wobbling in front of his nose.

This is the place what? he says.

Where they spent their honeymoon of course!

What do you mean, honeymoon? Where *who* spent their honeymoon?

He hadn't a clue what I was talking about so I had to tell him the whole story right from the start.

I see he says and kept on looking at me but I knew he wasn't listening to the story half the time. So there you are, I says. Now I have to find the boarding house where they stayed. Over the Waves it was called. Do you know where it is?

No, he says I know nothing about this town I'm only here on business.

I was going to say all right all right there's no need to lose the head Humpty but I didn't get a chance for next thing up he gets and wipes his mouth and away off muttering with half the breakfast still lying there on the plate after him. That was a lot of use. Then the girl came back so I asked her. She said she didn't know but she could find out. I suppose you'll be here for a while she says looking at the big pile of stuff on the plate. Now you said it I said and started into it with the fork. I was scraping up the last bit of egg when she comes back with the manager. I understand you're looking for someplace I know Bundoran like the back of my hand. Where's Over the Waves I says bedad now and you have me there he says and scrunches up his face and starts all this scratching. I'll tell you what though, I could find out for you. I got more tea and then back he comes with this old lad he must have been about a hundred years of age. This man knows every mountain in Donegal, he says and your man looks at me with a face on him: I'm famous!

Yes! he says, Its true I *do* know every mountain in Donegal! whatever good that was, knowing mountains. But I didn't care he could know about any mountains he wanted all I wanted was the boarding house. When I said Over the Waves his face lit up aha! he says don't I know it well, I pass it every day on me way down from the post office. There you are! beams the manager, what did I tell you and the girl in behind him saying don't forget me now like a magician's assistant.

The old lad hobbled along beside me on the esplanade he was a bit like the gardener in the school for pigs for he was all talk about Michael Collins too except that he said he was the worst bastard ever was put on this earth because he sold out the country. Now you said it I said, and what about De Valera? When I said that he was away off again but I wasn't listening to a word he said. I was all jiggy and sparky again all I could think of was Over the Waves Over the Waves that was where it all began. Your man was still going Free Staters, he says, I'd give them two in the head apiece. There's the place you want he says, stabbing at it with his stick, down at the far end there. Its a bit of a walk but sure you have your health it'll not knock a flitter out of you. I nearly knocked him over the railings into the sea I was so excited. I walked up and down past the houses I don't know how many times. I'd look in the window and then look away again. I went in behind a parked car and tried to scrape off some of the dried stew on my jacket. It wouldn't come off so I had to go at it with a piece of broken lollystick. I thought to myself: That's a good one because I think it was a lollystick me and Joe were hacking at the ice with that day. I think it was. I'm nearly sure it was. All you could see was brass pots and big plants big rubber plants and pictures of horses or yachts hanging in the shadows but it didn't matter the houses were still in a sulk and they weren't going to come out of it no matter what you did. Look at us, they said. You won't get better houses than us and look not a sinner comes to stay. I'll tell you what I'll do houses I said. I'll click my Time Lord fingers and then what? Streams of children running round the place shouting look at me look at me sliding down the banisters and everything! Click and away off with the chairoplanes in the carnival and the whirligigs of the carousel wrapping up the town like a present in bright musical ribbons. Sea! I'd cry, big foamy breakers roaring in to crash against the sea wall. Delighted shrieks all along the strand. Boats by the dozen way out on the horizon. Trips around the lighthouse roll up! Oh yes you did Punch. Oh no I didn't. Oh yes you did Punch! Oh no I didn't youse bunch of cheeky little bastards!

Bacon and eggs frying and the smells floating out through the open windows. Women with veins hobbling along this is the best holiday we ever had. Yes indeed thanks to Francie Brady – the Time Lord. That would be good magic.

I rang the doorbell, I sprang at it for I knew if I didn't I'd still be walking up and down when the summer really came round. No I'm sorry, its number twenty-seven not number seventeen. Oops sorry I said I don't know what made me say it like that oops sorry it was like Toots or Little Mo out of the *Beano*. I don't know how many houses I called to after that ten or eleven or twelve or thirteen maybe but I shouldn't have called to any for if I had looked right the first time I'd have seen it it was there all along. There was a nameplate with an anchor and a painted sailor man, and just over the door Over the Waves Rooms Available. I nearly ran away but I didn't I tidied myself up and coughed and scraped off the flysplats and the stew as best I could and then the door opens and there she was. I knew she'd look like that, a chain on her glasses and all.

There was no holding her once she got started oh she says

its nothing now to what it used to be. In the old days I had twenty or thirty people at a time staying in this house and I says ah you probably wouldn't remember them all then but no she says that's where you're wrong old and all as I am, I never forget a face. I have a great memory for faces there's not one person stood in this house but I remember. Then she goes way back right to the very beginning of the old days. But the best year we ever had she says was the Eucharistic Congress, glory be I didn't think there was that amount of people to be found in the country, the crowds that used to land on that railway platform. Then of course after the war we had a lot over from England. And do you know what it is, not one of them would ever give you a bit of bother, paid their bills on time, never any fuss. Its not everyone's like that, I can tell you!

Are you all right for tea there, she says. I said: I am indeed.

Ah you'll have another drop she says. All right so I said.

I've had my share of important visitors too in my day, oh yes. Did you ever hear of Josef Locke? She pursed her lips and looked at me. I had never heard of him in my life but I stared over the rim of the cup and went: *Josef Locke?*

Yes!, she said. Three times he stayed here.

He sang for me and all she says, inside in the parlour. Oh what a wonderful evening that was. We had a schoolmaster used to come every year from Derry, Master McEniff, he played the piano. The melodies of Tom Moore. Do you know Tom Moore she says?

I knew Tom Moore that worked in the chickenhouse but I knew that wasn't who she was talking about. But I could still say I knew him. I do, I says.

It was an evening I'll treasure as long as I live she says.

Then she was away off again, some actor that used to stay and say poems and recitations. The Green Eye of the Little Yellow God, she says. Yes, I said, and The Cremation of Sam McGee!

I remembered that from the night of Alo's party.

Correct! she says, all delighted and passing me the biscuits.

Yes, she says. I always had lots of guests from the entertainment world, always did.

I was sitting on the edge of the chair waiting for a chance to get the bit in about da singing for her. I forgot all about my tea waiting for it. Then she says to me what you want to see young man is my collection of photographs. I have photographs of nearly everyone that ever passed a night under this roof. I don't know how many photographs she had, maybe a thousand. All these lads with faded brown faces and wide trousers. Sitting beside haystacks with girls. Shading their eyes staring off out to sea. Picnics too. I kept going through them and through them but I still couldn't find any of ma and da.

Oh that's such and such she'd say he stayed here for a whole month. He was a judge from Dublin, she was a relative of such and such, all this. But still no da. When we had gone through them all she shuffles them and looks up: Now what did you say your father's name was again?

Brady I said.

Brady then she says again, there was a Lucius Brady he was a musician he played the piano and a very good singer he was too as I recall what was the name of the song you said your dad sang again?

I dreamt that I dwelt in Marble Halls, I says.

Hmm, she says, of course I know the song but I can't say it rings a bell. He sang it, I said, he told me. You left the key under the mat for them! *Mm?* she says all surprised then. Oh no I'd never do that! I'd never do that! I don't know how many times she said that.

No matter she says then, wait till we see. She went through a few more Bradys, I had to keep saying all the time: No, that's not him.

What did you say his full name was again? she says. Bernard Brady I said and she said it after me a few times shaking her head and it was only after I said *Benny* that her jaw dropped and she looked at me all different. From where did you say, she says, and when I told her she starts gathering up the photographs and humming and hawing. I says: He never stopped talking about the days here and the beautiful things and all that but all of a sudden she didn't want to talk about it any more she says I'd be as well gather up all these bits and pieces God knows I don't know where to start with this work. I said but what about da and that, you said.

But then she says oh I don't know, my memory's not what it used to be. She tried to make a laugh out of it. Old age is catching up on me she says ha ha. She was putting all the photographs back into the boxes and the album now and I said why will you not tell me, you said you'd tell me. She just shook her head. Please tell me I said I have to hear it I have to hear it no she said let me go. All I wanted to hear was something about them lying there listening to the sea outside the window but it didn't matter I didn't hear it anyway. When I said to her go on tell me you said you would she said: *Get your hands off me do you hear me!* What can I tell you about a man who behaved the way he did in front of his wife. No better than a pig, the way he disgraced himself here. Any man who'd insult a priest the way he did. Poor Father McGivney who wouldn't hurt a fly coming here for over twenty years! God knows he works hard enough in the orphanage in Belfast without having to endure abuse the like of what that man gave him! God help the poor woman, she mustn't have seen him sober a day in their whole honeymoon!

Then what did she do she said *I'm sorry* but I was in the hall when she said it it didn't matter now anyway I just closed the front door softly with a click. I went on ahead up the street who did I meet then only the manager. Oh he says did you find the place you were looking for. I did indeed I says and I gave him the thumbs up have a good stay in Bundoran he says I will indeed I called after him the wind was blowing I went into a shop and bought some fags I went down to the beach and smoked a few the sea was dirty and grey like a dishcloth there was a few boats I think there was three I smoked another fag some of the fags I just smoked half of them the others I smoked them all. I counted how many I had left in the packet. One two three I had three left. I went up the town there was a few people about they were going about their business there was a woman shopping and a council man in waders over a manhole and convent girls outside a cafe I bought a comb my hair was getting all tangled up. But the thing was that beside the shop where I bought the comb there was another shop I must have missed it on the way down it was a music shop. There was a dog hanging over the door, staring into a trumpet, trying to find his master's voice. I'm in here get me out Fido says the master. How says Fido. How do I know says the master just do it will you my best little pet dog? In the window anything you wanted. To do with music that is. A silver saxophone you could have that. Trumpets. Stacks of records and a red-cheeked woman with her hair flowing and a half-knitted scarf of notes curving out of her mouth. She wanted everyone to sing along. I would. I'd sing along. I went in and who's behind the counter only the music man humming to himself and writing out notes on a music manuscript like da used to before he stayed out in the Tower all the time. The music man looked like a telegraph operator click click message for the marshal in Abilene and all this, with a big gold watch strung across his waistcoat. I said to him: I know something about you.

Oh he says and what might that be?

You know every tune in the world I says. I'll bet you know every one.

Not them all he says with a smile but a fair few, I'd say I know a fair few. I walked around. Gramophones, how many, twenty maybe. All kinds. Big trumpets, little trumpets. Any kind you want. Then what did I hear only this gurgling and when I look over what's that old music man doing only pouring himself tea. Want some? he says. A spot of tea, he says. He had some good sayings that music man. His sayings made me so happy I wanted to cry. But then what! Out of nowhere comes these cakes, would you believe it butterfly buns! Fuck me, I says, how did you know? He just smiled and said there you are and the tea looping and gurgling into the cups say when he says. I still don't know how he knew but it didn't matter I was away off filling him in on ma and da and the potatoes and salt and the song and saying the rosary on the rocks and everything. So he played the trumpet he says, your father. Yes I says and I told him some of the tunes. Well if he could handle that solo he says about one of the songs he certainly knew how to play a trumpet! He sure did I says licking the cream off my fingers. Outside the town had turned into glass the colour of dawnlight. There were tinkling mobiles in the shape of music notes hanging from the ceiling tinkle tinkle pling was all you could hear. Stacks of records, one by one I went through them but you had to be careful they could fall to pieces in your hands. *Watch it Francie!* I said and laughed: *Don't worry, I will!*

John McCormack I knew him. Da conducted in the air when he came on, cut big swathes of air with his index fingers. I laughed again. Then I saw it and when I did I nearly fainted, I don't know why I'd seen it plenty of times before. My legs went into legs of sawdust. Trot trot goes the sadeyed ass pulling the cart and away off into the misty green mountains and the blue clouds of far away. And right over the picture there in big black letters EMERALD GEMS OF IRELAND. I flicked through the pages over and over reading all the names and when I went to pay the music man I dropped the coins all over the place then I went into the whole story about Philip and Joe and everything it was like a cavalry charge of words coming out of my mouth I didn't know where they were all coming from. You'd think you were finished then over the hill would come a whole pile more yee haa wait till you hear this bit too. And all the way through he listened to everything I was saying and you could tell by his eyes that he wasn't really thinking I wish this Francie Brady would shut up about Joe Purcell or anything like that I knew he really wanted to hear it. For then he says the best thing of all. But of course there's a far better book than that available now. There it is behind you. A much better book. It was called A TREASURY OF IRISH MELODIES. There was no ass and cart on the front of it just an old woman in a shawl standing at a half-door staring at the sun going down behind the mountains. So this is better than the other book, I says. Oh yes says the music man, much better. I want to buy it! I says, all excited and what did I do only drop more coins all over the floor. The music man thought that was a good laugh. He had no intention of selling it to me. He was *giving* it to me. Its not every day I meet someone whose father could play the trumpet like yours, he says. Isn't it enough that you like the songs? Then he went away off humming a new tune to himself and parcelled it up for me. I just stared at the music man when he was handing it to me. Just wait till Joe sees this! I said. But he didn't get excited. If they started hammering on the window shouting the aliens are eating all the children in the town what would he do? He'd say: Right so. I'll be with you in a minute. I'll just lock up the shop first. He was the best man I ever met that old music man I kept looking at the book over and over and trying to see Joe's face as I handed it to him I wasn't sure which road to take for the school I went the wrong way a few times what do you think of this book I said to them its good they said yes I said, its for Joe Purcell, *Emerald Gems* is nothing compared to this one.

The black road twisted in and out of the curly countryside like a ribbon at the end of it was Joe's school and what was he going to say then: For fuck's sake Francie, you've done it again! Hey Joe! I'd shout. Saddle up! We're riding out! Yee – haa!

I was getting as bad as ma. Whiz this way then whiz the other way. I'll do this no I'll do that. The whiz again. I know – I'll think some more about Joe and the old days. But then, more laughing. Big whorly clouds made of ink powder riding the sky and the music book stuck in my back pocket. Then the school rising up out of the fields with all its yellow windows gleaming – another house of a hundred windows. But this time it was different, behind one of them windows was Joe and when I thought that I leaped so high I could have headed the moon like a football. Francie Brady plays for the town he's forty yards out he's thirty yards out twenty ten yards out its a long ball and the goalie's missed it and yes Francie Brady has scored a goal for the town Francie has scored a goal the moon is at the back of the net!

I had been tramping for over an hour before I seen it and then soon as I turn the corner what happens. Out go the lights. Phut!, every last one. Hey – what the hell do you think you're at up there, turning off them lights? Leave them on! How am I supposed to find Joe Purcell! Hey! Did you not hear me!

Then all of a sudden I thought: This is something to do with Mrs Nugent. She's heard about me going to see Joe and she has some plan up her sleeve. She's told the priests to switch off all the lights so they can lie in wait for me and when I'm finished running round the place like an eejit looking for him, she'll appear out of the shadows standing there with them, smiling: So you couldn't find him could you not? That's a pity Francis isn't it and then I knew that would be the end I'd never find him then. But then I started breaking my arse laughing it was such a stupid idea. *Oh no*, I said, *this is one thing that Mrs Nugent isn't going to spoil!*

I'd thought some things but that was the daftest yet.

I went round the back and nearly walked into a big bin full of brock you'd think with me being King of The Brock I'd have been able to see that! I was in behind the kitchens. Grr says a dog.

Fuck up I said but I managed to get past him all right. I could hear the toilets hissing. Hiss hiss, we can see you Francie. I kept checking the book to see that I still had it in my back pocket. Where did I end up only in a room full of football boots and the smell of sweaty oxters. Curse of fuck on this and I had to start again. Dant-a-dan! Along the wall. Don't move! Six soldiers out of nowhere cocking rifles, up against the wall so we have you at last Mr Brady! No, none of that, only snoring priests and bogmen but where were they? Not in here nothing only an empty bed and a cupboard full of medicine bottles. I think I'll have a look at these I said and shovelled a few coloured pills into my hand out of a little brown bottle. Gulp down the hatch they went. I wonder what they were. I don't know. Whee, I thought I heard someone shouting from the other end of the corridor you take a left then the next right Francie and you'll find him no problem. I turned round to thank him whoever it was but there was no one there. Then the pill said: Oh that was just me Francie. Pill, I said, you bastard! Now now Francie said the pill for that I'll just have to turn your feet to sponge. Squish squeesh along the tiles. What's this the biggest bell in the world sitting under the stairs. I said: Mrs Nugent if you're in behind that bell you had better come out. I know you're in there Mrs Nugent you can't fool me.

Then I started laughing I couldn't stop myself. It wasn't an ordinary laugh either it was a bogman laugh the way they laugh at nothing with snots coming out of their noses still laughing long after the joke is over. I says I know what I'll do I'll give this bell a whack and see what happens. I'd say it'd make enough noise to waken every boarding school bogman in the world even the ones who are completely deaf. Ready steady – fuck off! If I did that they'd be down on me like a ton of bricks and maybe give Joe the boot into the bargain. Oh no you don't pill you'll not make a cod of old Francie that easy. Pill, I said – have manners!

I was in a right state now with all this laughing I couldn't stop. Hmm I says I wonder what tricks Joe gets up to in this place. Sliding down the knotted sheets out of the dormitory and away off to midnight feasts in the boatshed I'll be bound! I say Purcell you bounder! You are a perfect cad! For fuck's sake! I wonder is there any secret passageways I said. Fall against the knob of a banister next thing aaaaaaaaaaah! and away off down a black corridor full of cobwebs and the skeletons of dead bogmen boys.

Up the stairs I went what's this, a wooden door creak creak Our Lord Jesus appearing out of nowhere in the dark, hanging on the cross – hello yes what can I do for you? I'm looking for Joe Purcell Jesus. Straight on up to the top of the stairs. Right so Jesus thank you.

———

What's all this I said, a hundred sleeping bogmen! But not for long. Wait till they seen me and Joe in action!

Da-dan!

Flick – on goes the light blazes away and them all gone chinky-eyed and pulling the clothes round them: What's goin' on who's puttin' on the lights? I nearly said: why its me – Algernon Carruthers of course!

When I thought that I doubled up again and all I could see was them staring at me. They were all saying to the prefect who is he you do something about it its your job and all this but he wasn't going to do anything he had the blankets pulled up the same as the rest of them.

I thumped my thigh with the rolled up music book: *Joe! Where are you Joe Boy? I'm here! saddle up! We're ridin' out!*

I shouted it for all I was worth and then I shouted it again in case he didn't hear me. As soon as I said that all the things I had ever worried about floated away like silk scarves in the breeze and I knew all I had to do now was wait for Joe and we were off and this time we'd be gone for good. It made me feel so good I shouted again: Joe. Yamma yamma yamma! Yamma yamma yamma!

Then I said: Yee haa! Take 'em to Missouri men!

We'll ride out to the mountains Joe and there we can track for days. We can listen to the coyotes in the night. The coyotes baying at the moon because it makes them feel good they howl out anything they ever worried about. Then I did it. A-woo! A-woo! I closed my eyes and cried out across the prairie.

Then I looked up and who's coming the priest. It was Father Fox not because his real name was Fox but because he had a long snout and a hmm I wonder how could I trick this fellow face? Hello Father Fox I said, I'm looking for Joe Purcell. You're *what!* he says and I could see that Father Fox he wasn't such a nice old fox at all his face went all dark and his eyes didn't say I wonder how could I trick this fellow any more they said one more word out of you my friend and I'll take this collar off and I'll floor you by Christ I will and don't think for one second that I wouldn't. Father Fox I'm surprised at you! Don't say such things!

That's what Algernon Carruthers would have said. But I didn't say it.

I just said I'm looking for Joe can you help me please?

What did Fox say half to himself and half to the bogmen I can not believe it I just can *not* believe it! He shook his head and when the bogmen seen him doing that they did it too. I could hear doors banging and all this commotion and running on the stairs. Then two more priests came in and who had they with them only Joe Purcell.

Joe! I shouted. *Fuck!*

I knew I shouldn't have shouted that, but I did. Fox made a wind at me but I ducked. He tried again but that was no use either I sidestepped it he was only making a cod of himself. All I had to do now was walk right over to Joe and that's what I would have done only for what happened then who was standing right behind him only Philip Nugent. He was taller now a bit tougher looking but it was him all right with the hair hanging down in his eyes. He was staring at me in a way he never did before straight at me. As soon as I seen him everything started to go wrong because he wasn't supposed to be there. All the things I was going to say I couldn't remember what they were now then the priest brought Joe over and the way he looked at me my stomach turned over it wasn't Joe. Philip was still standing over by the door with his arms folded. I knew when it was all over what he would be telling them. That I had wanted to be one of them and had turned my back on my own mother. He'd laugh then and say: Imagine him thinking he could be one of us!

Joe said to me: What do you want?

No he didn't. He said: What do *you* want?

It was no use me trying to say I wanted us to ride out Joe I wanted us to talk about the old days and what we'd do if we won a hundred million trillion dollars maybe go tracking in the mountains I don't know Joe, it was no use me saying that for I knew it wouldn't come out right so I said nothing I just stood there looking at him.

He asked me again: What do you want me for? Are you deaf or something?

Then he said: Do you hear me. What do you want me for?

I never thought Joe would ask that I never thought he would *have* to ask that but he did didn't he and when I heard him say it that was when I started to feel myself draining away and I couldn't stop it the more I tried the worse it got I could have floated to the ceiling like a fag paper please Joe come with me that was all I wanted to say dumb people have holes in the pit of their stomachs and that's the way I was now the dumbest person in the whole world who had no words left for anything at all. All I had now was one thing and that was the music book. It had got all twisted up with sweat marks all over it I says don't worry Francie its going to be all right

I smoothed it out a bit and handed it to him some way or other I dropped it and the next thing the priest came in between us and says: *Look this has gone far enough! Is this fellow a friend of yours or is he not Purcell?*

I looked at Joe please Joe I was saying but he wasn't looking at me he was just saying I'm tired I want to get back to my bed its three in the morning.

Then Joe just shook his head and said: No.

Then he left he said something to Philip on the way out and Philip smiled. I stayed there for a minute I was still twisting the book then the priest said I think its time you were leaving Mr Brady. I said yes, yes Father and they brought me to the gate they said I was lucky they didn't call the police I said yes it was then I went off into the dark I had left the bike somewhere but I didn't know where. It didn't matter anyway I just walked I felt like walking that wasn't Joe I said I don't know who that was but it wasn't Joe, Joe is gone they took him away from me and all I could see was a pair of thin lips saying that's right we did and there's nothing you can do that will ever bring him back again isn't that true Francis Pig you little piggy baby pig and I says yes Mrs Nugent it is.

When I got to the town they were all running round saying the world is going to end. The first thing I seen was Mickey Traynor wheeling a statue of Our Lady up the street in a barrow did you not hear he says the world is going to end it was on the news last night its all over he says oh I know says I I know that all right you don't have to tell me *that*!

What do we care he says let them do their worst we have the Blessed Virgin Mary to protect us she spoke to my daughter she says she's going to come with a sign. For the love of God go along and listen to her young Brady in these times every man must look after his immortal soul!

He got a grip of me by the shoulder and says: Will you do that for me Francie I knew your father.

I know you did I says he was supposed to go up to you about the television but he didn't that's why I had to go and watch the octopus in Nugents. Right says Mickey I'd better be making tracks good luck now and off he went with the barrow.

I shouted after him: I don't suppose you'd be able to fix it now Mickey would you?

He didn't look round I knew he wouldn't be able to anyway it was too far gone after the kick da gave it. It was finished, that television. I should have thrown it on the dump by right for what was it doing in the coalhouse only taking up space. I went on up the street and who did I meet only the drunk lad. Come on into the Tower I says but he shook his head. I says what are you talking about and he says did you not hear about Traynor's daughter? I says I did but what the fuck do I care about Traynor's daughter come on in and I pulled out a fiver. No he says no I have to go on about my business the priest was down to see me he says I've to get into no more trouble. I've got into enough trouble through going about with you I have to go on up to see Father Dominic he says he might have a job for me. Excuse me he says pushing past me and away he goes with the raggy coat flapping behind him. Go on you humpy bastard! I shouted after him, you were glad enough of it when it was going!

I went in and bought a packet of fags and something to clean my jacket all they had was shampoo that'll do I says.

When I came out I seen Mrs Connolly going past on the far side of the street with a basin full of flowers. I waved to her but she got all red and stuck down her head and never let on she seen me. A loudspeaker whistled and screeched then a hymn started up. It was called Faith of Our Fathers. I listened for a while but it was only a fuck up of a hymn. I stood outside the home bakery and sang my own. It was about Matt Talbot, my old friend from the Father Tiddly days. This is more like it, I said, this is a real hymn!

> I love my planks the best of all
> In spite of cold and frost and rain
> And I love my cat I give him kipper teas
> But most of all I love my chains.

I sang a few more verses all about them saying to him: Do you want us to buy you a drink Matt? Fuck off with your-self!

I had a good laugh at that, sitting on the wall and shout-ing at them going by: Matt Talbot for president!

Then I sang more. I pasted back my hair and sang into a lollystick.

> *Well its one for the money!*
> *Two for the show!*

I sang that one. Then I sang:

> *When you move in right up close to me*
> *That's when I get the shakes all over me!*

I sang more. I shouted:

> *Francie Brady on Radio Luxembourg!*

Then I got fed up singing fuck this I said, fucking singing. I went into the cafe its you he says what do you want I says sausages rashers beans chips eggs all that. I'm sorry we're closing sorry but we got to close now. I bought a bag of Tayto crisps and went out to the hide. I tried to clean the jacket up with the shampoo but it was no use I used half the bottle all it did was make it worse then I fell asleep.

I woke up the next morning and went round to the slaughterhouse but it was too early I was waiting for near two hours before Leddy came how long are you here he says a good while Mr Leddy I said. Its near time you'd show your face around here or where in the hell were you! Oh I says I was off rambling. Rambling he says, you'd do well to ramble in your own time Brady I've a mind to kick you rambling down that road. Well says I you won't have to worry for that's the end of it it'll be all over now shortly. He pulled on his apron and says they have a half ton of shite round at that hotel you were supposed to collect it and they have my heart scalded now get round there today and fuckingwell see about it. Right so Mr Leddy I said.

Then we started into the killing and we were working right through till dinnertime. Then he wiped his hands on his apron and says I'm away to my dinner take that cart round now. And make sure and tell them tell them you'll collect on time next week. I will indeed Mr Leddy I says. When he was gone off down the town I took the captive bolt pistol down off the nail where it was hanging and got the butcher's steel and the knife out of the drawer. There was a bucket of old slops and pig meal or something lying by the door so I just stuck them into that and went away off with the cart whistling. So Traynor's daughter had been talking to Our Lady again, eh? They were all talk about her going to appear on the Diamond. I heard two old women on about it. We should be very proud says one of them its not every town the Mother of God comes to visit. Indeed it is not says the other one I wonder missus will there be angels. I wouldn't know about that now but sure what odds whether there is or not so long as she saves us from the end of the world what do we care? Now you said it missus now you said it. Everywhere you went: Not long now.

I went by Doctor Roche's house it was all painted up with big blue cardboard letters spread out on the grass: AVE MARIA WELCOME TO OUR TOWN. I was wondering could I mix them up to make THIS IS DOCTOR ROCHE THE BASTARD'S HOUSE, but I counted them and there wasn't enough letters and anyway they were the wrong ones.

Tell Leddy to collect this brock on time or its the last he'll get from us says the kitchen man and stands there looking at me like I was stealing something off him. I will indeed I said and started shovelling it into the cart. I shovelled and whistled away and made sure there wasn't a scrap left so there'd be no more complaining. Then off I went again on my travels. Everybody was all holy now, we're all in this together people of the town, bogmen taking off their caps to women, looking into prams and everything. This is the holiest town in the world they should have put that up on a banner.

There was a nice altar on the Diamond. There was three angels flying over it just in front of the door of the Ulster Bank.

I never saw the town looking so well. It looked like the brightest, happiest town in the whole world.

I went round the back swinging my meal bucket. I could see the neighbour's curtain twitching whistle whistle hello there Mr Neighbour its me Francie with my special delivery for Mrs Nugent. Then away she went from the window so I knocked on Mrs Nugent's door and out she came wearing her blue housecoat. Hello Mrs Nugent I said is Mr Nugent in I have a message for him from Mr Leddy. She went all white and stood there just stuttering I'm sorry she said my husband isn't here he's gone to work oh I said that's all right and with one quick shove I pushed her inside she fell back against something. I twisted the key in the lock behind me. She had a white mask of a face on her and her mouth a small o now you know what its like for dumb people who have holes in their stomachs Mrs Nugent. They try to cry out and they can't they don't know how. She stumbled trying to get to the phone or the door and when I smelt the scones and seen Philip's picture I started to shake and kicked her I don't know how many times. She groaned and said please I didn't care if she groaned or said please or what she said. I caught her round the neck and I said: You did two bad things Mrs Nugent. You made me turn my back on my ma and you took Joe away from me. Why did you do that Mrs Nugent? She didn't answer I didn't want to hear any answer I smacked her against the wall a few times there was a smear of blood at the corner of her mouth and her hand was reaching out trying to touch me when I cocked the captive bolt. I lifted her off the floor with one hand and shot the bolt right into her head *thlok* was the sound it made, like a goldfish dropping into a bowl. If you ask anyone how you kill a pig they will tell you cut its throat across but you don't you do it longways. Then she just lay there with her chin sticking up and I opened her then I stuck my hand in her stomach and wrote PIGS all over the walls of the upstairs room.

I made sure to cover her over good and proper with the brock there was plenty of it they wouldn't be too pleased if they saw me with Mrs Nugent in the bottom of the cart then I lifted the shafts and off I went on my travels again there was more hymns and streams of people up and down Church Hill with prayerbooks. Who did I meet then only your man with the bicycle and the raincoat thrown over the handlebars. He was all friendly this time he was a happy man Our Lady was coming he said. I haven't seen you this long time he says are you still collecting the tax? No I said that's all finished I'm wheeling carts now. You never thought you'd see the day the Mother of God would be coming to this town, eh? he says and looked at me as much as to say it was me arranged the whole thing. No, I did not, I said, its a happy time for the town and no mistake. A happy happy time he says and reached in his pocket to take out his tobacco puff puff what will we talk about now nothing I said the best of luck now I'm away off round to the yard right he says no rest for the wicked that's right I says no rest for anyone only Mrs Nugent in the bottom of this cart. But he didn't hear me saying that.

I let down the cart for a minute and went in to buy some fags the women were there over by the sugar only without Mrs Connolly. I got the fags and I says to the women its a pity Mrs Connolly isn't here I wanted to talk to her about what I said sure I was only codding! I said. What would I go and say the like of that to her for! Me and Mrs Connolly are old friends! Didn't I get a prize off her for doing a dance! A lovely juicy apple! I lit up a fag and puffed it ha ha they said ah sure don't be worrying your head Francie they said we all do things we regret don't we ladies. Yes I said especially Mrs Nugent and laughed through the smoke. Then they said: What? But I said: Oh nothing.

One of them twisted the strap of her handbag round her little finger and said there was no use in people bearing grudges at a special time like this. Now you said it I said, you never spoke a truer word.

Well ladies, I said, I must be off about my business there's no rest for the wicked indeed there is not Francie said the woman with three heads laughing away like in the old days. I had gone through that fag already and the shop was full of smoke I was puffing it all out that fast so what did I do only light another one. Francie Brady – I smoke one hundred cigarettes a day! Yes its true! Francie Brady says! No, it isn't. Only when I'm wheeling Mrs Nooge around. I stuck a little finger in the air and pulled on the fag like something out of the pictures. I say ladies – good day, I said and that started them off into the laughing again. Master Algernon Carruthers and his Nugent cart. OK Nooge let's ride I said, the Francie Brady Deadwood stage is pulling out. The drunk lad went by with another saint in a barrow and ducked down when he seen me.

Stop thief! Come back with that saint! I says and started into the laughing again. Stop that man! He's going to sell that poor saint for drink! Whistling away on I went my old man's a dustman he wears a dustman's hat. I don't know where all the songs came out of. Well its one for the money. I am a little baby pig I'll have you all to know. Yes this is the Baby Pig Show broadcasting on Raydeeoh Lux-em-Bourg!

Hello my good man. Fine weather we're having. What did you order? Two pounds of chump steak?

Or was it a half pound of Mrs Nugent?

Sorry folks, Mrs Nugent's not for sale! She's off on her travels with her old pal Francie Brady. I was passing by Mary's sweetshop so in I went and got a quarter of sweets, clove drops. I came in to say hello to my old friend Mary I said will you ever forget them old days Mary! Twenty years in Camden Town! What about that! What do you say we go inside and you can give us a song on the piano!

I lit another fag and went on talking away but Mary said nothing just scooped the sweets into the bag with a silver shovel and then twisted it the way she did spin twist and there it was a little knobbly bag of best clove drops yes indeed. Then she went and sat down by the window again looking out across the square. Look at that Mary! The same old clove drops! I said but she still didn't say anything just smiled if you could call it a smile. I knew who she was thinking about. She was thinking about Alo that's who she was thinking about. Don't worry Mary I said, your troubles are over Mary – Francie Brady the Time Lord is here!

But soon as I said it I felt stupid and I tried to think of something completely different to say but I could think of nothing so I just put the sweets in my pocket and went out the bell jingle jingle and the door closing behind me. Mary had the same face as ma used to have sitting staring into the ashes it was funny that face it slowly grew over the other one until one day you looked and the person you knew was gone.

And instead there was a half-ghost sitting there who had only one thing to say: All the beautiful things of this world are lies. They count for nothing in the end.

Even if that was true I still went round the lane where the kids were this might be my last chance I said. Sure enough there they were setting toy tea-things on an orange box and clumping around in the enormous shoes. Can I play I said. How can you play if you're big one of them said, clear off! There was a young lad sailing lollystick rafts out into the middle of a puddle. I said to him: What would you do if you won a hundred million billion trillion dollars?

Without thinking he looked at me and said: I'd buy a million Flash Bars. Well fuck me, I laughed, then off I went again and left him churning up the water with his stick and whistling some tune he was making up as he went along.

Where the hell were you says Leddy when I got back to the slaughterhouse yard. Oh, tricking about I says, well trick about in your own time he says I have to go on up to the shop, you take over here. Right, I said, that suits me, and I let down the barrow beside the Pit of Guts and asked Leddy where he'd put the lime. Clear off Grouse! I shouted and he tore off through the gate with a string of intestines. I got the shovel and slit open the bag of lime there was warm tears in my eyes because I could do nothing for Mary.

I'd say it was a good laugh when Mr Nugent Ready Rubbed came home that evening. Brr that's a cold one yoo-hoo! I'm home what's for tea dear? Dear oh dear that wife of mine she's so busy she hears nothing. The smell of scones and the black and white tiles polished so you could see your face in them. O she's probably just gone out to the shop for something never mind let's see what's on the telly. Here is The News. News. Mm, isn't it quiet around here since Philip went to boarding school? Mm, isn't it quiet around here since my Mrs went to heaven he'd soon be saying but he didn't know that. I wonder what it will be – rashers and eggs maybe or one of her special steak and kidney pies! But poor old Mr Nugent he'd have a long wait before he got one of them again. Ah yes, it was sad. And that is the end of the news. Hmm. Tick tock. I wonder where she could be. I wonder where my wife could be? Hello next door neighbour did you see my wife? No, to tell you the God's honest truth now I didn't. Oh dear said Mr Nooge. Tick tick and walking round the kitchen the silence wasn't so nice now over and over again just where is Mrs Nugent the invisible woman? Tick tock and I don't care about Maltan Ready Rubbed, where is my wife! Look at that old Mr Nugent and his big red eyes! Maltan Ready Rubbed – Its The Best Boo Hoo Hoo! That wouldn't look so good on the television. I wonder would she be upstairs? Do you think she might have gone upstairs and fallen asleep next door neighbour? Why yes she could have couldn't she? Let's go and investigate shall we? Good idea says Mr Nugent and off they go taking the stairs two at a time but then when they open the door what do they see all over the walls oh no Mr Nugent hardly able to stand and the next door neighbour don't look don't look!

Well she doesn't seem to be in there anyway ha ha perhaps the police might know why don't we ring up let me do it Mr Nugent. Sweaty fingerprints all over the telephone hello is that Sergeant Sausage I mean is that the police station?

I was whistling away when I looked up and seen Sausage and four or five bogmen police coming across the yard I never seen them before they weren't from the town. One of them kept looking over the whole time sizing me up trying to catch my eye to tell me *by Chrisht you're for it now boy!* but I just went on skinning and whistling. I don't know what I was whistling I think it was the tune from Voyage to the Bottom of The Sea. Leddy was standing in the doorway wiping his hands with a rag then looking over at me with a chalky old face on him. I heard the sergeant saying: *The neighbours seen him going in round the back of the house this morning.*

Next thing what does Leddy do only lose the head. Before the sergeant could stop him he had a hold of me and gives me this push I fell back against the fridge door *I hope to Christ they give you everything that's coming to you! I should never have let you darken the door of the place only I let myself be talked into it on account of your poor mother!* he says standing there shaking with his fists opening and closing. He tried to push me again but I managed to get a hold of his arm I looked right into his eyes and he knew what I was saying to him, Mr Leddy from the Cutting Up Pigs University you better watch who you're pushing Bangkok you were never in Bangkok in your life and you better watch what you're saying about my father plucking my mother or you'll get the same Nugent got would you like that Pig Leddy – Leddy the Pig Man would you fuckingwell like that!

Then I burst out laughing in his face he was so shocked

– looking I thought he was going to say O please Francie I'm sorry I didn't mean to say all that it was a slip of the tongue.

What could I say? Such a daft place!

Mr Nugent was shivery and everything I knew he couldn't bear to look at me. Where is she, said Sausage and the bull-neck bogmen got a grip of me two on either side. They had me now all right I wasn't fit to move a muscle. Oh I said, this must be the end of the world. I hope the Blessed Virgin comes along to save me!

Where is she? says Sausage again.

Maltan Ready Rubbed Flake, that's the one!, I said to Mr Nugent and I got a thump in the ribs. Then they said right turn this place inside out and that's what they did. They turned it upside down. Those bogmen cops. You could fry a rasher on their necks. How many rashers was that? Four. No – let's make it two rashers and two eggs instead if you don't mind!

I wonder is she in behind this half-a-cow? No, she doesn't appear to be. What about under this septic tank? No, no sign of her. Then they got hysterical. They had to take Mr Nugent away. What have you done with her? I said who and they got worse. They gave me a beating and took me for a drive all round the town. What had they draped across the chicken-house only THE TOWN WELCOMES OUR LADY. I said to them: She must be going to land on the chickenhouse roof and they stuck the car to the road with a screech of brakes by Christ I'll tear that blasphemous tongue out of your head with my bare hands says Sausage. But he didn't, then we were off again where to, the river. Is she out here? Who, I said again. After all that they took me back to the station and gave me the father and mother of a kicking. In the middle of it all what does one of the bullnecks say: Let me have a crack at him and I'll knock seven different kinds of shite out of him!

That finished me off altogether. I started saying it the way he said it. Seven different kinds of shoite! For fuck's sake!

The way they do it they put a bar of soap in a sock and I don't know how many times they gave it to me it leaves no marks. But it still knocks seven different kinds of shite out!

Where is she said Sausage, shaking. Castlebar Sausages – they're the best! I said. Hear them sizzle in the pan – Sergeant Sausage says!

Then they got fed up and said fuck him into the cell we'll get it out of him in the morning. I could hear them playing cards. Foive o' trumps! and all this. That's the besht keeerd you've played thish ayvnin'! I stuck my ear to the wall so as I wouldn't miss any of it. I heard them saying: I wouldn't turn my back on that treacherous fucker not for a second!

They kept me in the cell the whole of the next day they were waiting for the detective to come down from Dublin. I could hear them all going by in the street come over here you bastard I shouts to the drunk lad through the bars you owe me two and six the fucker away off then running like the clappers. Hello Mrs Connolly I shouted look where they have me now! Your man with the bicycle, I shouts over: This is what I get for not paying my pig toll tax! It serves me right!

Ha ha he says and nearly drove the bicycle into a wall. Who appears at the window of the cell then only Mickey Traynor and McCooey the miracle worker. I'm praying for you son, says McCooey. He had Maria Goretti propped up against a couple of haybales on the back of the cart he said she was going to bleed at the apparition. Then he says I hear there's been bad trouble in the town this past few days. How are you my son, he says, I'm praying for your immortal soul, never fear. Through the bars I could see Goretti gawking up at the sky with her hands joined. Observe her beautiful eyes, McCooey'd say, Observe the beautiful saint's eyes and then two red red rubies of blood would appear and roll down her white cheeks. Its sad Mr McCooey, I said. What, my son, he said, this vale of tears in which we are all but wanderers searching for home? No, I said, fat old bastards like you wasting all that tomato sauce. O Jesus Mary and Joseph says Mickey and reaches out in case he faints. You're a bad and wicked and evil man and you broke your mother's heart didn't even go to the poor woman's funeral! I said to him what the fuck would you know about it Traynor what do you know you couldn't even fix the television could you well what are you talking about! Do you hear me Traynor? Fuck you! Fuck you and your daughter and The Blessed Virgin! I didn't mean to say that Traynor made me say it the whole street heard me there they were all looking and crossing themselves oh Jesus Mary and Joseph then in came the bull-necks and the detective they gave me another kicking and says we're going for a drive after and you'd better start opening your mouth Brady or by Christ you'll get what's coming to you. I fell into a sort of sleep then after that and I heard Mrs Connolly and them all saying the rosary for me outside in the square. I looked up and there was Buttsy and Devlin looking in between the bars. You better pray they hang you says Buttsy what we're going to do to you we'll string you up like the pig you are. He was all smart but then he starts screeching *what have you done to my sister* till Devlin had to take him away. I said good riddance and read the *Beano* I got one of the children to get me in Mary's shop. General Jumbo he had some army, tiny little robot men he controlled using this wrist panel of buttons made for him by his friend Mr Professor. I used to think: I wouldn't mind having one of them that controlled all the people in the town. I'd march them all out to the river and click!, stop right at the edge. Then just when they were saying: Phew that was a lucky one we nearly went in there, Hi-yah! I'd press the button – in you go youse bastards aiee! and the whole lot of them into the water.

The next time Sausage came in on his own turning the cap round on his lap looking at me with these sad eyes why does there have to be so many sad things in the world Francie I'm an old man I'm not able for this any more. When I seen them eyes, I said to myself, poor old Sausage its not fair. All right Sausage I said I'll show you where she is thanks Francie he said, I knew you would. Its gone on long enough. There's been enough unhappiness and misery. There has indeed sergeant I said.

The new detective was in the front of the car, Fabian of the Yard I called him after the fellow in the pictures, and I was hemmed in between two of the bullnecks in the back.

Sausage was all proud now that things had worked out and he hadn't made a cod of himself in front of Fabian. It'll be all over shortly now Francie he says you're doing the right thing. I know Sergeant I said. When we turned into the lane he drove slowly to avoid the children what were they at now selling comics on a table it was a comic sale. They stood there looking after us I seen tassels pointing look Brendy its him!

We stopped at the chickenhouse and Fabian says you two men stay out here at the front just in case you can't be too careful. Right they said and me and the sergeant and him and the other two went inside. The fan was humming away and it made me sad. The chicks were still scrabbling away who are all these coming with Francie?

We waded through the piles of woodchips as we went along and I said to them it isn't far its just down here at the back. Fabian wasn't sure of where he was going it was so dark and when he walked into the light hanging in front of his face it went swinging back and forth painting the big shadows on the walls and the ceilings. I think the chicks must have known what was going to happen for they started burbling and getting excited. I said fuck who put that there and made on to trip and fall down. Watch yourself says Sausage its very dark and when Fabian came over to help me up I had the chain in my hand it had been lying there under the pallets where it always was. I swung it once and Fabian cried out but that was all I needed I tore into the back room and bolted the door. I didn't waste any time I threw the chain there and flung open the window and got out then ran like fuck.

I don't know where all the policemen came from but they were combing the country for me high up and low down.

I could see them moving out across the fields and shouting to each other: Any luck? and Have you searched the other side of the woods yet?

It was a good laugh listening to all this I could see everything from inside the hide and old Sausage would he have kicked kicked himself stupid if he knew that he was standing right beside me twice.

They brought more police in you could hear them poking about night noon and morning and the sniffer dogs wuff wuff on the bank of the river time was running out for the deadly Francie Brady! Oh no it wasn't it was running out for fed-up Fabian and his men for all they had found was a dead cat in the ditch and you could hardly take that back to Scotland Yard. Well done Detective Fabian! You didn't catch Brady but you did catch this – a maggot-ridden old moggy! Congratulations!

In the end they said he has to be in the river so out the frogmen police went and dragged it there was reporters and Buttsy and Devlin and half the town all waiting to see me coming up covered in weeds and dirt but all they got this time was an iron bedstead and half a mattress. They came back a few times after that poking bits of sticks in bushes and muttering to themselves ah fuck this he's gone then they just slowly drifted away and then there was only me and the river hiss hiss. Hey fish! I said, youse are lucky youse didn't tell youse bastards! then out I went onto the main road there wasn't a sinner to be seen so off I went towards the town whistle whistle I was back in action. There was an old farmer humming away to himself and his bike lying up against the ditch. Tick tick tick and off I went and soon as I turned the corner wheee freewheeling away down the hill round the lane by the back of the houses in I went da-dan! I'm home! What's this ma used to say? I've so much tidying to do I don't know where to start, I rubbed my brow and stood there with my hands on my hips. I just don't know! Such a smell there was in the place! Not only had Grouse Armstrong been in but every dirty mongrel in the town. Everywhere you looked there was dog poo! In the corners, smeared on the walls. I gathered up as much of it as I could and put it all in a big pile in the middle of the kitchen. Well, I said, at least that's a start! Now – what about those mouldy old books! I lifted up one of them. What's this? The Glory That Was Greece! To Benny 1949.

I turned a few of the pages and it all broke up in bits in my hands. I threw them all on the pile one after the other. There was a heap of clothes lying in the corner. A handful of earwigs fell out of the pocket of da's Al Capone coat. There was skirts and odd shoes and all sorts of things. I threw them all on. Then I went out to the scullery and got plates and knives and any other things that were lying around. I wiped my hands. Dear oh dear this is hard work I said. And I haven't even touched the upstairs yet! I didn't bother going through the drawers I just turned them upside down. There was letters and calendars and bills and stuff like that. Then I went upstairs and got the bedclothes and anything that was left in the wardrobes. What about us? said the pictures on the walls. Oops, I said, silly me! I nearly went and forgot all about you didn't I?

There was one of da pressing the mouthpiece to his lips. On you go, I says. Then the Sacred Heart with his two fingers up and the thorny heart burning outside his chest. Do you remember all the prayers we used to say in the old days Francie? He says. Oh now Sacred Heart I says, will I ever forget them? May the curse of Christ light upon you this night you rotten cunting bitch – do you remember that one?

I do, He says, raising His eyes to heaven, then off He goes what about this I says John F. Kennedy the man himself. What about me says Pope John the twenty third do I have to be dumped too? I'm sorry Holy Father I have to or else I'll get into trouble with the rest so on you go it'll not be long now. I had a hard job carrying the telly over I wanted it on the top but I managed it. The guts was still hanging out of it, wires and bulbs all over the place. The records were still under the stairs but I only wanted one I threw the rest away. I plugged in the gramophone it was working as good as ever then I carried it out to the scullery and put it near the sink. Right says I, now we're in business.

I got the paraffin from the coalhouse and threw it round everywhere but mostly on the pile, Spin spin goes your head with the smell of it here we go I says and then what happens.

No matches! No fucking matches! Oh for fuck's sake! I said.

When I got out into the street I couldn't believe it what's going on now I says. It was like the bit in Gone with the Wind where they burn the city. Fellows with halves of legs and some with none at all only a bit of a stump. Traynor's daughter was bucking away on the Diamond between two nuns, with her mouth all suds. The drunk lad was directing traffic with a new tie on him. *This way to the Mother of God, my friends!* They were far too busy waiting for her to be bothered about me running round for matches. I went into the shop thank you very much Mary I says its goodbye now I'm afraid but she didn't say anything she just sat there.

When I got back to the house I locked all the doors and then I lit a couple of matches. Soon as they fell on the heap up she went whumph!

I put on the record then I went in and lay down on the kitchen floor I closed my eyes and it was just like ma singing away like she used to.

> In that fair city where I did dwell
> A butcher boy I knew right well
> He courted me my life away
> But now with me he will not stay
>
> I wish I wish I wish in vain
> I wish I was a maid again
> But a maid again I ne'er will be
> Till cherries grow on an ivy tree.
>
> He went upstairs and the door he broke
> He found her hanging from a rope
> He took a knife and he cut her down
> And in her pocket these words he found
>
> Oh make my grave large wide and deep
> Put a marble stone at my head and feet
> And in the middle a turtle dove
> That the world may know I died for love.

I was crying because we were together now. Oh ma I said the whole house is burning up on us then a fist made of smoke hit me a smack in the mouth its over says ma its all over now.

———

That's what you think! says the voice and when I look up who is it.

Oh for fuck's sake! I said – Sausage!

Ah Francie what were you at for the love of God! he says, twisting the cap in his hands.

Fabian was behind him with the one eye closed giving me a dirty look let's see you try to escape now!

Every time I woke up there was a different bullneck standing by the bed.

I was in a bad state, there was no doubt about it. I looked in the mirror.

What's this? I says.

All you could see was bandages, it was like the Invisible Man.

Aiee! I says. Come on now says the nurse *come on!* or I'll have to send for the orderly.

After a while they gave me a set of crutches I was hobbling around on them when this bogman in a dressing gown says to me: What happened to you? Your face is all burn-ted!

I told him the whole story about the orphanage going up in the middle of the night and all the children getting out except one poor little boy. I couldn't stand the screams I said we could all see him standing at the upstairs window help me help me!

So you went back in to get him? he says with the lip hanging.

I just shrugged no no tell me tell me he says so I told him about me and the little lad jumping from the top floor and all that. When I was finished he had tears in his eyes. He was so mad to give me a cigarette that he dropped a scatter of them on the floor. He could hardly steady his hand to light the fag for me. Puff puff through the bandages all you could see was the fag and the two eyes looking out. That bogman, he couldn't get giving me enough fags. *And what else?* he'd say then with his mouth open.

Then one day in comes Fabian walking like John Wayne and I could see by the way he looked at me he meant business. OK you sonuvabitch move we're ridin' out right you be now Mr Fabian sorr!

So off went me and Sausage and Fabian of the Yard I could see Sausage as white as a ghost in the front, in case I'd make a cod of him again but I wouldn't for I knew that was what pokerarse Fabian wanted, to be able to show off and give out to Sausage. Leddy had the place all locked up but the manure heap was still warm from the morning kill. Here we are I said and Sausage says: Right, dig!, and hands me the graip. How can I dig sergeant with these hands and I lifted up my swaddled stumps.

He was nearly going to say: There's nothing wrong with them hands you're only making it up but then he saw Fabian staring at him with his *well what are you waiting for you country bumpkin* face on him so he spat on his hands and starts digging with the graip. I was sorry now I had gone near her with the lime I was afraid if she was gone they wouldn't believe me and the whole thing would start all over again come on Francie and we *know* and all this. But there was no need to worry for after a while I knew by the sarge that he had hit something and sure enough when he pulled out the graip there stuck on the end of it was part of a leg and Mrs Nugent's furry boot hanging, Fabian wasn't so smart then. Oh Christ!, he says, *bwoagh!* and gets sick all over his foot.

Gammy Leg the court man thought he was all it limping up and down tell me this tell me that I'll tell you fuck all I said.

Oh! was all you could hear in the gallery what did I care I didn't care let them say it. But after Sausage told me that if I ever said that again I'd be in real serious trouble all right then I said. So when he said did you do this did you do that I said yes I did. And I would have kept on saying it only he started on about the money. Comes right up to me there in the box: It was a cold-blooded, premeditated, and deliberate crime – one that had been cunningly planned and thought over, and above all, it was a murder perpetrated for the meanest and most contemptible of motives – for the purpose of robbery and plunder! I had a good mind to make a go at him soon as he said it but I could see Sausage glaring at me no don't Francie so I just said what would you know about it Gammy Leg you don't know what you're talking about I never robbed a thing off the Nugents the only thing I ever took was Philip's comics and I was going to give them back I swear you can ask Joe. Sausage showed me papers *Brutal pig killing – sensation in court!*

There was a drawing of me standing there and underneath *Francis Brady is a pig*.

Fuck this I says even the papers are at it now but there was another bit I didn't see; *Francis Brady is a pig butcher in a local abattoir.*

I said to Sausage: Will they hang me? I hope they hang me.

He looked at me and says: I'm sorry Francie but there's no more hanging. No more hanging? I says. For fuck's sake! What's this country coming to!

———

232

But Sausage was right, there was no more hanging and a few weeks after that there we were all off again me and the sergeant in the back phut phut away off down the road to *another* house of a hundred windows. But this time there was no ho'ho h'hee they'll put manners on you here or any of that stuff, we just talked about ma and da and the old times in the town and when we said goodbye on the steps he said to me there's a lot of sad things in this world Francie and this is one of them.

Goodbye sergeant I said, right says Fabian and the bull-necks then they were gone off down the avenue in the patrol car and that was the last I seen of my old friend Sergeant Sausage.

They took my clothes the pair of fuckers nearly tore them off me come on come on they says. Then they gave me this white thing it tied at the back. What's this I says Emergency Ward Ten?

One of them gives me a dig in the ribs and says you needn't think you'll get away with that kind of lip here its not old women you're up against now Brady.

I know I says then I managed to get away from him: You don't fool me! I shouted. You're trying to trick me! You're going to put me into a mental hospital!

He got a bit red under the eyes and I could see him clenching the fist. Then I laughed: Its all right I said, its only a joke, for fuck's sake!

That was all a long time ago. Twenty or thirty or forty years ago, I don't know. I was on my own for a long time I did nothing only read the *Beano* and look out at the grass. Then they said to me; There's no sense in you being stuck up in that wing all on your own. I don't think you're going to take the humane killer to any of our patients are you?

Humane killer! I don't think Mrs Nugent would be too pleased to hear you calling it that, doc, I said. Oh now now he says that's all over you must forget all about that next week your solitary finishes how about that hmm? I felt like laughing in his face: How can your solitary finish? That's the best laugh yet.

But I didn't. I just said that's great and the next week he introduced me to all these bogmen making baskets and fat teddybears. Is there anything you want, says the doc. Yes, I said, the *Beano Annual* and a trumpet. There you are he says the next day. So now I have a trumpet and if you could see me I look just like da going round the place in my Al Capone coat. Sometimes they have sing songs in the hall and they ask me for a song. Go on!, they say, you're a powerful musicianor! You're the boy can sing then off I go and before long they're all at it, that's the stuff! The Butcher Boy by cripes!

You're all enjoying yourselves says the doctor yes I says, doing the bogman tango. Out with the backside, up with the nose.

One of them comes up to me one day I was hacking at the ice on the big puddle behind the kitchens and says what's going on here or what do you be at with this ice? I'm thinking what I'm going to do with the million billion trillion dollars I'm going to win, I says. So you're going to win a million billion trillion? he says. That's right, I said. Then he leans into me and whispers: Well if you'll take my advice you'll tell none of the bastards in here. They'll only fill you full of lies and let you down.

Oho! I says, don't you worry nobody's letting me down again!

Nor me either! he says, now you said it!

Then he said give me a bit of that stick there like a good man and the two of us started hacking away together beneath the orange sky. He told me what he was going to do when he won his money then I said it was time to go tracking in the mountains, so off we went, counting our footprints in the snow, him with his bony arse clicking and me with the tears streaming down my face.

AFTERWORD

Pugnacious, pataphysical – with either adjective possibly being apt, I considered, on the publication of *The Butcher Boy*, only to find that while the former was routinely applied, the latter was but on a single occasion recruited. Sadly, at this remove, the location escapes me, and – with my apologies – I quote from memory: 'This novel would appear to be suggesting that, in human affairs, things are somehow pataphysically fixed, so that they can never come out right.'

Pataphysics is the French absurdist concept of a philosophy dedicated to studying what lies beyond the realm of metaphysics, intended as a parody of the methods and theories of modern science and often expressed in nonsensical language. Now whatever about parodies of scientific methodology – of which, I'll concede, there are few in this book, that being territory I have always have been more than willing to cede to Flann O'Brien and his particular General Jumbo boffin, Mr de Selby of *The Third Policeman*, it is surely incontestable that *The Butcher Boy* has more than its share of wild and absurdist, quite nonsensical language. Which, in earlier drafts, in fact it didn't possess – reading perhaps like some stilted conflation of John McGahern and, in recent times the criminally overlooked John Broderick, with a faltering nod towards the crimson grace of Flannery O'Connor. But in this, its final, published and complete incarnation, there can be no mistaking the fizz-bang cannonball shot of commedia del arte and the Dudley D. Watkins (Oor Wullie, Jimmy and His Magic Patch) *Beano* comic Corporal Clott-style occluded world and word-bubble dialogue, defiantly insisting on its snowglobe blurry hermetically sealed circularity. With its shift into the adult world attempting something of a stylistic symmetry in its mimicry of the comparably lurid tabloid sensibilities of Samuel Fuller, in particular *The Naked Kiss* – part melodrama, part sensationalism and part surreal, evoking a nightmarish cartoon nether-dimension that is also fiercely real and recognizable and absorbing to watch. Omnipresent also is the riverrun prose not only of James Joyce but the French writer Dujardin from whom he slyly appropriated it, and that of Davis Grubb, author of *Night of the Hunter*. With, always underneath, the symphonies of Balfe's *The Bohemian Girl* (I Dreamt I Dwelt In Marble Halls), sacred Victorian hymns and numerous giddily musical confections of the early 1960s – none of which really ought to belong but impertinently earned their place, solely on account of that very impishness and their childlike, vertiginous, soap-bubble faith – providing perhaps a necessary counterweight in the process to a story which essentially relocates the Manson murders to a small Irish village, complete with its 1940s Abbey Theatre cast, including the long-suffering mother, no end of rain, a gifted and wounded, unreliable father, not to mention the blustering, ubiquitous plum-cheeked clergyman. But who had to be there, however exaggeratedly, because they are real, and belong just as much to life as it proceeded during this period as to any arguably overly familiar representations of it on the stage. With it being itself, of course, a cliché to suggest that some clichés become clichés simply because they are true.

The Helter Skelter tune of which the aforementioned, disappointed Spahn Ranch habitué was so enamoured, and which so shockingly orchestrated his grotesque choreography on that appalling night when he ended the sixties dream, is not entirely without significance, and within the text there is indeed an awareness, an acknowledgement of a Wintry congruence which might exist between that brace of cleft, convulsive souls, Charles and Francie. With the somewhat colourless spiritual and linguistic landscape of the Irish runs depth-charged in a controlled explosion of sixties psychedelia.

Pigs as a metaphor for the inheritance of malignant, perhaps colonial shame had been on my mind for quite a long time – subconsciously, to a great degree: ever since I starred, at four years of age, in a convent primary schoolroom in *Na Tri Muice* – the story of the Three Little Pigs, in Gaelic, in what was known at that time as High Babies. As far as I can remember, I was the one who lived in the house of straw. Which Wile E. Coyote made short work of with some TNT in a television cartoon I saw much later – the proper way to do things, he reckoned. No 'I feel your pain!' for Hanna-Barbera. At a pinch, if you were so moved, you might suggest that the essence of *The Butcher Boy* is perhaps best expressed by the image of Wile E. Coyote sunk in a big raggy armchair holding back tears as he flips yet another page of Greek tragedy over.

But I didn't come close to snaring the above suggested theme until close on thirty-three years later. Which ultimately came about when the wavering, jostling notions which concerned me least were, if not relinquished, certainly subdued – and the subject of the world and its almost medieval bafflement, hurt and suffering as a parody of itself was allocated steadfast, steel-spined hegemony. 'Why is there so much pain in the world?' asks Laura in arguably the greatest motion picture ever made, David Lynch's *Blue Velvet*, in the final frame of which a mechanical robin chews up a cockroach. Trapped in a world which is the real thing and simultaneously a saturated version of itself, in the end I allowed the awful beauty of the blood-soaked ballad which gives it its theme – 'The Butcher Boy', in its 1960s version by The Ludlows – and, without faltering, stammering or second-guessing, allowed the sad hilarity to seep out from its many psychic wounds, fashioning in the process a humble creation which is not, I have to say, to me so much Gothic as a Roger Corman B-movie with the colour turned up full, and which closes in an uncompromisingly limpidly melancholy minor cadence of individual and communal heartache, parting its hands in appeal and yearning, as it poses a question to which I then didn't have the answer. Just as, regrettably, I do not now – and have no inclination to suppose I ever will. But if it's hard to cry out then sometimes maybe writing helps – and there's always the chance someone else will overhear, and recognize, the echo.

Patrick McCabe
2014